Loving LUKI VASQUEZ

Lou Sylvre

Dreamspinner Press

Published by
Dreamspinner Press
4760 Preston Road
Suite 244-149
Frisco, TX 75034
http://www.dreamspinnerpress.com/

Loving Luki Vasquez

Cover Art by Reese Dante   http://www.reesedante.com

ISBN: 978-1-61581-913-3

Printed in the United States of America
First Edition
June 2011

eBook edition available
eBook ISBN: 978-1-61581-914-0

For Orv Nimister, a sweet man, passed on, whose wit still makes me laugh. And for Derrick Bushnell, a beautiful man, met in passing, who shared his Snickers and his dazzling smile.

Acknowledgments

For invaluable contributions in bringing *Loving Luki Vasquez* to life, I thank Elizabeth, Lynn, Ginnifer, and all those who played a part behind the scenes at Dreamspinner Press; artist Reese Dante for an inspired cover; and friend and fellow writer Rena Mason for unflagging support and the occasional reality check.

Prologue

Oak Flats, Nebraska, 1982

A MUD-SPATTERED *pickup in the front yard of a weathered house. Summer-gold hayfields rolling back farther than the eye could see. In the west, a sinking sun screened by a line of trees—cottonwoods and willows. Under those trees, a band of children just into their teens, whooping and laughing in that way that kids do in the summer when night is just on the edge of the next breath.*

Luki ran faster than all the rest, and then looped back to taunt them. Excitement like electricity ran through him. Something about this day, this hour, this prelude to night, was special. "Maria," he yelled. "I'll race ya!"

It started a stampede, all seven of the boys and Maria, the one girl who always hung out with them, running as if they could fly, thrashing through brambles and over sticks and stones as if they couldn't feel them. Out onto the Old Granary Road, onto the bridge, right over the rail and into the river, just as they'd done hundreds of times before.

Luki swam underwater for as long as he could hold his breath, which was longer than anyone, except maybe Maria. When he came up, laughing and spitting, and slicked his hair back out of his eyes, all of the other boys had gathered at the shore, whispering, or maybe arguing. Maria hadn't even gone in, and now she was worming her way down the steep embankment from the road to the river.

The sun sank under the skyline, and the river turned dark, and Luki felt a chill run through him.

"Hey, Luki, c'mon over here, man." It was Ronny Jemison, the boy that was a bit taller, a bit rougher, a bit meaner than any of the rest. Maybe the leader, if they had been a gang. *"We've got something for you. C'mon."*

Ronny scared him when he was like this. Luki had seen the bully push Little Jimmy down the bank, yank Maria's hair hard enough to put her on her knees, kill birds and frogs and rabbits—anything that lived—just to be killing. But, scared or not, Luki knew he had to choose: go and fight and maybe get hurt, or be deemed a coward and so get picked on—probably for the rest of his life.

So Luki went.

Before he quite made it safely to dry land, Ronny smacked him hard in the face with a balled up fist, and yelled one word, spit it at Luki as if it was made of acid and would flay him.

"Faggot!"

Chapter One

Washington State, 2010

BRIGHT clothes, sunburns. Summer had arrived, and Port Clifton was awash in tourists. Since Juan de Fuca Boulevard constituted most of the town, they had nowhere else to go. They chattered and milled about, and Sonny Bly James wasn't in the mood for chatter or milling because he was worried about his nephew, Delsyn, who always stayed gone for days, but who should have come home by now. Sonny quickened his long-legged strides and slid through the crush, trying to disturb the air as little as possible on the way to his truck.

Then he saw a man.

Which in itself wasn't unusual, but this man, an islander, maybe Hawaiian, by the look of him, lounged cool and beautiful in loose summer whites, half-sitting on the fender of an ice-blue Mercedes, a strip of sand beach and the blue straits for a backdrop. Dark chestnut curls shining; straight, white teeth softly teasing a lush, plum-red bottom lip. His eyes, startling pale blue against brown skin, roved all over Sonny; the islander made no effort to pretend otherwise, and besides, Sonny could feel them. Their touch trickled over him like ice water, exciting every nerve he had, even those he'd never heard from before.

Which scared Sonny, a recluse by choice—and, he knew, because he'd always managed to be socially… well, clumsy. So, he turned to the weapon that had been his first line of defense since adolescence, when all the reservation had noticed that their star young grass dancer didn't mind being gay: a smart mouth.

"What are *you* looking at?"

Even though the islander had responded by looking away, Sonny knew he hadn't—couldn't have—intimidated him. The stranger might have been a few inches shorter than him, but judging by his physique, and despite his laid-back manner, Sonny guessed the man could have dropped him with a cold look and a slap. It would have been less of a blow if he had. Instead, he freed his lower lip from his teeth and spoke.

"I beg your pardon."

Sonny wanted to let a whole raft of words spill out, starting with "I didn't mean it," and ending with "so kiss me, now." But the man's attention had turned away. A baby in a stroller dropped a floppy brown bear at his feet. The young mother looked frazzled, at her wit's end, carrying another child and trying to keep a third from making a dash down the boulevard. The islander squatted down—a graceful move— and picked up the bear. Right before Sonny's eyes, his icy exterior melted, and though he didn't smile and couldn't pass for cheerful, he somehow seemed kind. He handed the stuffed creature back to the baby, who seemed to like him. She expressed her gratitude by spouting a number of syllables that all sounded a lot like "da."

Sonny, angry with himself for blowing his chance to meet this chill but beautiful stranger—who might be trying to hide a kind heart— pretended he hadn't seen. He turned his faux-stoic shoulder and walked away. A little shaky, perhaps; already sorry. Three strides and he heard a voice, unexpectedly scratchy, even hoarse.

"Hey."

Sonny turned.

The man took a deep, lovely breath, flashed his cold-fire eyes at Sonny, and said, "I have coffee most mornings at Margie's. In case you're interested."

MARGIE'S it was, then, the very next day. Sonny had weighed the wisdom of that, thinking it might be better if he didn't seem so anxious. *But hell,* he thought, *I* am *anxious. Nothing about me is un-anxious.*

He took the truck—which his Uncle Melvern had left him when he died a year ago and which functioned as a good luck charm. After he pulled over to the curb a half-block from Margie's, he forced the clutch to cooperate, wrestled the column shift into first, and shut the engine down. Sort of. It kicked and spluttered, backfired, and groaned to death. He really, really hoped that the man he had come to meet had not heard that. He wanted to make a good impression. He crashed his shoulder into the door to get out, slammed the door twice to shut it, then paused to look in the side-view mirror. Some other person spoke out of his mouth—or at least that's how it felt. "Sonny," it said, "here's your chance. Don't blow it."

Great. A confidence builder.

The wooden sign attached over the arched brick entry said "Margie's Cup O' Gold," but nobody ever called the cafe anything but just plain Margie's. The elegant door—leaded glass set in oak panels—had been pushed open and held there with a shoe. All that stood between Sonny and whatever fate awaited him inside was a wooden screen door, the old-fashioned kind; it might have been there since the block was built in the 1890's. He crossed the threshold wearing a smile for Margie, then reached back just in time to stop the screen from slamming behind him. "Hey, Marge," he said, maybe not quite as loud as usual. He glanced around lazily, as if he weren't looking for the man he'd come to think of as "the islander." He didn't see him. He let out a long breath that he must have been holding, wondering if he felt disappointed or relieved. He walked, casually he hoped, across the expanse of black and white parquet floor.

"Well," Margie said, hand on hip and scolding in ringing tones. "Hello, Sonny. You're here awfully early."

"Margie, usually people don't give other people a hard time for being *early*."

"Shush, Sonny Bly. So what do you want? Never mind, I already know. You and your fancy coffees. What's wrong with a good old-fashioned cuppa, eh? Now that young man that came in a little earlier—real nice looking fella; I think you'd like him—now he just ordered coffee, black and sweet. There's a man that knows what he likes, I say."

She'd nearly finished making the latte by the time she stopped. That was one thing about a conversation with Margie. Sonny never worried about what to say, because he was pretty sure he'd never get a chance to say it. But this time she had him a little dumbfounded. She'd said, "that nice fella" with a sly glance out of the corner of her eye. Sonny figured she was on to him, but he couldn't decide whether that was good or bad.

She cleared up those muddy waters as soon as she handed over his latte. "He's around the corner, dear. The last table. Don't worry, you look fine."

Which left Sonny absolutely certain he should have worried more about how he looked.

There he was, the islander. Same skin, same lips, eyes, even hair. Of course. But the rest of him was dressed in a posh business suit, a light gray, summer fabric so finely tailored that he might have been born in it. "So why the getup?" Sonny asked.

"Ah," the stranger remarked. "A way with words."

He didn't have to say that. Sonny was already giving his forehead a mental smack. He stared at his coffee for what seemed like, maybe, a hundred and twenty-four years. He'd all but decided to bid an embarrassed farewell and beat a retreat, when the islander spoke.

"I have to go to work in a while," he said. When Sonny looked up he added, "That's why the getup." No smile went with the words, but his eyes danced, like they were laughing—or maybe teasing. He reached halfway across the tile-topped table, holding out his long-fingered, manicured hand.

Sonny stared at it.

The islander said, "I thought maybe introductions would be a good place to start. I'm Luki. Luki Vasquez."

Embarrassed again, Sonny blushed, which—he knew from experience—made his off-brown skin look purple. But in an act of sheer bravery, he put his own dye-stained and calloused hand out and took hold of Luki's. Somehow, what felt like gibberish came out sounding like his name. "Sonny James."

Luki leaned back when the handshake was done, draped his left arm casually over the back of the chair… revealing a bit of leather strap that might be part of a shoulder holster and something sort of gun-shaped half-hidden under his jacket.

"Is that what I think it is?"

Luki pulled his jacket back and showed him what was under there. Or some of what was under there, and not necessarily what Sonny wanted to see.

"Is that what you thought it was?"

"I'm afraid so. Police?"

Luki shook his head. "Used to be, sort of—ATF. Not anymore."

"ATF?"

"Alcohol, Tobacco, Firearms."

Sonny said, "Oh." Thinking he'd probably heard of such an organization, sometime. "What now?"

"Security."

Security? Sonny's mind raced. Luki couldn't possibly have meant he was one of those people that walk around the factory at night. That wouldn't make enough money for a man to feed himself, never mind buy a suit handmade by the angels of heaven. What kind of security work might be so lucrative? He imagined Luki running alongside royalty as they headed for the limo, staving off the paparazzi."What, like bodyguard?"

Luki's voice, low and raspy but sweet, tightened a bit. Apparently he hadn't expected to be quizzed about how he paid the bills. "Yes, from time to time. And property—gems and what not. Investigations, sometimes. What about you? What do you do?" The look he shot Sonny was almost a glare.

The most honest response would have been, *"Please, don't look at me like that,"* but belligerence is a tough habit to break. "I play with yarn."

"Yarn?"

"And string."

"String."

"Yep," Sonny said aloud. Silently, he told himself he'd probably gone too far. He wasn't sorry that Luki's cell phone, attached to his belt in a stylishly businesslike manner, buzzed just then.

Luki glanced at the number, looked up, and caught Sonny's eyes with an entirely unreadable gaze. He set his hand on the table, preparing to rise. "Sorry," he said, "I'd better go."

"Alright," Sonny responded, his voice faint. A wish that he'd spent this time with Luki getting to know him a little, rather than engaging in subtle verbal warfare hit him so hard that it took his breath. Heart pounding, acting on either bravery or desperation, he put his hand on Luki's where it lay on the table. Luki's hand turned and grabbed hold. His thumb washed across Sonny's knuckles; his fingers promised Sonny's palm a kiss, which struck remote bits of anatomy like lightning. Sonny tried to put some of his chagrin into a smile. His lips had gone dry, and he licked them. "Luki—" He stopped, surprised at how the name filled his mouth with something sweet. He laughed a little and went on. "Maybe we can try this again?"

Luki stayed silent, worrying softly at his bottom lip—again.

Sonny stopped breathing.

"Yeah," Luki said, with that already familiar *something* in his eyes. "I'd like that. Tomorrow?"

Sonny's confidence underwent significant restoration as a result of that promising end. He smiled a farewell to Luki and sat a few minutes longer to contemplate and sip the last of his tepid, but still delicious, raspberry latte. Getting ready to leave, he stood, slid his feet more firmly into his flip-flops, and patted his back pocket, as always, to make sure that indeed his wallet was still there. He took a step toward the door, but stopped when he heard conversation around the corner. He'd thought Luki must have gone out the back door to the parking lot, but there was no mistaking his voice.

"The man plays with string, Margie."

Step one, Sonny thought, *deflate ego.*

"Oh, yes he does," Margie said. "And he does it better than anyone I know. Would you like to see?"

Step two: remember who your friends are.

"Not today, Margie. I have to go. Some other day, maybe. I'm sure it's spectacular."

Step three: write off potential romance as a loss for tax purposes.

Footsteps. The back door opened, closed. Sonny came out of hiding to find Margie standing with arms crossed and a raised eyebrow.

"Well?" Margie made words like that into whole dissertations, having a talent for saying more when she spoke less.

"The man plays with guns," he mumbled.

"Quite competently, so I've heard. Any word from Delsyn?"

Sonny didn't mind changing the subject, but thoughts of his too-long-absent nephew hardly cheered him up. He shook his head.

"Don't worry so, dear. He'll come home."

This time Sonny nodded, wished Margie a good day, and started for the door.

"He wants to see your work sometime." Which, of course, did not refer to Delsyn.

"Don't bother, Marge." Hoping to convince himself that he didn't care, he added, "He wouldn't know crimson from scarlet if they jumped up and shouted their names."

THE next day, Sonny talked himself through some considerable misgivings and went to Margie's as arranged. Luki didn't show. After an hour and 2.8 lattes, he left. He didn't say a word, but Margie did. Of course.

"His work is unpredictable, Sonny. He should have told you that."

"No big deal, Marge."

"He doesn't live here, you know. Leases one of those condos up the street, temporarily."

"Luxury, I'm sure."

Margie raised her eyebrows. "I expect so. Anyway, he said he lives in Chicago, has a business there, but he can run it from anywhere.

It takes him all over the world, I guess, and right now, he has a job here."

Sonny remembered how closemouthed Luki seemed. "You got him to say all that?" But of course Margie could get a signpost talking if she had a few minutes to spend. She didn't answer, but she did keep talking.

"He likes it here, said he's tired of Chicago, tired of always being on edge. Decided he'd stay a while, maybe not work so hard."

"Why are you telling me all this, Margie?

"Because you want to know."

LUKI glanced in the mirror for a minimal look before leaving his condo. He'd dressed more casually than he generally did when working—which in the past had been always—but today his face looked even more grim than usual. He didn't like to see it, anyway. The scar that ran straight down the left side of his face from scalp to chin made him ugly, and he knew it. And he knew that, try as he might to distract people with perfect clothes and beautiful curls, that scar scared people and turned them away. Everyone except kids.

And Sonny James, maybe.

Which explained the grimmer look.

He'd been working, a nasty job that involved a wife trying to get her jewels back from a former trophy husband who, it turned out, had full access to a lowlife but dangerous security force of his own— exactly the kind of job he hated the most, though it paid well. He couldn't help missing his date... sort of date with Sonny, but Sonny had no way of knowing that. He'd called Margie late that first day and asked for Sonny's cell. She didn't think he had one, she said, for practical reasons. That left Luki baffled, and then before he could ask for his landline, things started happening outside. "Tell him I called," he'd said. Three days ago.

"Maybe I'll be lucky and have a chance to explain," he told his reflection.

He walked the four miles to Margie's for exercise. And because he didn't think Margie's would be open this early anyway. Not being someone who could remotely be called a "morning person," he'd never paid much attention to what time things opened. They were always open before he got there, except when he had to get up for work, in which case he didn't go have leisurely coffee with a beautiful... exceptionally beautiful man.

I can't believe it, he thought. *I've got freaking butterflies in my stomach. Cigarette.*

He had one in the first mile and hoped the next three would blow away the smell of smoke. *I should quit.* Not knowing why he thought St. Christopher might help in a situation like this, he touched the medal he always wore on its chain. *Let him be there.*

Right. Because I'd certainly be there if someone stood me up without a word and didn't show up for three days....

Sonny didn't appear at Margie's that day, nor the next, nor the next, despite Luki getting there early—though admittedly later each day. Margie said he hadn't been in after that first day, and when he asked where Sonny lived, she laughed. He hadn't expected a laugh, but he hadn't really expected an answer, either—other than the usual, "It's not my business to tell you that."

Instead: "You'd never find it, Luki."

"I'm a detective."

"Well, if you can detect yourself around the forest, through the bog, and over the back roads, then you'll do fine. He lives about an hour out of town—not because of distance, because of the roads. Hardly ever comes to town, to tell the truth. One of those reclusive artist types, you know?"

No. He didn't know. When would he have had a chance to know what "artist types" do with their off time? "What about his phone, then?"

"Well, I don't know...."

"I'm sure you have it."

"I do, and I've got your phone number too. Do you want me to just hand it out to any looker that asks?"

"If the looker is Sonny James, yes." He meant it, but it didn't look like Margie even heard it. She'd already walked away, heading for a table newly filled with four tourists.

Luki left, resolving not to come back with his hopes in the air again. Why he had done it in the first place mystified him. He never pursued relationships. Went out of his way to avoid them, in fact. He liked a tryst as well as the next guy, had honed his skills at sex the same way he perfected his marksmanship and tai chi. But relationships? No; single instances, adding just enough class to keep them from being sordid. He found the idea of a relationship dangerous.

Sonny James threatened his well-being. Better left alone. So he told himself, but after he walked out Margie's door, he turned around and walked back in.

"You said you'd show me some of his work sometime. Can you do that now?"

SONNY couldn't get his mind around weaving. This happened rarely. Actually, it happened never, but this time thoughts of Delsyn's absence loomed so large, he scarcely had room in his mind for anything else.

Almost true, he thought. Delsyn left room for one other subject: Luki Vasquez.

He'd reached an impasse in his thinking on both subjects, so in disgust, he moved away from the loom and into the rough-floored mudroom, which he'd set up with tubs and flasks and boxes of ingredients—even a long rack for stripping bark and a freezer for storing bags of exotic, color-yielding insects. He'd dedicated the space for making and using dyes, and that's what he set about.

He had a project in mind, something he wanted to do that, for once, had not been commissioned. To be honest, he had two in mind, but one involved a sore subject, and he chose not to think about it. The project he applied himself to that morning nearly matched his mood, though perhaps a little brighter. It needed a big sky that duplicated the color and feel of the cloud-strewn mornings these last few weeks.

Colors just a hair off from what was called for could change a piece completely, even ruin it—Sonny knew that better than just about anyone. Creating effective, precise dyes had been the core of his doctoral work, and the subject had become a mainstay in his rare academic appearances. Being the kind of man that rarely does anything the way anybody else would, he'd developed a quirky but relaxing way to get every hue, tint, and shade exactly right. And now seemed a good time for relaxation.

Before dawn, he gathered swatches of silk cloth, dyed and set two days ago in a range of hues from off-white to beige to various grays. After tying each onto its own slender pole, he carried them to the beach at the edge of the straits. Hiking east up the beach, he stopped when he found a place that seemed right and had some high rocks to watch from. He planted the poles in the sand and climbed to his perch just in time for the light to show.

The job involved a lot of doing nothing. Or so it would seem from the outside. In reality, he observed and noted and carefully recorded, all in his brain. But when he saw Luki Vasquez running along the shore, he knew that if the islander saw him, he'd think he was lazing about. Strange, though, for all Luki's "I'm a professional bad guy" attitude, he didn't spot Sonny there until he came upon the silk flags fluttering in the breeze. He turned to scan the beach but still didn't see him. When finally he did, he stood for a minute, inscrutable, then walked toward Sonny's rocks.

"Hey," Sonny said.

"Hi."

Silence. A promising start. Sonny scooted over on his rock. There was room for two. "You want to sit?"

Luki climbed up and cleared his throat a few times before speaking. "I was working."

"You do that a lot?"

"Not as much as I used to. I'm trying to cut back."

By the sound of his voice, Sonny would have sworn the man was smiling, but when he turned to face him, he didn't see any expression more mobile than ice. At first. Then it peeked out, that tiny, shy little bit of something sweet behind his eyes, in the set of his mouth. A smile? Maybe so.

"What are you doing?" Luki stared at the flags as if trying to decode a hidden clue.

"I'm testing dyes, colors."

"Aren't they all pretty much the same?"

Sonny sighed, pretty sure this new acquaintance would lead nowhere. He wondered briefly what Luki wanted out of him. He suspected it would be a quick fling before he returned to his real life in Chicago. Maybe he had a lover there, though Sonny's intuition told him not. Anyway, the last thing Sonny wanted was a one-nighter. He avoided them. That habit, coupled with his lack of the time needed to find love—or have any real relationship—had left him alone and even shyer than he'd been when he started out. And, he knew, probably the most inexperienced twenty-nine-year-old man, gay or not gay, this side of the moon.

But he had Delsyn to worry about, and that took up too much of his mind and heart to make room for lovers anyway. Now that he'd grown up enough to realize that Delsyn's well-being couldn't be expected to take care of itself, he would gladly devote himself to doing the caring if only Del would stay home. He wouldn't, never did. But the boy knew he needed to come home every two weeks, maybe three at the most—his life might depend on it. That's what Sonny needed to think and worry about. Not Luki Vasquez.

"No," he answered. "They're not the same." He jumped down from the rocks, gathered up his poles, and strode away, affording Luki a wave.

RIVER sounds climbed the muddy bank where Luki stood shivering in moonlight so bright it glared, and he had to shield his eyes. He knew there were other kids in the water, though he couldn't hear them, could barely make out the dark shapes of their heads, like shadows. He heard a call from a short distance off to his left, and when he turned his head, there was another shape. A boy, and something gleaming silver in the air.

Again he heard his name. "Luki, come on over here. I've got something for you."

"Not again, no," he whispered to himself.

"Yes," Ronny said. *"Again, and again, and again...."*

Luki cried out, woke, and rolled instantly off the bed and onto his feet. Sweat soaked him, and the left side of his face burned as if newly slashed. Fear, then grief took their brief turns with him, each like a punch to his throat, cutting off his air. He hurried past them and embraced rage, stood in its white-hot flame until, for this time, it burned itself out.

He knew the drill, knew the dream, knew how to shake off its remaining shards.

Seconds after he woke, he gauged the light and estimated, *morning.* Which, he knew, demonstrated his brilliant powers of deduction.

"Better than Sherlock Holmes."

As an alternative to testing his detective skills, he looked at the clock. Eight thirty. Still early by his standards, but he never contemplated going back to bed. He stumbled into the bathroom to vomit—an old and bothersome reaction—not even trying to hold it back this time.

Thanks to his invisible housekeeper, who came every day in his absence, somehow always knowing when he'd be gone, he had coffee ready to brew by the cup. He brushed his teeth so he could enjoy the taste and did just that. Two cups of black and sweet, into the shower, out again in no time. He put on his old and ragged clothes. Yes, he had some. He remembered Sonny's blunt question. *"Why the getup?"* He almost smiled, almost wished the intriguing... frustrating and intriguing man could see him now.

Meanwhile, he got out three handguns of various sizes and capabilities, placed them in a case designed for just that purpose, and added ammunition. He kept his firearms, always, clean and in perfect condition. None of his weapons were intended for sport. Intimidation, protection, and defense constituted the mainstay of his profession and of his habits; a life, even his own, could depend on them. And honing all his skills, working them to stay in top form, fought off the dream and the havoc it would otherwise wreak. Guns and targets this morning, and then perhaps tai chi—which he considered the best and deadliest of his martial arts.

By the time he'd driven to the range outside of Port Angeles, reassured himself, and impressed his fellow shooters, the need for breakfast finally caught up, so he stopped at Front Street, a corner restaurant that served steak and eggs seasoned and cooked to perfection. On the way back to Port Clifton, he set his phone on speaker and delegated the day's work to his various staff, using his fabulous office admin as a go-between.

"They won't listen to me, boss. You know that."

"Contrary, Jude. I know you put fear in their hearts every time you speak, and they wouldn't dare go against you. Make my nefarious plans your orders, and they'll get it done."

"Are you coming back soon?"

"No."

"That's all I get, just no?"

"Yes."

After an exasperated groan, Jude hung up. For the second time that day, Luki almost smiled. Which made him think maybe he *should* go back. Port Clifton was turning him soft.

FOOD digested, business taken care of, cigarette half-smoked, he decided to go straight down to the beach. He could have gone home. He had plenty of room in his condo, or on the balcony, for tai chi. He had a key to the top floor gym, a luxurious space that boasted a three-sixty view. But luxury had never seemed right for tai chi, and, Nebraska child that he was, saltwater still fascinated him. Besides, this was the closest he'd ever come to a vacation. He might as well at least make a pretense of it.

He drove a little way past town to a stretch not lined by houses and not crowded with people—in fact, it looked deserted. Perfect. For the first part of his tai chi practice, he always worked carefully and slowly through forms; for the next part, he "fought" target posts of various sizes, each about two inches in diameter. In early days, the posts had been wrapped with padding and duct tape, but once he'd mastered the art, he left them bare. The "give" had to be in his own hands, his own stance, and that's what imbued his blows with deadly force.

He took the targets out of the car, removed his shoes, and walked across the beach to the edge of the water, where the wet sand provided a perfect base. After he'd set his poles and taken a minute to perfect his state of mind, he began the first form, working thoughtfully, slowly, aware of every muscle, every move.

By the time he'd finished, the sun had risen almost midway. With heat and exertion, he'd broken into a profuse sweat. He turned his face into the breeze, let it riffle his curls, took his shirt off, and tossed it to hang on one of his targets.

A dot in the distance moving up the beach toward him. A person. Sonny, no flags in sight.

Crap.

Oh well, no problem. If there was anything he knew how to do, it was shut out emotional disturbance. He'd just continue with his practice, maybe work another form first, as if Sonny weren't there. But with Sonny's long legs, he covered a lot of distance in a short time, and now he'd come almost close enough for eye contact. *My God, the man is beautiful.*

"Hey," Luki said.

"Hi."

"Nice out, huh?" *Oh, yeah. Great. Talk about the weather.*

Sonny ignored the comment.

Thank you, universe.

"It's like dancing."

The conversation seemed like some kind of mirror image of the last time they spoke, when Sonny was checking out colors, which certainly weren't all the same, or so Sonny informed him, leaving him to feel foolish. Nice thing was, now they were in his territory. But he had no taste for retaliation.

"It's been called that. Tai chi."

"Oh. Yeah. I've heard of it. Sort of dancing that can kill. Seems exactly right."

Luki didn't know what he meant by that last remark, so he stayed silent.

"It's graceful, the way you do it."

Luki remained at a loss for a response. *Was that a compliment?*

"I've even thought about trying to learn it. But I could never get away from my studio—or maybe I should say get my studio out of my head—long enough for anything like that."

Luki still said nothing, but now he subtly eyed Sonny from head to toe—a pleasant undertaking but one with purpose. "You're in good enough shape to do it well."

"I suppose."

Luki didn't know how he could speak and hold his breath at the same time, but it felt that way. "I could teach you a little," he said, "right now."

To his surprise and nervous delight, Sonny agreed after only a second's hesitation. Soon Luki had him barefoot and mastering a perfect opening stance. From there, he taught him some traditional warm-ups—not part of the forms but a good way to get the feel of the art. Though his long, loose limbs gave him some trouble and made Luki want to secretly and fondly laugh, and though Sonny giggled— *yes, giggled*—at a few of the early warm-ups, he attended well and learned fast.

They'd reached the last of the warm-up exercises: Pushing Chi. A little more complicated than the ones that came before, it took focused coordination. When Sonny could Push Chi with acceptable grace, Luki decided to introduce him to at least part of the Chen form: First, he revisited the simple but all-important Opening Movement. Then, Pound the Pestle, Lazy Tying Coat, and Six Sealing, Four Closing.

Single Whip led into White Crane Spreads Its Wings, the name of which made Sonny adorably... *all right fine, adorably* happy. The sequence involved motions that at first felt counterintuitive. Like probably every student in the centuries tai chi had been around, Sonny needed help with it. As he would with any other student, Luki stood behind him, using his own hands to guide Sonny through the move. He wondered if he could get away with teaching him all the rest of the moves in just that way. Perhaps for hours. Every day. For a long time.

As he was teaching and wondering and probably even almost smiling, a wind rose up, splashing spray and sand and whipping Sonny's long hair at Luki's face and right into his mouth. On the word "open," appropriately enough.

Sonny spun around, gathering up his luxurious baked-earth red hair. Before Luki had a chance to close his mouth, Sonny kissed him. A passionate, seeking sort of kiss. A kiss that Luki instinctively returned, though kissing wasn't a large part of his intimate life, and especially not kissing on the beach.

As suddenly as he started it, Sonny ended it, leaving Luki bereft... frustrated and bereft.

Sonny turned away, refusing eye contact. "I'm sorry," he said. "I shouldn't have done that." Without any further explanation, he stepped away.

Luki knew fear, could spot it from afar and pick it out in a crowded room. Right now, it ran hot through Sonny's veins. He reached for Sonny's arm. "Sonny, what...." *What are you afraid of?* he ended the question silently. Sonny had already gone.

Luki hated roller coasters, both the mechanical ones and the emotional. In response to hating it, he relaxed completely, letting his tension be soaked up in the wet sand. Then he took that emotion out on his targets. Using tai chi *fajin* in a rapid-fire assault, he took every one of those posts down before they knew what hit them. Especially the last.

"You never even saw me leap, you stupid post."

Chapter Two

"I KISSED him, Marge."

"Yeah, he told me."

"He told you? When?" Sonny's stomach was balled up somewhere around his throat.

"Just a little while ago," Margie answered, "when he came in for coffee."

"He shouldn't have told you. That was personal."

"You told her too," Luki said, coming around the corner from the other side of the room.

Margie hummed.

Sonny turned around to walk out.

Luki stepped in front of the door. "Whoa! Just a minute. Have coffee with me."

"You're blocking my way."

"Just trying to get a chance to speak to you."

"I don't like having my way blocked."

Luki stepped aside with a dramatic flourish. "Have coffee with me."

Margie tried to hide a hearty laugh behind her hand with absolutely no success. Fleeing toward the stairs that led to her over-the-store apartment, she said, "I'm going home for a bit, guys. If anyone comes in, help them or call me—or hey, just lock the door and turn the sign over. Sonny, serve yourself."

"I don't know how to make a latte."

"Try just coffee, black and sweet," Margie said, "or with a little cream."

Margie brooked no disobedience, generally speaking, so while Luki locked up, Sonny poured coffee. He was still deciding on the cream when Margie's scream, a scuffle, and a crash of glass like a Chihuly chandelier in an earthquake came from upstairs. He stood frozen for an instant, then dropped his cup in the tub and ran. Luki had already made the stairs, and by the time Sonny got there he was pounding on Margie's door.

"Marge!" Luki yelled once, didn't really wait, and went in. Sonny had taken the stairs three at a time and was right behind him. His instinct was to push past, but Luki had drawn a gun—from somewhere—and held it out in front of him just like a cop on television.

But the main event was over.

Margie stood dumbstruck in the middle of the room, staring at the wall. What was supposed to be on that wall was a tapestry of Sonny's making, an intricate weaving depicting Margie's two grandchildren blowing bubbles in dappled sunlight under a canopy of green. What hung on the wall now were shreds of silken warp still clinging to broken weft. New graffiti in red and black decorated the empty spaces between.

FAGGOT.

Over and over, one word written at every possible angle. Sonny wouldn't have thought it possible to rattle Luki but, though his arm was around Margie as she sobbed into his shoulder, he looked as pale as Sonny felt. Possibly, he was shaking, but only seconds passed before he recovered.

He took a couple of deep breaths through flared nostrils, put his hands gently on Margie's shoulders, and stood her back away from him. "Margie," he said, speaking softly but in firm tones. When she looked up, he assured her, "I'm going right now to find them. You'll be all right here."

Sonny took that as his cue and stepped up. His arm took the place of Luki's, sheltering Margie. Whose home had been invaded, whose property had been destroyed, and whom Sonny claimed as friend, a very dear one.

LUKI moved to the large bay window, which looked out west toward the water. Jagged shards jutted from the casement and carpeted the floor. Why a vandal would have taken this route to flee he couldn't imagine—there were two sets of stairs, and the other window had a fire escape. And if they did choose this way, why break it, when they could have just opened it? Given that, he guessed he was dealing with someone lacking in criminal experience and almost certainly young.

He leaned out carefully and spotted the culprits immediately—as he'd expected, a couple of boys, both dressed in ratty, baggy sweats. One of them limped, trailing blood, and the other pulled him along but clearly didn't want to have to wait for him. Injury or no, they were moving fast and soon disappeared around the corner to the south, into an alley. Luki crossed the room in a few strides, slid the smaller, south-facing window sash up, and folded himself through it. He took the fire escape in leaps, a much faster route than doors and stairs.

He caught up to the boys as they disappeared around the blind alley at the next corner, snagged first the taller, uninjured one, and then the other, and swung them around to bump faces. Before they had time for the stun to wear off, he shoved them toward a brick wall, the back of a tavern if the content of the refuse bins was anything to judge by. Their heads hit the wall, but not hard—Luki wasn't out to hurt them, only stop them. The biggest of the boys came up with a switchblade from the depths of his hoodie.

Luki raised an eyebrow, surprised that the kid would have this particular weapon, but he lanced out a designer shoe and tapped the kid's wrist in just the right place. The hand went limp; the knife clattered to the ground.

He stepped closer, leaning over the nervous, yet still belligerent, teen. Deliberately he used his size, his ice-cold eyes, and his scarred face to intimidate the boy. But all the while he was trying to put these boys together with the crime they'd obviously just committed. It didn't quite fit.

"We didn't do anything," the smaller boy spoke up, perhaps trying to sound tough. If so, he didn't pull it off.

"Really?" Luki snatched the soiled pack off the younger kid's back, turned it over, and shook out the contents. Three cans of spray paint, a poultry knife, and nothing else. "Cuz, interestingly, these cans of paint are just the colors recently used to desecrate the home of my friend—"

"That don't mean nothin'." The bigger boy spat the words out, though he must have known his argument was ridiculous. "Thousands of people have that paint."

Luki went on as if the kid had never spoken. "And this… string," he said, thinking of Sonny. "These pieces of string that found their way into your backpack, tangled around this kitchen knife, look an awful lot like they came from a certain artwork that was destroyed in that home, which used to hang in the exact spot where some really ugly words were written with paint exactly like that."

This time the smaller, probably younger boy spoke up. Luki tilted his head, listening, as it appeared, respectfully.

"But we didn't… we wouldn't have… there's a man—"

"No! Shut up, Jackie! Don't say anything!"

Jackie didn't listen to the older boy, although to Luki it seemed obvious he wasn't used to such defiance. Probably the other one hadn't stopped to think that his yelling only served to let Luki know that Jackie spoke the truth. They were both scared, which was exactly what he needed them to be. He didn't let up on the intimidation, which he pretty much created just by looking at them.

"There's a man," Jackie said. "He gave us the paint and he told us to do it."

Luki continued to look at Jackie, who might have been shaking. He started to think he should back off. Maybe the kid had a heart murmur or severe asthma. And there was something about him….

The other boy opened his mouth, "No, Jack—"

So much for lightening up. Luki switched his gaze, shot a visual ice-dart or two at him, who very sensibly shut his mouth again, obviously miserable but silent. Luki took a deep breath, wishing he had a lit cigarette between him and the salty air. He returned his attention to Jackie. "And?"

"We do what he says, Josh and me, because he could get us in a lot of trouble—"

"I did it!" Josh suddenly yelled, his voice breaking on the last word. "It wasn't Jackie, it was me."

Luki let him know he had his attention, and the kid went on.

"I made him stay outside, down in the street. I did it, just me. Leave my brother alone."

Luki dropped his gaze for a second or so. "Quite noble, Josh. But you're lying." He caught the boy's eye, and then turned back to Jackie. "Go on. You were saying, get you in trouble?"

"And, this time..." He stopped to swallow, started kicking his heels against the brick wall. "He said he's bored with us now, said if we did this, then he'd leave us alone."

Luki started to sweat, hoping it didn't show. A horrible kind of recognition crept up his spine. A voice inside said, *yes, Luki, you know this story.*

"I never wanted to do it—Josh neither. But we thought it would be worth it."

Luki let the silence hang, riffling through a mix of emotions. What they'd done left him wanting to lash out, teach them to keep their hate words safe inside their slimy brains. But to begin with, he knew he'd never do that, never use his considerable potential for violence against them. No matter what their crime had been. To top it off, the explanation he'd heard so far forced him to listen. He hated times like this; it frustrated him to no end to have someone do something truly despicable, and then have it turn out they might be human.

"Tell me about this man," he sighed, and pointed to Jackie. "You first."

But the older boy yelled again, in an ugly voice, yet with a face full of fear. "No, Jackie, you little fucker. Don't say another word."

"Don't call me that," Jackie said. But otherwise, this time, he did as he was told.

Luki paced for a minute or so, a few steps each way, hands behind his back. Halfway through the fourth pass, he stopped just in front of Josh and met his dark, defiant eyes.

He kept his voice low, partly because people listened hardest to a whisper, and partly because he'd screamed the day he got the scar on his face, twenty-eight years ago, and ever since it hurt just to speak loud. He never yelled.

"You know I can hurt you," he said. "Right?" He felt like an ogre, but he hoped stepping up the intimidation a notch might get him some information.

"You can't threaten us! We know our rights. Just take us to juvie, if you want."

Without a word, Luki snapped two pairs of nylon cuffs on the boys, locking them to each other in a figure eight fashion intended to make them very clumsy if they tried to run. When he pointed them back toward the alley entrance and said, "Move," they had trouble even walking. He marched them back the way they'd come and right up to the back of Margie's building.

Josh pulled as hard as he could, shouting and trying to pull Jackie with him. Luki held on to him and kept walking. The boys had no choice but to stumble along with him, but Josh continued to yell.

"You're supposed to take us to juvie! You can't make us go here!"

Luki preferred not to rouse the neighborhood. He put a hand on Josh's shoulder as if in a friendly fashion, then dug his fingertips under the collarbone, pressing the length of his thumb into the base of Josh's neck. The move was almost invisible yet caused a great deal of pain. "Young man," he said, leaning close to his other ear, "be quiet. Be quiet or you're going to find yourself in way deeper shit than you're standing in now. And if you can't do it for your own sake, then do it for your brother."

Josh sniffed and nodded. Luki marched them up to the door, got out his cell phone, and called Margie. "Can you let me in the back door? I've got them. It's a little complicated, and I want a private place to…," he hesitated, thinking the word interrogate seemed like overkill. Finally he said, "… talk to them."

"Sonny will come down, Luki. You're okay, though?"

Luki smiled, at least in his head. "Yeah, fine. Thanks for asking."

Sonny let them in wearing a surprised look, apparently for Luki, followed quickly by a glare that would put any one of his agents to shame, thankfully intended for the boys and not for him. He could see gears turning in Sonny's mind, and for a minute he thought he'd have to put himself between Sonny and the boys—a position he certainly didn't want to take. He breathed a quiet sigh, relieved, when Sonny turned on his heel, said "Margie's alone," and disappeared back up the narrow stairs.

Luki pushed the boys along a narrow hall to a storeroom and office at the rear of the Cup 'O Gold, switched on the overhead lamp, and sat them down on a tatty plaid loveseat pushed up against the wall.

"I'd regret having to do you any harm, boys. Do you think I'll find myself with such regrets if I take your cuffs off?"

Nothing.

"Josh?"

"No," he said, head down and voice sullen.

Luki meant what he said. He really didn't want to hurt them. With Josh's persistent belligerence, he weighed the situation carefully. In the end he decided that if he could just get to the bottom of that belligerence, find out where it came from, he'd probably find a whole different Josh underneath, and maybe he'd be able to make sense of what the brothers had done too. He retrieved his cutter from the belt pouch and snipped off the cuffs. He sensed Jackie's tension, then felt Josh stiffen, no doubt acting on the mistaken belief—one held by at least half the human population—that a stiff back made for a powerful attack. He waited.

Smart enough not to attempt getting physical, Josh lashed out once again with his tongue. "Why did you bring us here? You were supposed to take us to jail!"

"But you see," Luki said, "I'm not a cop. I'll leave it for you to decide if that means you should be less afraid of me or, perhaps, more." He let the boys chew on their fears for a minute or so. The worst he might do to them would be turn them in, but they didn't know that. When he judged the time to be right, he prodded. "What's it going to be, boys? Who is this man?"

"He never said."

"We don't know."

They both spoke at once, which tended, Luki thought, to give credence. "All right. Tell me what you do know, then. What does he look like? Have you seen him before?"

Once the boys started talking, they let everything out in a rush, talking over each other and speaking so fast Luki had to stop them and make them take turns. In the end he learned everything they knew, but it wasn't much. The mysterious "creep" had a stocky build and dark hair—a white man who wore glitzy chains and diamond rings but drove an old, dented van.

"This isn't the first time he's sent you on an errand," Luki said.

"No," Josh answered.

"Always the same thing?" After both boys shook their heads, Luki asked, "What, then?"

Josh looked away. Jackie hung his head.

"Things you're ashamed of," Luki sighed.

"He made us—"

"No." Luki held up a hand. "Don't tell me that. Tell me where you met him, how you know when you're supposed to meet him and where."

But they didn't know. The first time, he'd had someone pick them up off the street and bring them to a building in Bellingham, a city up the coast, just south of the Canadian border. They knew the building because sometimes they'd snuck inside to sleep or sheltered under one of the broad doorways. It was built around the turn of the twentieth century, fashioned after a castle with crenellated walls and arched doors. People called it "the armory" because in one of its incarnations, it had served as one.

They hadn't seen his face clearly because he stayed in the shadows—easy to do inside that building. "Just call me Mr. K," he told them, holding up a knife to clarify the meaning.

"We don't know how he finds us, but he does, no matter where we go."

Mr. K knew where the boys were from. He knew their father's name. And he had Jackie and Josh so frightened that talking about him started Josh sweating and Jackie shaking.

Luki asked the obvious question. "What does this man have on you? You said he knows your father?"

After a bleak silence, it was Jackie who spoke. "He'll make us go back. It's... it's because of me."

"No, Jack, it isn't because of you. Jus' some people are creeps."

"Like Mr. K," Luki said, fishing for something that hadn't been said. He had a feeling he was going to hear something he liked less than everything else he'd heard that day. His stomach churned.

Jackie wrapped his arms around his stomach and leaned over them, apparently having said all he was going to say for the moment.

"Yeah, like Mr. K," Josh said, belligerent again. "And like the police in the town where we come from, and like the stupid perv in the park in Seattle, and—"

"Josh, stop!" Jackie's face was screwed up into a ball of misery, tears and snot, red shame and anger, but especially fear. He jumped to his feet and struck out at Josh, but Luki caught his arm.

"Sit down, Jack," he said, guiding the boy gently back to the couch. "I'm not going to hurt you." He handed the boy his very white handkerchief, with only a moment's regret that it would never be the same. He looked back toward Josh and nodded.

Josh stared at Jackie as if begging his forgiveness. "And like our dad."

Luki did not want to hear what he knew was coming. His gut threatened to rise up against him. He licked his lips, breathed deep for fortitude. Still, he prompted, two words that scratched his throat as if his larynx was lined with tacks.

"Your dad."

Josh nodded, and apparently he knew Luki's words were an invitation—or maybe an order—to continue. "Jackie's—"

"Queer," Jackie shouted. "I'm queer! I'm a fag. I'm an abomination to the Lord." The anger that had spurred his outburst drained away, and, looking hopeless, he drew his knees up to his chest and hid his face behind them.

Luki considered saying *me too*. He decided against it. With the shape the boy was in, he thought it might scare him more, rather than comfort him. But he didn't quite understand why it had been so hard for him to say it. There was, unfortunately, no shortage of gay teens on the street. *"I'm an abomination to the Lord,"* he'd said. Luki sighed and shook his head.

He pulled a hard-backed chair next to Jackie, sat, and waited for the young man to look up. When he had his eye, he said, "I can see you don't want to hear your brother tell me about your dad. If you'd rather, I can have you wait somewhere else, or you can tell me yourself. But I should know if you want me to be fair about what you guys did upstairs, and I won't do anything with that piece of information that will hurt you. That's my word. A promise."

"Josh can tell you," Jackie whispered. "Some of it I don't remember. Usually."

Luki stepped over to the water cooler, filled two paper cups with water and handed one to each of the boys. Jackie gulped it like medicine, but Josh didn't touch it. Luki scooted the chair back a ways to give Jackie some distance, and then nodded for Josh to continue. He waited, but he thought if he wasn't careful he might puke before the story ended.

"Our dad," Josh said. "He found Jackie with a boy—they were only holding hands and talking. I was supposed to watch out for them, make sure nobody surprised them, like. But I spaced out... I don't think it could've been very long—"

"It wasn't your fault, Josh." Jackie came out of his cocoon to reassure his brother.

"Dad jumped out of the car and started whipping Jackie with his belt, the buckle end. He turned around to give me a couple of licks, too, then threw Jackie in the car. His back was bleeding all over the back seat. He's got scars." He stopped for a moment, eyeing the long scar that bisected the left side of Luki's face.

Luki felt the old wound burn and smelled blood. It startled him for a moment, until he realized the blood he smelled was Jackie's. He'd forgotten about the cut. He found the business's required first aid kit, took out some peroxide, salve, and bandages, and sat down in front of Jackie again. "Let me see your leg."

As he began to inspect the cut, he glanced back at Josh. "And? You were saying…"

"He locked Jackie in this room; it's kind of a cellar out back of the house. It wasn't the first time he'd put one of us in there, so I knew the way to get in when the door was locked, by sliding through this vent. So after dark, I went out and sat with him until he stopped shaking and fell asleep. He was leaning up against me, see, so I couldn't leave. Besides it's a lot harder to get out than it is to get in. After a while, I couldn't stay awake either.

"Next thing I knew, he was there, screaming, and flailing that belt buckle again. 'Oh, so you couldn't stay away', he said to me. 'Well good. I'm going to teach your brother why it's not a good idea to go around kissin' boys, and you get to watch.'"

Luki waited while the boy struggled for breath, struggled against the tears that fell anyway.

Jackie was quiet—numb, Luki thought—and he directed his words to him.

"He raped you."

Jackie nodded, looking a little sad but otherwise showing no emotion.

But Josh was in agony. "It made me wish I'd never grow up to be a man."

"Don't wish that," Luki said. "Never wish that." He turned away, concentrating on taking deep breaths. "Give me a minute."

He hurried toward the tiny washroom across the office, leaned over the toilet, and retched. Which he hated. Unfortunately, over the years he'd gotten used to it, but it didn't do much for his tough-guy image. Worse thing about this time, though, was that now every time it happened again, it would be all mixed up with the smell of peroxide and visions of another boy's nightmare.

When he turned again, Josh was passing the loaned handkerchief back to Jackie.

In turn, Jackie held it out to Luki. "This corner is still clean."

"Thanks," Luki said and gingerly made use of it, to be polite. Then he rinsed and spit and popped a breath mint.

The boys were sixteen—"almost seventeen"—and fifteen. Their hometown, a place they never wanted to see again, was in the northwest corner of Kansas.

"Your last name?"

"Royce."

"Your father?"

"Mariano," Jackie said. "Mariano Royce."

Luki gnawed softly at his bottom lip, thinking. "So, if you could have what you wanted, what would it be?"

"Safe," Josh said.

And Jackie, "Stop running."

Luki nodded. "Okay. I'll hook you up."

LUKI'S spectacular leap to the window and acrobatic exit jarred Sonny from his shocked state. He squeezed Margie's shoulder and passed her a strip of silk he pulled from his pocket. He always had things like that with him, mostly because he forgot they were there. It was a strip for testing dyes, but it was clean, and Margie seemed a little calmer after she used it to blow her nose.

Sonny asked, "You okay?"

She nodded, but then started crying again and said, "Oh, Sonny, I'm so sorry."

"You're sorry! What on earth for? You're sorry some jackass vandalized your home and scrawled hate words on your wall?"

"But, Sonny, all your work, hours and hours, your beautiful work."

"It's just string, Margie." He hoped she'd stop crying if he could make her laugh.

"String?" A smile played around the corners of her mouth, even though the tears were still flowing.

"And yarn," he said, smiling.

"Yarn." This time she giggled. She dabbed her eyes with the clean end of the cloth, and when she looked up the fresh tears had stopped.

"Come sit down, Marge. I'll make you some tea."

They settled at the kitchen table—one of those sixties style ones with the marbled Formica and a metal rim. Marge cradled her teacup in two hands; Sonny sipped at a glass of water. Street noise drifted in. It seemed unusually loud, but the reason didn't click for Sonny until he felt the breeze from the windows. One open, one smashed. It sobered him.

"They must have come up the back stairs," Margie said. "I always leave it unlocked. I should've locked it."

"C'mon, Marge. We're in Port Clifton. This kind of stuff never happens."

"Well," she said, sounding a lot more like herself. "I guess it does now, right, young man?"

Sonny didn't answer except to raise his eyebrows. "I'll go down and lock the door now. Sit tight, I'll be right back."

When he came back, she changed the subject. "I suppose we should call the police."

Sonny thought about it, dusting off the pristine tabletop. "I don't know, Marge. If you want to, I guess. But I have a feeling we should wait for Luki to get back. Since he plays with guns for a living and all—" He stopped to smile at her. "I figure he'll have a good idea of what to do. What do you think?"

They waited. Margie wanted to start cleaning up, but again, Sonny discouraged her. Their wait ended soon; muffled footsteps at the back door drifted up through the windows. Margie's phone rang; she let the machine pick up, but when Luki's voice came through, she answered.

Having been told Luki was waiting, Sonny went back down the stairs, feeling repetitious, and this time unlocked the door. Luki ushered in two guilty-looking teens. They also looked scared, dirty, and hungry, but Sonny wasn't inclined to feel sorry for them. He took the wisest course he could think of and headed back up the stairs.

Twenty minutes later, maybe less, feet clambered up the stairs, and then Luki's muffled voice came through the door. "Marge, it's me."

Sonny didn't wait for Marge's direction. "Me" was not completely honest. Luki wasn't alone out there on the landing. He had brought those boys up with him and Sonny was leaning toward outrage. He hoped that reaction showed in his face as he swung the door open.

Luki, however, simply directed the teenagers to take off their filthy shoes and go sit on the kitchen chairs—recently vacated by Marge and Sonny. When he took his own shoes off as well, he looked at them and shook his head, presumably mourning their now filthy condition.

He turned around and faced Marge and Sonny, who stood in front of the desecrated wall. "They," he said, indicating the boys with a tilt of his head, "did that." He pointed at the wall. "They're going to fix it, do a lot of apologizing, and then I'm going to get them somewhere safe." Walking toward the kitchen, he ended with a question. "Do you mind, Marge, if I get us something cold to drink?"

Margie said, "Of course… oh, no, never mind that, Luki. Let me get it. I've got some nice, sweet, iced tea."

Despite her bustling, Sonny thought she seemed confused. Which was the way he felt. Or maybe flabbergasted. But if he was flabbergasted, it was in an unfriendly way, and he glared at the boys. It gratified him to see them hang their heads and shuffle their feet under the table.

Luki cut into his thoughts. "Mr. James, it would be good if you could stop glaring. They're scared of you."

Sonny thought of a number of responses, but what he said was, "Scared of me! I should think they'd be a little more scared of you."

"Yeah, they were." Luki walked across the room, sank down into an armchair, and ran his hands through his curls. "But they saw me puke. That tends to puncture the image."

Sonny looked back at him, incredulous. How could he be flip over something like this? He ignored the niggling little reminder from the depths of his brain that he was the one who could be, would be, deliberately flip about damn near anything. It was a survival skill. But now, this time, his rare temper began to ignite, his heart thumping a little harder, his breath coming a little faster. He opened his mouth, prepared to speak as soon as he found words for what he wanted to say.

Luki must have sensed what was coming because he snapped his eyes open and met Sonny's gaze. But instead of the anger or condescension Sonny expected, he found that the blue eyes had gone a little dim. They held only sadness, mild and perhaps a little weary.

Luki chewed softly on his bottom lip, then drew in a deep breath. "Sonny," he said. "We barely know each other, and you don't have any reason to listen to anything I say. But it would mean a lot if you could... trust me, maybe even work with me. I'll explain. Just not right now."

Their eyes locked, and Sonny felt silence take the room like snowfall.

Margie apparently could take only so much of that. She jumped in. "Well, of course we'll work with you, Luki. You just tell us what needs doing and..." She trailed off. No one was listening, not even the boys.

Sonny's eyes remained locked with Luki's. Finally he tipped his head in a slight nod. "Yes," he said, but the only sound was on the sibilant.

Luki smiled then, in the back of his eyes. Or at least Sonny thought so, and something happened; something comfortable lodged itself under Sonny's ribcage. Yet another surprise.

Luki redirected his gaze toward the table, and Sonny let his eyes follow. The youngest of the two guilty boys glanced up briefly. His eyes were full of fear but, just barely, they met Sonny's. Call it gaydar. Call it what you like. Sonny read that young man instantly. In light of that piece of information, considering the nature of the boy's crime, the situation made no sense at all. Sonny had agreed to trust Luki. He sincerely hoped the islander knew what he was doing.

He turned back toward the horrid wall. Reaching up to remove the hardware and the murdered remains of his tapestry, his gift to Margie, his hard and heart-born work, he shook his head.

His heart bleeding, he whispered, "But they can't fix this."

LUKI hated to see Sonny suffer the way he was. Hurt and anger hung on him like a thrift-store suit. When he took down the remnants of his work, he moved so stiffly that it seemed his spine might snap. He laid the hanger and its mournful threads gently in a corner and crouched beside it, chewing the back of a knuckle. Luki thought perhaps he understood a little. Not sure he should, he came to stand beside him and touched his back.

"I'm sorry, Sonny. It was beautiful."

Sonny stood up, all the stiffness gone, back to his usual grace. But his eyes, at first, said *what would you know about it*. He looked away and then back, and in that short instant, the message changed completely. Bereft. One more time he looked away, this time at the hate written all over the wall, and the anger that filled his eyes then held disbelief in equal measure. Luki wanted to comfort him, instinctively lifted his arms to hold him—not far different from the way he'd held Margie earlier to comfort her.

But Sonny said, "It's nothing." And walked away.

Margie apparently experienced a rush of motherly energy and bustled in the kitchen. To Luki's chagrin, when she was done feeding the boys and it was time for the repairs to begin, things only got worse for Sonny. He had painted the wall in the first place, and he was the only one who knew how to fix a wall, so he'd have to be the one to gather what was needed and teach the boys to do the job.

He prepared to go down to Margie's outside storage to get the leftover primer and paint, as well as the tools to apply it. He started out the door but must have realized he wouldn't have enough hands to bring it all in. He turned back, and Luki expected maybe he would ask for his help, but he scanned right past him.

He nodded toward Jackie. "You. Come with me."

The boy followed, but his face was flushed and slick with the sweat of fear, and Luki thought it might have been the bravest thing he'd ever seen. As he disappeared out the door, Josh started to go after him. Luki put an arm out to stop him.

"I'm not going to leave Jackie alone with that man!"

"He's not going to hurt him, Josh." Luki realized then that his own first reaction had been to protect Jackie, as well. He'd had to convince himself that Jackie was safe with Sonny. Nevertheless, he knew it to be true, knew he'd placed his trust in the right place.

"Of course he's not," Margie said. Her back was to them while she washed dishes, but she must have had the traditional eyes-in-the-back-of-the-head. "Luki Vasquez, I can understand this young man's worry for his brother, but I can't believe that look on your face." She turned around to give him something close in nature to the evil eye. "You *know* Sonny can be trusted!"

Luki did know that, had just got done thinking about knowing that, but he couldn't understand how Marge knew what he knew, and why she should think he must know Sonny could be trusted when clearly he and Sonny hardly knew each other. He scratched his head, then tried to rearrange his curls unobtrusively. Josh sat down rather hard in the chair he'd recently vacated, also looking a bit perplexed.

Luki said, "I'm going outside for a minute, Marge."

"You smoke too much."

Feeling entirely defeated, he said to Josh, "Stay here." Mostly just so he could feel in charge of something.

A few hours later, when the writing on the wall could no longer be seen, the mood in the room began to lighten. Not having to look at the word he hated more than any other in the world, Luki found himself watching as the repainting progressed. Sonny seemed to breathe easier as he taught the boys the way to get the paint evenly on the wall. He coached them naturally, as if teaching kids to paint was what he did every day, or as if teaching was in his nature.

Luki thought it beautiful.

Not much later, they made plans. Luki had decided to send the boys to his uncle, who still lived in Luki's childhood home in Nebraska. When he called, Kaholo didn't let him down.

"Hey, Mili," he said, using the nickname he'd given Luki when he was too young to remember.

"Hey, Uncle." Luki could see him clearly in his mind, a big man with gentle brown eyes, black, wavy hair—gray now—cut short, a smile forever in his voice. A man that Luki missed every day of the twenty years since he'd last seen him. "I need a favor. It's sort of a big one."

"Oh, anything, no problem. What do you need?"

"Can you put a couple of teenagers up for a while? Two boys, brothers. They're in a bit of trouble they don't deserve, I think. They need to be somewhere safe."

"Well, sure, that's not no big favor. Just give me the details and send 'em over."

SONNY felt better for a while with his attention fixed on teaching the boys to do things right. The calm state held while he covered Margie's broken window temporarily with plywood. But by the time they sat at the table to discuss Luki's battle plans in hush-hush tones while Josh and Jackie lounged in front of the TV in the next room, *sullen* had rolled over him like a steamship. When Margie went to take cookies and hot chocolate to the two young criminals, which reminded Sonny of Martha Stewart's prison stay, he turned to Luki with a challenge.

"You said you'd explain. Do that now."

Luki didn't use a lot of words, but the story came clear in Sonny's mind. Still, something had been left unsaid. One detail bothered him. "Jackie. He's afraid of me. He was afraid every time I picked up a tool in the shed. Why?"

With no more expression than he would have used to remark on the weather, hands on the table perfectly still, Luki said, "His father raped him."

Sonny answered in kind, ignoring completely the knife twisting in his gut. "Oh, yeah," he said. "I see." He got up to draw a glass of water from the tap. "You want some?"

"Yeah, that'd be good. Thanks."

"So your plan is…?"

"I'm concerned that this 'Mr. K' jerk can always find them. I'd like to try to confuse whoever's watching them, but I'm not sure how to do that. I thought maybe we could… We?"

"Yeah, 'we' is fine, for the time being. Go on."

"Maybe it'll be a little harder for them, whoever they are, to stay on the boys' trail if we put them on the train instead of a plane. Especially if we have that train bound, say, for Iowa instead of Nebraska, have the boys get off quietly at some podunk stop in South Dakota, and have Kaholo meet them there."

Sonny nodded slowly, hoping he looked thoughtful. It all seemed a little too James Bond to him.

"And I'll put some of my agents on the train with them, and some around Kaholo's place. I've already got some on the way here to keep an eye on Margie."

"You have agents."

"Yeah," Luki said. "That's why my business is called an agency."

"Oh. Yes, I see."

Luki opened his mouth to continue, but Sonny felt it was time to point out a glaring flaw. "But they, whoever they are, know the boys are here, no doubt. So all they have to do is follow them, or us, wherever we go."

"Yes. I haven't figured that part out yet."

"Maybe split them up."

"Pardon?"

"You take Jackie west down Hood Canal. I'll take Josh east across the floating bridge and the Narrows and head south on I-5. Have your… uh… *agents,* meet us separately at different places in Olympia. They can take them to the train station separately, like their parents, or something. You know, in disguise or whatever."

"We would call that undercover."

"It might not fool whoever's following them completely, but it might slow them down."

"Yeah," Luki said. "That's not a bad idea. I mean, if you don't mind helping."

"Sure. And send 'em to the Res. White Rock. I've got some people there. No love lost, really, but they'll get the boys off the train and meet up with your uncle. Won't hurt to have your agents there, too, I suppose. Undercover and all."

Silence slipped in. After a pause, Sonny chuckled and shook his head.

"Why are you shaking your head?"

"It's all pretty James Bond, eh?"

"Mm. Double-oh-seven, sitting right here."

"You never smile."

"No."

Sonny lifted his eyes from the table and looked at Luki to find Luki looking back at him. For the first time, they sat silently, looking each other straight in the eye, neither dropping his gaze or looking away. Though it seemed to stretch, it couldn't have lasted more than a minute. It ended when Margie came back to sit at the table, having seen to the young felons' comfort.

They made their plans, then. Sonny would wait with Marge and the boys while Luki ran back to his place to pick up a few things. Then Luki would come back and stay the night. After a morning filled with elusive maneuvers, they'd separately head south in the afternoon.

Sonny itched to get back, ridiculously hopeful that maybe Delsyn would be home, having snuck in just because Sonny had spent the last few hours thinking about something else. He didn't say that, of course, but when Luki got back, he stood quickly and headed for the door. "See you then."

"Give me five bucks," Luki said.

"What?"

"It's my fee. If you've hired me, I have a lot more freedom to work the case."

"Your fee is thousands of dollars, I'm quite sure."

"My fee is whatever I say it is. I'll get five bucks from you and five from Margie. Paid in full. Okay?"

Sonny dug three wrinkly dollars out of his pocket. "This is all I've got on me."

"Okay. Forty percent discount."

Money exchanged, they fell silent. But instead of stepping once more toward the door, Sonny stood leaning on the back of a chair, burning to ask a question.

"What?" Luki asked.

"The armory—are you going up to Bellingham to check it out?"

"You know the place?"

Sonny nodded, barely. Luki seemed to be waiting for more, but Sonny kept quiet. Finally, Luki said, "Day after tomorrow."

Chapter Three

"THANK heaven that's over," Luki said to his empty car as he eased off I-5 to Highway 101 on the way from Olympia, with its odd little train station, back to Port Clifton. He loaded a Smokey Robinson CD into the player, listened to the first sweet bars of "Quiet Storm," and settled in to think about all the things that didn't make sense about the whole incident, which he now thought of as *the James case.* Why he didn't call it *the Margie case*, or *the Cup 'O Gold case* he didn't know. He just didn't.

Cigarette, he thought. No, he'd stop for one up the road a bit, when he got out of Olympia.

Why, he wondered, *were those boys being followed? Why were they singled out for—*

His cell buzzed. Sonny.

"I'm broke down."

"Excuse me?"

"My truck. It quit."

"THAT truck is a piece of junk, Sonny." Luki didn't know why he said it. He hadn't minded going back for him. He liked having him there, relaxed and close, legs possibly a bit too long for true comfort in the Mercedes' passenger seat. And Luki could smell him. Clean sweat and a hint of soap, and something else that belonged to him.

Maybe I'm just pissy because I want a cigarette. But he wasn't about to stop for one. Smoking was a weakness—and he didn't want Sonny to see it. Mr. Robinson sang out from Luki's top-of-the-line speakers, "…power source, tender force… turn me on…." Luki reached over and switched it off, not sure why he suddenly didn't want to hear one of his favorite songs. "Can't you afford something nicer? Something more reliable?"

"It was my uncle's before he died."

That brought Luki down a little bit. He worried about Kaholo dying, sometimes. His uncle was his last link to a childhood ripped out of him way too early in the space of less than an hour. Sonny spoke again, brought him back to the moment.

"But yeah," he said, sounding a little annoyed—justifiably. "I do all right, money-wise."

"Your art sells?"

"For thousands, sometimes."

Luki thought of the size and beauty of the wall hanging that had been slashed to bits that afternoon. He hadn't even considered value. Had the crime upset him that badly, then, that he forgot everything he knew about his job? He sighed. "The one in Margie's house?"

"It was a gift."

"But if you'd sold it."

"Couple thousand, maybe."

Luki chewed his bottom lip, until he saw from the corner of his eye that Sonny was watching him. "Would you have preferred that we call the police?"

"Margie and I talked it over." Sonny somehow made that sound a little snide. "We decided to wait and see what you said. We trusted you."

He trusted me. A lump lodged itself in Luki's throat at the thought. He couldn't understand it. What was new? Hundreds of people had trusted him, had gladly put their decisions in his hands. He chewed his lip until he was sure he could keep the ice in his voice. "Do you want me to cover its value?"

Sonny snorted, apparently even more annoyed. "Luki, I said I have plenty of money. I don't need yours."

And Luki, to his own mortification, popped off: "So if you *want* to drive around in that rust bin, what *do* you spend your money on?"

"That's rather impertinent."

"I know." He smiled, mostly inside, at the schoolmarm sound of Sonny's retort. Still, he had it on the tip of his tongue to apologize when Sonny spoke up.

"Impertinent. Did I really just say impertinent?" He laughed out loud, which seemed like a special talent to Luki, who almost never did. "Anyway, I don't spend it, really. A few things I like, but mostly it just sits in the bank. But you've got money too. What do you spend it on?"

Luki held his tongue between his teeth, willing himself to keep his mouth shut.

"Besides nice cars," Sonny added.

And guns, Luki thought.

"And designer suits," Sonny observed.

And cigarettes, Luki thought, really wanting to smoke one. "That's it, for the most part." Words seemed determined to spill out against his will. "Except for buying what I need to do my job as best I can, I spend it on barbers and clothes and whatever I can buy to make it so I don't have to use up time looking in the mirror."

Crap! Why did I say that? At least he hadn't said *"look at my scar in the mirror."* He gave thanks that his scar was on the left side, where Sonny couldn't stare at it. Except that the man was scrutinizing him so thoroughly he could probably see clear through. Luki tried to remember exactly how Sonny had looked at him, that first moment on the street, when their eyes first locked. At the time, he'd felt he might have been dealt a miracle. Sonny didn't look at his scar—almost as if he didn't see it at all. Not counting children, everyone stared at his scar. And why shouldn't they?

It was ugly.

While he waited for Sonny to speak, Luki let his protective ice drop into place, habitual armor against threats to the heart. He tried to think ahead of Sonny, to anticipate anything he might say and plan how he might respond to save himself from one more wounding.

But Sonny turned away, saying nothing. He quietly rested his hand on the back of Luki's seat, and though unfamiliar, Luki recognized comfort. With not even a touch, Sonny's hand warmed him through like a crucible, where fear and attraction threatened to transform into something new. If that happened, he would have no idea what to do with it. Just like, at that moment, he had no idea what to say.

He was glad when the rain started coming down. Not a rare event at all in the region, but it made a moonless night darker and the road—which curved itself between rain forest and Hood Canal—treacherous. Hairpin turns and crazy drivers who obviously knew the road better than him, not to mention the odd log truck here and there. His skills were up to it, but conditions required his attention, and conversation ceased—thus Luki's relief. Sonny seemed content with silence too. That was good. If Luki were to allow friendship, it would have to be with someone who could be quiet.

Sonny broke that silence after a time, though, speaking softly. "There's a little store on the right hand side, up here not far. Right after you cross the Hama Hama. If you stop, I'll get us some coffee."

"Hama Hama?" It was, for Luki, close to making a joke. "And didn't we just pass a place called Liliput?"

"Yup," Sonny said chuckling.

Luki smiled, for real, not broadly, but enough to stretch his scar. Which didn't hurt, he noticed. And it surprised him how good it felt to make someone laugh. Could get to be a habit.

Like smoking, which he managed to do while Sonny was in the store getting coffee. He popped a mint and went to some lengths to brush the smoke smell away before coming out of the shadows to rejoin his graceful, long-limbed passenger.

Another hour and they made it to Jefferson County. But now Luki understood what Margie meant about forests and roads. He felt a little foolish, maybe selfish, when he realized that when Sonny had come into town just to have coffee with him, he'd driven at least an hour to get there. Maybe more, as there was a cut-off from the cut-off. The first cut-off had been narrow and completely hemmed in by second-growth firs. The second stage cut-off was gravel, and more pothole than roadbed. After a bouncing eternity, they pulled up in front of Sonny's home... rustic home. A charming cabin with a shed tacked on. Or perhaps the other way around.

Despite himself, Luki yawned.

Sonny opened the door, but he didn't move to get out. "It's a long drive, still, to Port Clifton."

"Yeah."

"You're tired."

"Oh yeah."

"You could sleep here."

Christ! Luki's heart threatened to break through his chest wall, shocked by the revelation, sudden insight, epiphany, that he had been waiting for that invitation, hoping for it.

Maybe Sonny took his silence for hesitation. He squirmed a bit, tightened his ponytail. "Look," he said. "Just sleep, if you want. There's an extra bed, a great couch; we can figure it out. I'd feel better if you weren't driving for another hour plus, over bad roads, alone, as tired as you are."

Luki had stopped listening at "if you want." He gave Sonny a long, cool look in the cruel light of the overhead lamp. He nodded. "But," he whispered, "what if I don't want?"

The words were scarcely louder than breath, and Sonny might easily have misunderstood, but he didn't. "I'm thinking we could figure that out too."

NOT twenty minutes after Sonny led Luki through his front door, the man was asleep. Sound, snoring asleep. Sonny came out of the bathroom after taking a quick shower and nervously brushing his teeth way too long, and found him sprawled on one side of the bed, fully dressed except that his belt had been loosened and his cufflinks dropped on the bedside table. Sonny felt complimented; he couldn't imagine Luki making himself so vulnerable just anywhere, with just anyone.

Except that Luki's left hand hung off the bed about a half inch from his gun, which lay loosened in its leather holster.

The man did *not* look comfortable. Beautiful, but not comfortable. From as far away as his long arms would allow, Sonny touched his shoulder, and when that got no result he shook it. Luki's eyes popped wide open, and Sonny leapt back. Luki didn't actually wake up, and soon his lids fell closed over the startling blue irises once more. Still, he looked damned uncomfortable.

Sonny couldn't do much about the clothes, but he thought he could at least take Luki's shoes off. Question was, could he do it without getting shot? A deep breath and he stepped forward to give it a whirl, on consideration deciding that even tired and sleepy, Luki was probably too good at his job ever to shoot someone without really meaning it. As carefully as he could, he lifted each foot, loosened the laces, and slid off the shoes to find—of course—designer socks.

"'anks," Luki mumbled.

Sonny jumped at the sound, smiled at his own foolishness, and grabbed a blanket from the foot of the bed. But he couldn't make himself climb in.

"Luki," he whispered. And nearly set off at a run when Luki's eyes snapped open again. They didn't blink, and they didn't follow Sonny when he moved. Once more, apparently, still asleep. Sonny took a chance anyway. "The gun makes me nervous."

To his surprise, Luki rolled slightly left and pushed the weapon under the bed, then rolled the rest of the way to lay on his left side, slightly curled. His long lashes brushed his cheek, and his eyes twitched under his lids, watchful in his dreams. Sonny, in turn, watched him. For a long time. Wondering how the islander had so quickly become dear to him. And annoying. They'd only kissed, and not even that, really.

Yet.

Sonny smiled, lay down, and snapped off the light. He pulled the light blanket over both of them, but kept a little bit of distance. Luki wasn't his to hold.

Yet.

THE clock had shown one a.m. when Sonny switched off the lamp. When he heard Luki knocking around the room, it said 4:35. He started to drift back to his dreams when he heard a clunk followed by an "ouch." He got out of bed to help Luki find a light and the bathroom. His house was like a maze, further confused by boxes of dyestuffs, bags of wool, swatches of silk, and skeins of fine gauge yarn. A stranger could get lost and never come out.

"Wait, Luki," he said. He crossed the room to switch on a nightlight, helped Luki find the right hall, and pointed him to the door. Luki almost disappeared into the room, but he turned back suddenly.

"Can I shower?"

Sonny smiled. "Of course."

Luki came out—damp curls framing his face, towel wrapped around and tucked at his waist, and the ultra-ice look back in his eyes. How could that kind of chill be a turn on? Sonny couldn't say but, bottom line, it was. He got up and walked over to Luki, but when he got close, he could only stand there, goose bumps running like winter over his skin. Luki stepped close and used Sonny's hair to pull him down to his lips, not rough treatment, but not to be refused. His kiss was long, soft, slow. Not, after all, the least bit cold.

Insistent, Luki guided Sonny back to sit on the bed, and then sat beside him and pulled him close. His kisses pushed and Sonny's pushed back. Their seeking hands roamed everywhere, following each other to share a touch, exploring alone. They tasted sweat, licked nipples into knots of pleasure, touched and tickled and teased. The exploration could have gone on all night.

But Luki's breath burned hot on Sonny's skin, their erections hard and close and touching. Their play was sweet, but Sonny didn't want to wait. As if he read Sonny's mind, or the change in his breath, Luki laid him down and stretched alongside him, ran his hands once more over Sonny's skin, kissing him hard. Sonny clung to him, kissing back, claiming Luki's lush, sweet mouth, giving himself in return.

The taste of Luki's mouth was so good, like sweet, hot spice; Sonny wanted more, had to have more. He pulled away and touched

Luki's lips, gasping a little when Luki, eyes locked on his, pulled his fingers into his mouth with a strong suck and licked them.

Sonny laid his length over Luki's body, buried his face in Luki's neck, kissed, licked, nipped, and then followed his strongest desire downward until he reached Luki's hard penis, glistening already with slick pre-cum.

He tasted. He savored. And then he feasted.

In the midst of gluttonous abandon, he looked up to find Luki's hooded gaze on him, his lips slightly parted, a sheen of sweat over his face and shoulders. He watched for a moment, Luki gazing back at him the whole time.

"Damn, Sonny," Luki breathed, and then took hold of his shoulders to pull him away, pull him toward him, pull Sonny's mouth into his. Sonny lay over him, still sucking at Luki's lips, breathless, nervous, beneath it all hoping that he hadn't been, wouldn't be, clumsy, wouldn't disappoint. When Luki pushed him back, he feared he'd already done just that. But Luki's breath came hard, sweat beaded on the fine, dark hairs that covered his upper lip. His eyes blazed—Sonny thought with desire, but behind that, impossibly, calculation.

Their loving suspended, Luki searched Sonny's eyes until Sonny felt he had not a secret left in the deepest fold of his brain. He knew that Luki read his limited experience. Though he'd kept it that way mostly on purpose, now he wished with his whole heart that he'd been a lush, a diva, a perfect slut.

After a moment, that not-quite smile of Luki's that Sonny had come to recognize appeared in his eyes. He laced his strong fingers into Sonny's hair and rose up to meet Sonny's lips in a long, soft kiss, keeping possession of his gaze all the while. "Sweet, so sweet," he whispered. And then, his lips still moving against Sonny's: "You can have my ass."

Chapter Four

NOT the kind of person to worry, Sonny put yesterday's crime and related events out of his mind, letting only sweet sex and the man he'd shared it with flicker through his thoughts. He concentrated on the sheen of dawn newly broken over the straits of Juan de Fuca. He never tired of the scene, every day unique, every morning a study in the possibilities of color and movement, light giving form to everything it touched. Sometimes he watched from the water's edge; sometimes he ducked nearly naked into the always-frigid water and emerged in a corona of jewel-colored waves.

This morning, he watched the unfolding day through his broad kitchen window, whistling low, and breathing in the heaven-sent smells of fresh coffee, hash browns, and sizzling bacon. He'd woken up curled around Luki, gazed down in awe of the man's beauty, and thanked whatever god or angel liked him enough to give him last night. He'd thought about waking his lover. Might he hope for an encore?

But his eyes had filled with other images and his fingers itched to make use of them. He rolled out of bed, warmed up a cup of yesterday's coffee, and padded in sweats and sandals to his studio at the back of the house, leaving all the doors open so Luki could find him if he woke. As always, his workspace housed multiple projects in various stages of completion, most rolled or protected by a canvas drape, but some bare to the light, lending their colors freely to the large, rectangular room. Sonny draped those now, even the one with the big sky colored like a northwest sunrise. He wanted, needed—or so it felt—to start this brand new project, and he didn't want the colors in his mind to be distracted by any other palette.

A little breathless, needing to bring order to his unbridled vision, he followed well-practiced steps to begin the task of housing the ephemeral in fiber and dye. He chose the loom he'd use and strung the weft with tough, colorless silk. All the while he thought about mixing dyes and testing yarns, determining a place to start in his search for precise colors, perfect textures. Before his vision faded, he made sketches. He created the subject from several angles to help him give the final tapestry depth and dimension. He added the backdrop, the light, and touched the paper with color.

His first flush of energy spent, the imperative to *begin* satisfied, he stepped back and took stock of what he had done. "It's decent work, Sonny," he whispered. He smiled and nodded, a habitual acknowledgement that could be called a self-directed pat on the back. He liked what he did. It wasn't a job. He breathed it.

But his coffee had gone cold. A new pot was in order, he thought. And while he was in the kitchen, why not breakfast? And so, now, the smells of coffee and bacon, dawn outside the kitchen window, and Sonny whistling while he worked.

Until Luki clomped past the long row of shelves and counters that served as Sonny's kitchen and stopped at the open door, clutching a Navajo blanket around his shoulders and wearing Sonny's unbuttoned jeans—too tight for his muscled cheeks and too long for his legs. Sonny stood two feet away, stalled in the act of cracking eggs, slack-jawed at Luki's appearance. Especially after Luki turned to face him, eyes apparently too bleary to bear their usual chill, with a cigarette dangling out of his mouth.

After an almost visible effort to summon the energy to raise his eyebrows, Luki rasped, "What are *you* looking at?"

It took Sonny a minute to see that Luki's eyes held something close to a sleepy smile, and—weak as it was—a minute longer to get the private joke. He smiled back. "Coffee," he said, not a question, and poured a cup.

"God, yes," Luki sighed, not exactly a thank you, and pushed open the screen.

Sonny called out to his retreating back, "Will you eat?"

"I always eat," he answered, already mincing his bare feet through the sand and sedge that made up Sonny's front yard. A sizeable drift log sat cattycorner to the house, a hundred yards or so closer to the straits. When Luki first reached it, he sat hunched in the blanket looking strangely sad and vulnerable, even timid. After a time, though he kept the blanket, he began to look more awake. Sonny saw a brief flame, and then white smoke drifting downwind in a loose-knit cloud.

A twinge of apprehension troubled Sonny, though he couldn't have named the reason. He did his best to ignore it, called up courage and, with breakfast holding in a warm oven, wiped his hands on a dishtowel and took his own coffee out to sit beside Luki—upwind of the smoke.

He started to sit, but Luki held his hand out, pushing against his hip.

"Wait." He drew his pistol from the waistband of his borrowed jeans.

Sonny's heart beat inordinately hard, but all Luki did was lay the gun beside him on the other side, lay the blanket down, and pat the log. Sonny took that as his cue, and sat. "You smoke," he said, and then congratulated himself for brilliance.

"Yup, cigarettes," Luki said, sounding almost angry and grinding out the remains of his latest in a pool of sand caught in a knothole.

Something was happening that Sonny didn't understand, but instead of pursuing it he pretended he didn't notice. He tried for a change of subject. "You brought your gun."

"I always bring my gun."

"You seem... tense."

"I'm always tense."

"Oh, well yes," Sonny snapped. "You always eat, you always bring your gun, and you're always tense. Do you always treat people you just slept with as if you wished they'd disappear? Usually act like the person whose bed you just crawled out of is worth less than the cost of your attention, worth less than guns, less, for God's sake, than your freaking cigarettes?"

Luki tensed, his fists opened and closed, which possibly should have made Sonny nervous, but he felt pretty sure that if Luki were about to commit violence, he wouldn't signal in advance. But Luki still didn't look at him, and when he spoke, his voice sounded as if he could barely squeeze it past a rock in his throat.

"I don't wish you'd disappear," he said. "And there is no usually."

"What do you mean, there is no usually?

"I mean," he answered, spacing the words apart like he resented every one, "that there aren't people I just slept with, and I don't crawl out of people's beds. I mean that I've never before slept the night in someone's bed and no one has slept in mine. I sleep alone and where I'm—"

Sonny waited. When the next word failed to come, he asked, "Where you're what?"

"Never mind…. And when someone wants me, and I decide to let it happen, I keep my gun where I could reach it before they could, and maybe another weapon. And I never get so caught up in the moment that I lose my grasp on the skills that make me a weapon. If the person I've decided to have sex with doesn't like that, they don't have me. In any way."

It seemed like a very difficult set of words to respond to. Perhaps, Sonny thought, he should just get up and go back into the house. Throw Luki's designer shoes, etc., out the door and lock it. But he would be the first to admit, he never knew when to leave well enough alone, and besides, he'd made breakfast. "Last night when I told you the gun bothered me, you pushed it away."

"My point exactly."

"Damn, Luki!" The shout leapt from Sonny's mouth without permission, but once it was out there he realized that all he wanted to do was finish the sentiment. "To hell with it."

He was already walking away.

LUKI took the last drag off his second cigarette, collected his butts, and began to walk toward Sonny's home. Last night, it had seemed like a run-down shack. Then it had seemed like shelter—a foolish idea for Luki Mililani Vasquez. Now he dreaded going in, feared that it would draw him in with its charms and never let him go. But he kept walking, knowing that what must be done, must be done, and hoping he'd find some way to take leave from Sonny and at the same time undo the pain he'd already caused.

Sonny had left the door open, and when Luki walked through, he found him standing in the kitchen, glaring at him. Luki looked directly at his companion for the first time since he'd left the house. "What about your truck, Sonny?"

"To hell with my truck! I can get my truck. What about the armory?"

Luki looked away again. *I need another cigarette*, he thought, not at all understanding why he didn't want Sonny to know that, why it had mattered in the first place, especially why he still cared, when obviously this thing between them, which hadn't even really started, was over. "I take it," he said, not directly answering Sonny's question, "that it's not just *my* cell phone that doesn't work out here?"

"No. No coverage. Low-tech, low class, but I make do."

God, Sonny. Cut me just the tiniest bit of slack. But then, why would he? Luki had never meant to be cruel, but he had been. Somehow, the sex last night plus the cut this morning added up to betrayal, and if there was anything Luki knew, it was just how that felt. He was sorry, wanted to apologize, might have gone down on his knees to plead forgiveness if he didn't think it would make things worse in the end. Because he couldn't hang around. He couldn't let this thing develop—whatever it would have been. His guard would slip. He'd be lost.

"Then can I use your phone? I have to check on Margie," he said, keeping his voice flat, letting it chill. "And the boys. They won't be at Kaholo's yet, but they were supposed to call my cell. I'm hoping they left a message." *Because, you see,* he added silently, *I care about people, Sonny.*

"For the life of me, I can't figure out why you care."

"Of course I care! I'm a jackass, not a monster." He looked away, bewildered. It hadn't taken even a minute for him to lose control of the situation—of his own mouth, even.

"Eat," Sonny said, dropping a plate in front of him on the oak countertop. "Maybe it'll help you feel better."

He wanted to shout: *I feel freakin' fine!* But when Sonny filled his cup with hot coffee he only said "Thanks." He probably couldn't have eaten, even though he felt like he might starve, if Sonny had not set his own plate a little ways down and across the bar and sat down to join him. Once he started, he dug in with nearly his usual level of gusto, communicating with Sonny only to pass the butter, trade the pepper for the salt, and share the Tabasco. Just as he ate the last of his potatoes, Sonny slipped another egg out of the pan and onto his plate, rolled on a few sausages, and filled the empty spots with more potatoes.

"Thanks," Luki said when his plate was clean. "It was good. And yeah, I do feel better."

"I'm glad."

"So, I started to say earlier, after I make sure everybody's okay, I'm going to put out some feelers, set some things up. Then after I stop by my place, I'm going to Bellingham. To the armory." *And smoke cigarettes all the way.*

"I'm going."

"No."

"Yes, I'm going."

"You can't."

"You can't stop me!"

Luki *could*, technically, stop him, though it might be ugly, and he was sure Sonny knew that. What he was probably betting on was that Luki *wouldn't* stop him, if push came to shove. And he was right. Luki hoped he could bluff.

"Luki, whatever you think about me, however sorry you are for… *sleeping in my bed…* last night, you can't push me out of this. That was my work cut to shreds yesterday. Doesn't it seem likely that when the writing on the wall said 'faggot' it meant me?"

It did seem likely, though something about that didn't jive, something Luki hadn't quite been able to put his finger on. Probably because his preoccupation with Sonny, *and thus with sex and cigarettes,* muddled his brain to the point he couldn't even do his job. But he *wanted* to do it well, which was—

"Why, Luki?"

"Because my being a jackass doesn't mean I don't care!" *Oh, great, Luki. There you go again—extract heart, slap on sleeve.* "Because I don't quite understand this crime, and that means I have no idea how dangerous it will be, and I don't want... I don't want you hurt, Sonny. Think what you will, I want you safe."

THE Keystone ferry dock, which would have dropped them at Everett, was not in service. *Damn it!* So, Luki ventured south, with Sonny feeding him directions. All of which seemed to point him in the wrong direction, since he wanted to go north. He wondered how people who lived in the state full time could stand it.

"Take 20 east," Sonny said, "south on 101 for a short time, then south... or maybe it's west, on 104. Take the floating bridge over Hood Canal...."

Blah, blah, blah. Luki kept his ice-cold face in place and drove where Sonny pointed him until they got to the Kingston ferry dock, where he learned smoking was *against the law* on the ferry. At Edmonds, they picked up I-5 and finally, *finally,* headed north.

"At least," Sonny said, "we're north of Seattle. You won't have to drive through downtown."

Blah, blah, blah.

"Too fast."

"I'm going four miles over the speed limit."

"Not your driving. Last night."

"It was a long day." Luki's voice scratched like it was dragging over shoals, worse than usual, and he shoved his free hand through his curls, for the moment too weary to care that they wouldn't fall just right. He kept himself fit and healthy—if you didn't count an occasional cigarette—and for the most part he felt young, even younger than he was. Days like today, he felt his age plus decades. He wondered if Sonny would have something to say about it. He seemed to have something to say about most everything.

And, sure enough…

"How old are you?"

Luki smiled despite himself, though he knew the expression would be invisible to anyone who didn't know him well. "How old are you?"

"I asked first."

Luki sighed, shook his head, and gave in. "Yes. Yes you did. I'm forty-one."

Sonny didn't look surprised. Luki found that annoying.

"Twenty-nine," Sonny said.

"Baby."

"Old man."

Luki spared Sonny a quick glance, only the second time their eyes had met since Luki passed through the kitchen door that morning on his way out for a cigarette and an argument.

The moment, precious as it was, passed. A brief silence followed, during which time Luki concentrated on navigating around a slow-moving motor home and avoiding being the unwilling cause of death for a young motorcyclist weaving through seventy-mile-per-hour traffic as if it stood still. But Sonny had more to say.

"It might explain some things."

Luki, still annoyed and wondering if Sonny thought forty-one should be the age of mandatory retirement, nevertheless had to concede he had a point. "Might," he said.

Quiet reigned again, while Luki begrudgingly slowed the Mercedes through Everett and Monroe. Speeding up again on open road, almost a straight shot through almond orchards and across boat-filled sloughs before a rise took them over the languid Stillaguamish River.

"Stillaguamish," Luki said, reading the road signs.

"Yup." A brief smile. "And up here a ways you'll see Tulalip."

"Heavens. I'll be on the look out."

"And down south you'd see Skookumchuck, and Chehalis, and on the coast Quileute."

Luki said, "They're pretty names, though, aren't they?" *What am I talking about! The man is going to think I've taken leave of my senses.* But his mouth pressed on, ignoring his brain completely. "I mean, some of them roll right off the tongue, have a rhythm, you know?"

He felt a little breathless after saying that, as if he'd stepped out on a crumbling bridge. He felt Sonny's eyes on him, but when he stole an instant from the road to glance at him, Sonny's eyes only held surprise.

"Yeah," Sonny said very quietly. "They are. They do."

Otherwise setting his features into his deliberately habitual freeze, Luki chewed softly at his bottom lip, once again considering his options. He could *light up a cigarette,* even though he still didn't want Sonny watching him smoke, and he never, ever, *ever* smoked in the car. Or, he could drive on while his nerves sizzled to crispy fragments. Or, he could reach over and somehow, in some way, touch the man sitting not two feet away. *The choice could very well kill me all on its own,* he thought, only kidding a little bit.

Sonny took the decision out of his hands. "Except Liliput," he laughed. "I've never been able to get behind that one."

Luki let an almost silent chuckle slip past his lips and took a deep and grateful breath. Sonny reached his hand halfway across the distance between them and turned it palm up. An invitation. Luki took it, and their fingers entwined, and it felt so comfortable that he didn't even wish for a cigarette. And when they disengaged because he needed to shift gears, it didn't feel awkward at all.

"Stop here?" Sonny asked, when they approached a rest stop north of Tulalip.

Cigarette, Luki thought, and steered the car off the freeway.

BACK on the road, they didn't touch again, but the silence between them had a more companionable tone. Still, Luki could feel Sonny's nervousness. It wasn't hard to do—Sonny, he observed, was a fidgeter. He chewed his lip and then chose to break the silence, *just because,* which was something he almost never did. He observed, "Chuckanut."

Sonny's laugh bubbled.

Bubbled, Luki thought, shaking his head. *What am I becoming?*

When Sonny's laugh was done bubbling, he said, "Yup. Chuckanut. That's a good one, eh? But hey, what about your name— Hawaiian? Or is it like Saint Luke but fondly."

"Neither," Luki answered. "Basque, as my last name might suggest." It wasn't the first time he'd been asked, but his annoyed tone wasn't sincere, and he could tell Sonny knew that. "I was named after my father's grandfather. 'Luki' means—" He stopped to look quickly over the top of his shades at Sonny, drawing another smile, this time deliberately.

"Yes?"

"Famous warrior."

"No."

"Yes. But I do have a Hawaiian name. My mother gave me my middle name. Mililani."

"What does that mean, man with gun?"

"Smart ass. No, you'll like this even better. Heavenly embrace."

"Ah," Sonny said. "That is perfect."

He wasn't joking, Luki realized, and it made him a little self-conscious. *Cigarette,* he thought, even though he'd just had one. Which annoyed him because he never smoked this much before he'd met Sonny. It was like Sonny was a big, man-shaped, flashing, neon sign that said "SMOKE HERE NOW." He shook his head and tried to take his mind off it with a question of his own. "And how'd you get to be called Sonny?"

"It's from Son, which is supposed to mean star in some native language." Smiling, he added, "But really my mom picked it out of a baby name book. And Bly means high—same story."

Sonny laughed again, which Luki rather enjoyed. *If I could find a way to inhale that,* he thought, *it might work better than cigarettes. But until then....*

"But Mom meant well," Sonny added. "And at least they sort of go together."

"And they fit—the meanings fit you.... Well at least the star part. I don't know about the..." *Babbling!*

"If you say so," Sonny said, just as if Luki had made perfect sense.

Silence took hold again, more or less easy, and Sonny eventually dozed. Luki smiled, thinking about why Sonny didn't get enough sleep last night. But his head rested on the window, and every time they hit the smallest bump, his skull knocked against the glass. Luki felt an unaccustomed—and not altogether welcome—tenderness and managed to reach across and behind Sonny and his seat belt to stuff his own tailored jacket between the glass and Sonny's head.

He hoped Sonny didn't drool and in almost the same instant wondered if he should go ahead and light a cigarette. He decided to think about the case he was working instead, which he'd done far too little of since last night. And it needed thinking about. Something just didn't quite fit, and it was probably staring him in the face.

What did he know? A tapestry—made by Sonny, a gay... wonderfully gay man, given as a gift to Margie, a talkative... very talkative and caring woman who runs a coffee shop. A man with one, a lot of bling; two, an old rundown van; and three, a soul that should surely rot in hell, goes by the name 'Mr. K'; he coerced two innocent... painfully innocent boys to desecrate the woman's home and the artist's work.

What the hell? What sense did it make? *Would it make more sense if I smoked a cigarette?* Maybe, but he'd probably never find out. He settled for chewing his lip instead.

The question was, why there? As Sonny had pointed out, the "F" word painted all over the wall did seem to be aimed at him. But Luki would bet gold bricks that Sonny had work hanging in large, open venues—galleries and public spaces. So, if the aim was to hurt Sonny, why order the invasion of a tiny home and commit the crime where nobody would ever see it? Why…?

Oh, hell. Hopefully it'll make more sense after I see what's up at this armory building, maybe get hold of the creep.

He dropped an Etta James CD into the player, turned it down low, and tried not to think about why Etta's sultry tones singing "At last, my love has come along" sounded so much better than usual. *Maybe having someone else in the car changes the acoustics….*

STUCK in a blackberry bramble in front of the locked and probably molded shut basement entrance to the armory, which Sonny had assured him was always open and the best way to sneak in, Luki paused for breath and turned to look at his equally stuck companion.

"Remind me," he said, "how I ended up bringing you along."

"I appealed to your softer side."

Luki used the cover of dark night to secretly roll his eyes. Although he knew he was on shaky ground after his extraordinary behavior over the last few days, he decided to try to play it off. "What makes you think I have a softer side?"

"Because," Sonny said, embracing the cliché, "I appealed to it, and I'm here."

Luki sighed. A million thorns had wormed into his shoes, under his arms, even into his curls. He could move neither forward nor backward without shredding most of his clothing and some of his skin. And his cigarettes, damn it, were *a block away in the car.*

"Wait," Sonny said, alleging that he had greater experience with Northwest style brambles. "Hold on a sec and I'll help you."

Looking the other way while Sonny began to disengage him thorn by thorn, Luki gave thanks for the dark. He refused to think about how ridiculous he would look if seen. Great clothes. Perfect hair. Stressed out, scar-faced, frustrated smoker, gun-toting security agent and general badass standing waist deep in blackberry vines while an artist rescued him from thorns.

"Ooph," Sonny said and stumbled backward. A series of exclamations followed, accompanied by rattling vines and scrabbling hands and feet.

Then: "Shit, what was that?"

Feet thumped hard on concrete. A muffled cry. And what sounded—to Luki's unfortunately practiced ear—like a body slumping against a wall.

Fueled by adrenaline, Luki freed himself from the vines in zero seconds—not at all sure how he'd done it. A short but steep slope gave way from blackberries to ancient ivy and ended in a low sandstone wall. Beyond that wall was a three-foot square landing in a down stairwell, probably leading to the famed basement door.

Luki shone his penlight—its size deceiving, as it cast a generous circle of light— and saw Sonny crumpled in the corner.

He jumped down to help him to his feet. Sonny accepted the help, and that surprised him. "Are you all right?"

"I suppose I will be. Stop shining that in my eyes."

"Sorry," Luki said, though he'd been shining it in his eyes on purpose, looking for signs of head injury. He didn't find any, but as the beam descended, he saw blood. On Sonny's arm and hand. On the stone where he'd fallen against the wall. On his shirt.

"Turn around, Sonny," he ordered after he had him fairly steady on his feet.

Sonny didn't turn around. He saw the blood, and said, "It's not serious."

By the time Luki argued him into letting him look at the wound, blood seemed to be everywhere. "What did you cut yourself on?"

"I don't know. You're the detective."

Luki rolled his eyes, an act he felt quite free to exaggerate under the circumstances. He shone the light around on the ground, the stone walls, even down the next flight—though that revealed nothing more than the first few steps. He couldn't see anything that might have caused a cut that would bleed like that. Something didn't make sense. Again. He thought maybe it was something cosmic—maybe things that happened around Sonny never made sense.

"Sonny," he asked, "what made you fall?"

"I just tripped, I guess."

Luki didn't like the feel of this event, was itching to investigate, but Sonny was bleeding. He turned the light back toward the wound and leaned in to take a closer look. Whatever had made the cut had bitten deep and left a ragged edge. The wound bled but didn't gush. Not immediately life threatening, but when Luki used the flashlight's beam to probe the cut, he was pretty sure he saw something shiny lodged inside. In any case, it needed cleaning and stitches, more than a few.

"Damn, Sonny."

"I know. I don't know what possessed you to let me come along."

Sonny's smart mouth remained intact, obviously, but he looked a little shaky. In fact, he wrapped his arms around his chest and started to shiver. Not a good sign. Probably shock at this point, rather than blood loss. Luki guessed that when the shock wore off Sonny would be in more than a little pain.

That happened sooner rather than later. Weighing the risks, Luki decided not to let him sit here and wait for Medic One, but instead took him—mostly against his will—back to the car. He fetched a towel and a blanket out of the trunk, laid the seat back and got him settled in, and then wadded the towel against the wound and had him turn sideways to keep pressure on it, hoping that wouldn't drive the foreign object deeper. The blanket he draped over Sonny for warmth; he clutched it but still shivered. Luki sighed, pushed a strand of Sonny's long hair back out of his face with more tenderness than he knew he owned, and he would have leaned in to kiss his cheek. Except, as usual…

"Give me a minute," he sighed and stepped away a few yards. He concentrated on deep breaths, which he knew was stupid because it never helped, and then he retched. *Damn it.*

He spit twice, lit a cigarette and took three quick drags on the way back to the car, put it out and popped two tiny, supercharged breath mints. He started the car and took an appraising look at Sonny.

Sonny tried to smile. "Puking punctures your tough-guy image."

"Yeah," Luki said. "Are you up to answering one more question?"

"Mm."

"Did that cut happen on your way down the hillside—"

"No," Sonny interjected, much more emphatically than Luki expected. "I'd already landed on the stairs."

Implications, Luki thought. He'd have to sort them out, but not now. He looked at Sonny again, and his mouth went dry. "Hospital?"

"No."

"I'm not asking for your preference. I'm asking for a name. Maybe directions."

"St. Joe's. Squalicum Parkway. You'll see the signs."

Which response, devoid of argument and sarcasm, let Luki know how much hurt Sonny was trying to hide. He hadn't a clue where Squalicum Parkway was, so he consulted his GPS, put the car in gear, and eased as gently as possible off the shoulder and onto the road. When they got down the steep hills to the parkway and he no longer had to shift every hundred yards, he reached out and took hold of Sonny's hand. He gave it a squeeze for comfort. Sonny squeezed back, hard.

Luki wasn't sure what that meant, but he didn't let go.

BELLINGHAM seemed like a small city, but it had a good-sized hospital, a fact for which Luki felt grateful. Sonny's check in went smoothly if you didn't count a belligerent drunk crashing into him in the hallway and a forty-five minute wait that would have been longer if Luki hadn't quietly influenced the process.

Then the paperwork started, which incidentally gave Luki an opportunity to learn some things about Sonny. One, he'd been born in Frankfort AM, (West Germany), was a US citizen by birth, and was an enrolled member of the Confederated Tribes of the Yakama Nation. Two, his next of kin was Delsyn James, a nephew, which suggested that no members of his immediate family survived. Three, he named Margie as his emergency contact, so Delsyn must either be a child or not available. Or both. Four, when they said they preferred to have two contacts, Sonny shook his head.

Luki thought perhaps he should offer, and that thought surprised the hell out of him. Still, he leaned forward to whisper his offer in Sonny's ear.

Sonny might have been feeling unusually vulnerable. He smiled and started to shake his head. But then he turned to meet Luki's eyes; after a moment he nodded "yes" instead. Luki gave his information, not sure why it made him feel good to do this, like it washed away some wrong or another. Sonny started to shake again as he signed consent forms releasing the hospital to share information with him or Margie. Luki squeezed his lover's shoulder, hoping to reassure him. And then, notwithstanding the sex of the night before, he wondered when he'd begun to think of Sonny as his lover. And why.

LUKI'S hatred of hospitals, he knew, stemmed from fear. Possibly it *was* fear, thinly disguised, the product of a single incident a long time ago. If it had been anyone else needing medical care, he would have left them there, gone somewhere a good distance from the facility for a hot meal, and come back to pick the unlucky patient up at curbside. What was different when it was Sonny?

He gave up thinking about it and sat next to Sonny, leaning forward, elbows on his knees and trying hard to maintain his cool facade.

After another hour of bleeding, Sonny's name was called for his turn with the professional staff. It came just in time. Luki had already brought the staff's attention to the facts that one, Sonny was having such pain that he was sweating, and two, Sonny was still losing blood; by now his lips had gone almost blue. He was just about to make his point in a much stronger way, which very well might get him jailed but almost certainly would also get Sonny the attention he needed.

Nice that such extreme measures wouldn't be necessary. Sonny had remained conscious and was not voluntarily giving up Luki's hand. For the last hour, Luki had passed up the opportunity to smoke in order to let Sonny hold on to him, for whatever reassurance that provided. Yes, he found his own behavior alarming.

He kept hearing his own words: *I'm a jackass, not a monster.* Maybe it was true, after all. Perish the thought.

By the time his turn came, Sonny could barely stand on his own, never mind walk, and even Luki didn't think it would be wise to drag or carry him, so he advised the apparently blind nurse that a wheelchair might be in order. Another five minutes, then, while they waited for Sonny's ride. Luki bent once more to Sonny's ear.

"Do you want me to go back there with you?"

Sonny's answer, spoken between labored breaths, was a question. "Are you offering or hoping I'll say no?"

Why did that hurt? Luki chewed his lip for maybe two seconds. "I wouldn't have asked if I wasn't offering."

Apparently Sonny would find a way to be a smart-ass even to his last breath, when that time came. As if he had heard Luki's thoughts, he threw the words at him. "You're a jackass, Luki, not a monster." Then, before Luki had a chance to respond, or possibly retaliate, he said, "Yes, stay with me. I don't like to admit it, but this scares me a bit."

What Luki didn't like to admit was that the tenderness that overcame him upon hearing Sonny's response scared *him*, more than a bit. At that point, staying with Sonny ranked as the number one bravest thing he'd ever done. But once he committed himself to the idea, he defended his position fiercely. When a nurse's aide hinted none too subtly that he should leave, Luki treated him to a frightening icy glare. From the expression on the man's face, he hadn't lost his touch. Luki stayed right where he was, bedside.

They removed the metal shard, which apparently hurt like the fires of hell despite the anesthetic they'd applied and the morphine they'd started in Sonny's IV drip. The bleeding increased from an ooze to a flow, but not—thankfully—to a pulsing gush.

Irrigations. Gauze. Two units of packed red cells. Sonny's face looked much less corpse-like. Morphine killed the pain, mostly, but left him nauseous. Which meant more drugs, which meant Sonny should have been sleeping the sleep of the thoroughly loaded, but he wasn't. He nodded off now and then, but he could still argue.

"No," he said, a simple response to the doctor's statement that they would get an abdominal CT to make sure no veins or organs had been nicked.

She said, "Mr. James, if—"

"No."

The doctor gave Luki a pleading look, apparently thinking he might have some pull with her patient. "Sonny," he started, "it's not go—"

"No."

Sonny snored for a few seconds, during which the doctor and Luki shared an exasperated look. But when Sonny's eyes fluttered open he asked, "What, Luki?"

"Let 'em do the damned CT."

"Okay."

Luki had been right. The pictures didn't take long. When it was over, it was time for stitching, which took longer, required more people than Luki would have guessed, and turned out to be grueling. For him, not Sonny. Sonny seemed mostly happy now, when he was awake. Apparently, however, the cut had been deep enough to snag a muscle— the lattisimus dorsi, Luki knew, as it was something he habitually worked out. Fortunately, only an inch or so of the broad muscle had been injured, and only a top layer of fiber.

Three sets of stitches. An hour of observation. Luki's head filled with a bewildering list of instructions and cautions. Sonny released in his care. *In my care!*

The wound, they said, should heal quickly as long as it wasn't reopened. The drugs would wear off, but they prescribed pain medications along with antibiotics. Luki thought it unlikely that Sonny would swallow narcotics after the first twenty-four hours. He wasn't sure how he'd come to know Sonny well enough to make that judgment.

He felt out of his depth—with emotions, with medical instructions, and with the whole idea of taking care of another human being in any way except to keep them from harm by violence. Knowing Sonny would be miserable trying to endure a three-hour ride home—

and he still hoped to check out the armory before the trail cooled beyond benefit—he stepped out to call a hotel. But before he left the room, he gazed fondly at Sonny and smoothed the younger man's hair back, then unabashedly planted a kiss on his forehead.

What am I doing?

Feeling he needed some practice at his usual impersonation of an icicle, he glared at everyone he came across on the way out to the car where he'd *unbelievably* left his cell phone. Except for a child in a wheelchair. He smiled at her, and she smiled back. Children never saw his scar.

Chapter Five

FAGGOT.

In red crayon, capital letters, written three times on the passenger-side window of Luki's ice-blue Mercedes. His personal ice shield dropped in place immediately as he scanned the parking lot. He shook with anger and fear and devastation, but only inside.

No one in sight looked to be a possible culprit, but when he looked for clues, he found a half-smashed hypodermic and a scratch on the door, possibly where someone tried to catch the syringe as it fell. He produced from the inside pocket of his jacket a small baggie with cotton swabs and a few other items, paraphernalia of his occupation. He shook out a swab and bent to soak up some of the liquid still pooled in a curve of the plastic syringe, then brought it to his nose for a quick sniff.

Heroin.

Cigarette, Luki thought, and made good on the idea.

He took off his jacket and laid it on the hood, took off his shirt and with angry vigor used it to clean the offending word from the window. It left a ghostly impression in grease. He felt like crying. He didn't.

When he pulled the car up to the hospital entry, he saw the nurse's face, knew she registered the telltale remnant of the cursed word, and hated her for seeing it. Irrational. He didn't care.

He stayed silent as they drove away.

After a minute, Sonny said, "I see it, you know."

"Yeah."

"You're pissed. You're beyond pissed."

"Oh yeah."

"Not me, so much. Maybe it's the drugs. Or maybe I'm scared instead. It can't be coincidence. Somebody is… following me?"

They'd come to the traffic light on the corner of Samish Way and Bill McDonald Boulevard, which could vie for first place as the longest red light in the world. Luki took the opportunity to glare at Sonny, really hating the fact that something as frivolous and dangerous as compassion could cut into his well-justified, cold anger.

"*You're* scaring me now, Luki."

"You're scared of me?" Luki had spent most of his life cultivating a look and manner that would scare people, but now, even though he'd thrown that look out there, the idea hurt. He waited for Sonny's answer, praying for something that wouldn't cut too deep.

"Scared *for* you," Sonny said, his head lolling against the back of the seat. Fading, he said it again, "Not of you, Luki, for you."

Some time passed, once more in silence. Then Sonny moaned and said, clearly doped to the hilt, "I think I'm going to be sick, but it's okay."

As snores followed the announcement almost immediately, Luki only smiled. Which did worry him a bit. Since when did anyone over the age of seven make him smile? But Sonny did, way too often. Made him want to smile and made him want to smoke. He wasn't sure either one of those things was good for him, wasn't sure Sonny was good for him at all.

But regardless, he wanted Sonny safe. It ate away at him that he seemed to be failing at that—the one task at which he was supremely capable. Of all the people he'd watched over, why must it be Sonny that he couldn't keep from harm?

Driving down the hill into Old Fairhaven, a place full of small shops and cafes that must be charming during the day but was all dark at midnight, he patted his pocket for smokes. He had enough to last, even with Sonny around.

The hotel loomed square and solid on the corner, flush up against the sidewalks. Luki counted five stories up and secured underground parking. That was why he'd chosen it. He'd asked for a room on the fifth floor and VIP parking, which, of course, he got. He felt a little calmer—some things perhaps were going right.

At the final red light, he glanced over at Sonny, taking in the sight of him with unaccustomed familiarity and a warmth that he might have to call fondness. But as the light changed and he turned his eyes back to the road, he caught a glimpse also of the window, the moving light revealing and hiding the words like apparitions. Shades of hate.

This far into the night, no valet waited, so Luki parked the car himself. He shut down the engine and sat in the silence and looked again at those pale ghosts. "I'll find him, Sonny," he whispered. "I'll find him."

SONNY heard Luki say it, though he didn't let on. *"I'll find him."* Something about the words, or maybe more the way Luki said them, helped. Sonny had begun to feel wobbly—and not from the pain meds. Fear had sprouted yesterday from the ruin of his work, the desecration of Margie's home. It had doubled, maybe tripled, when he'd come out of the hospital and seen the remnant—still visible after a diligent effort at removal—of the same hateful word scrawled on the car window.

He'd been feeling out of his element, like a sailor on a horse ranch. Sonny Bly James may have had a rough start in life, but now he played with yarn, he watched the sky, he didn't own a television, he lived where cell phones went silent and seagulls wouldn't shut up. He kept to himself, mostly, and when he did stick his head up into everybody else's world, he did it with a smile. He might skim through life mostly unattached—except for Delsyn—but he didn't run over people, and it had been long years since he'd left enemies in his wake.

He wasn't used to being the target of anybody's anger, let alone hate.

Being with Luki helped.

What was it that made him feel close to a man he'd known less than two weeks? Besides sharing one amazing night of sex. *He slept in my bed.* Sonny hadn't known then what an extraordinary event that was, but he understood now. They hadn't known each other long, but the last couple of days and nights they'd shared had been far from usual, filled with every emotion from fear and anger to compassion and companionship, all with passionate highlights. Under those circumstances, he knew, people showed what they would and could usually hide.

Sonny excelled at observation. He didn't miss the way Luki smiled underneath his mask. That he feared friendship more than he feared enmity. That he wanted it, cried out silently for it, anyway. That Luki wanted him, and not only in his bed—or some bed. But, all that said, Luki seemed to be armed to the teeth even when he wasn't armed at all, and Sonny had never seen anyone so at home with the idea of defensive violence.

So when Luki said he'd find the hater, Sonny knew he would.

And when he said, *"I want you safe,"* Sonny believed he could make it happen.

GETTING Sonny from the car to the elevator to the room turned out to be much easier than Luki expected. Sonny's nap apparently had cleared his head of a few opiate cobwebs. Propping him up from time to time got complicated, as Luki carried assorted weapons as well as the bag he always kept in the trunk with fresh clothes and hair conditioner.

Fortunately, Sonny walked alongside him, for the most part self-propelled, though he did look a bit comical. Tall, lanky people on drugs seem to have more arms and legs than they can safely use.

"Just lean on the wall for a minute," Luki said, jiggling the key card in hopes of making it work.

Sonny guffawed—yes, guffawed, which was a word Luki never expected to use even in his thoughts—apparently thinking Luki had fed him the funniest line since "Who's on first?"

But even though Luki thought he should be annoyed, he wasn't. Being seriously annoyed with Sonny would require some special skill that he, erstwhile icicle of the century, didn't have.

Inside the room, Luki quickly took stock of all the furnishings, doors, windows, views, accoutrements, and all other things that might be used as weapons—as defense or by an intruder. Satisfied overall with security, he also took stock of comfort. Though a single room rather than a suite, it had plenty of space, furniture that made sense— except for the second king bed—appliances to make food or beverages hot or cold. And, thank the saints, a shower.

Which he and Sonny shared for practical reasons. One, they were both covered with everything from road dust to drool; two, Sonny needed help in order to keep his wound dry as per medical instructions; and, three, Luki needed to keep Sonny in sight to assure himself that Sonny was safe. Which he suspected was overkill.

Sonny, wavering as Luki helped him out of the shower, turned greenish, shook his head slowly, and brushed Luki out of the way. He barely made it to the toilet before he heaved, falling to his knees and clutching the bowl like a lover. Luki pulled Sonny's long hair back out of the way and held his forehead.

What am I becoming?

"Retching is *my* job," he said as Sonny rinsed his mouth.

Sonny did his best to smile. "Yeah. Ruins the happy-go-lucky-artist-guy image."

He couldn't eat, wouldn't take any pain pills, only wanted to brush his teeth and sleep. While he did, Luki called one of his Los Angeles agents, currently on a job in Seattle.

"Kim, it's Luki."

"I know." She laughed.

"Shut up," he said, which, as he'd expected, made her laugh harder. He couldn't for the life of him understand why he kept such a frivolous person on the payroll, except perhaps that she had great instincts, good connections, and could really kick ass. "Listen, I want you to put away what you're doing down there and come up to Bellingham. I don't want you to give me any shit, seriously, about this next part. I want you to get my car washed—"

Luki held the phone away from his ear while Kim treated him to several exclamations, each creatively using profanity. When she quieted down he set her off again, thinking he might as well get it over with all at once. "And buy some clothes—"

He waited until she wound down to tell her what to get and what size. He had his own clothes, but Sonny had arrived at the hotel in a T-shirt with a Sisters of Providence logo, and jeans stiff with dried blood. Finally, when Kim was thoroughly pissed, he topped it off with, "and because I write your paycheck."

Silence. Seething silence, Luki thought.

"And because I can't do it myself at the moment. When you're done with those things, which I will thoroughly appreciate, scope out a building called the armory here in Bellingham. Get familiar with the immediate area. Then get some sleep."

"Okay, Mom."

"Look, Kim, I need some help up here. I need someone I can trust at my back tomorrow, and you'll be a damn good someone in that respect. I'd prefer it if you're at your best, which means sleep."

"You're sleeping too?"

"Yes, as soon as possible. Let me know where you're at in the morning—"

"But not too early."

"Exactly. Let me know, and I'll be in touch. Job is probably around dusk, tomorrow."

With Kim more or less mollified, he made another safety check, then felt Sonny's face for temperature.

God! Have I turned into my grandmother?

Then, *finally,* he went out to the balcony for a smoke, leaving the slider open a bit just in case and hoping the smoke would go the other way. Leaning back on the low balcony wall he gazed through the glass. Inside, an electric fireplace threw orange light and blue shadows over the room, casting Sonny's shoulders in bronze.

Luki found himself imagining the rest of Sonny's bare skin glorified in that light. He went back inside and stood at the foot of the bed, couldn't help it, stared at Sonny's sleeping form, chewing his lip.

"What are *you* looking at?" Sonny asked, apparently not sleeping and always the jester.

Luki almost laughed. Sonny seemed to be trying to find some moisture in his drug-dried mouth, so he took him a glass of water. Sitting on the edge of the bed, he watched him swallow.

Sonny managed to deposit the water glass on the night table without a major spill, then met Luki's eyes again, more serious this time. "What are you thinking about?"

Luki waited, feeling his breath go scarce, his heart insisting on heating his blood. "You," he said. After his treatment of Sonny that morning, speaking his mind now felt like a frightening plunge. "I'm thinking about putting my mouth all over you."

Sonny returned his gaze. Faint, sober smile. No jokes, no words.

Luki leaned over and kissed his mouth, sweet and soft. "Yes?" he asked.

"Yes."

Luki started with another kiss, sucking honey from Sonny's lips. He visited tender, fleshy earlobes, dusted the lightest of kisses over fluttering eyelids. He feathered his lips and tongue over the line of Sonny's jaw and down to the dip at the base of his throat.

Sonny moved as if to participate. Luki held him back, gently pushed him down.

With tongue and teeth and lips he paid tribute to every beautiful curve and hollow and rise of Sonny's body he could reach without causing his wound to hurt. He kissed the hollows behind his collarbone, gently nipped taut nipples, poked his tongue into the dip of his navel. Then, the miraculous valley inside each hip—there he started at the fold of Sonny's thigh and blazed a trail of kisses to the place that made Sonny dig his hands into Luki's hair.

Once more, on the other side.

Sonny shifted again as if to participate, but Luki took hold of his hands and paused to meet his eyes. "No," he said. "Be still."

Sonny's belly clenched and he gasped, as if he thought the words, all by themselves, were sex play. His prick had hardened to the point that the tight skin pulled it almost flat against his belly. Luki ignored it, except to run his tongue beneath to collect the pool of pre-cum that had gathered there, brushing across the head of Sonny's penis in the process.

Downward again, inside the thighs, behind the knees, the sensitive toes and arches. Slowly, then up again, until he came once more to the center of Sonny's excitement, pleasure, and despair, and began to address the heat arising there. He spread Sonny's legs, burrowed his hands beneath his ass to hold him still.

Sonny grabbed at his hair again, said, "Luki, please."

"No," Luki said. "Wait."

Thick, wet lips, the flat of his tongue, a long, light kiss. He teased at the small, diamond-shaped tenderness just behind the head of Sonny's penis, circled the smooth coronal ridge with his tongue, closed his mouth over the taut, curved head. Pleasuring. Or perhaps, judging from Sonny's struggling breath, torturing.

"God, Luki, please," he panted.

"Wait," Luki said.

He stroked the length of Sonny's cock, squeezing, and with thumbs gathered the lubricant that emerged. Again cupping Sonny's ass in his strong hands, he used the now slick thumbs to massage the sensitive rim of his anus, sucking at his firm testes before moving his mouth once again to his erection.

Sonny felt good to him, tasted sweet. Luki rejoiced in every touch he applied to Sonny's gorgeous skin. But what drove him on his quest was a deep, unfamiliar desire to please at all costs. Luki applied all his experience and skill, relentless, merciless, demanding, but slow and sweet. Sonny's breathing became ragged and his grip on Luki's hair turned desperate, insistent, almost violent.

Luki dropped his mouth over Sonny's shaft, opening his throat, and then sucked upward, slow and hard, at the same time pushing his two thumbs just inside, just past the pliant opening.

To Luki's overwhelming pleasure, Sonny responded just as intended. He moaned long and low, almost silent, and the first hard pulse of orgasm shook him, splashing semen against Luki's swollen lips.

After a while Sonny's breathing calmed. Luki flared his nostrils to draw in the smell of Sonny's sex, like saving it up, and rose to his knees.

Sonny looked spent. Not necessarily in a bad way, but Luki hoped he hadn't overtaxed him, what with his injury and all. He moved up next to him, handed him the water glass, and propped him up to drink from it. Not at all sure what to make of his own feelings, Luki nevertheless curled up around Sonny, cradled his head and kissed the top of it.

Sonny said, "You?"

"No. Another time. This was for you, Sonny."

Sonny pulled his head away to look at him. After a time he whispered, half asleep, "You're smiling."

"I guess I am. I'll probably have to rectify that."

"Punctures the tough-guy image."

"Almost irreparably. Are you hurting, now that you're awake and not being driven into a sexual frenzy? Do you want some more pain meds?"

Sonny hesitated. "Yeah, I think so."

Luki extracted himself from his cozy situation reluctantly, then resisted the instinct to rush after Sonny, who had rolled off the bed and set off for the bathroom.

Damn, Sonny, what if you fall! Damn, Luki, give it a rest!

Sonny made it back in one piece and, breathing again, Luki brought him his pill and plumped his pillows and helped him lay down without straining his injured muscle and pulled the blanket up and....

"What are you doing, Luki?"

"I'm tucking you in."

"Tucking me in?"

"Yes." He hoped he was managing a cold and intimidating expression. "You have some sort of problem with that?"

Sonny laughed hard enough that Luki worried about his stitches—*what the hell is going on with me*—and kept laughing when Luki turned the lights out and stepped to the balcony to smoke, flopping on a cushioned wicker chair with one leg draped loosely over the arm.

Sonny fell silent, and a moment later his drowsy advice floated out to the balcony. "You should quit."

"News," Luki said. He found the night air, the lights on the water, the faint noises of traffic a lot more satisfying than would usually have been the case. He suspected he was still smiling, even though it wasn't stretching his scar.

Sonny's low, buttery voice came again, softly, from the edge of sleep. "Luki?"

"Mmm."

"Uh… thank you?"

Luki smiled some more, which should have alarmed him but didn't. "You're welcome, sweetie," he said. "You're more than welcome."

Chapter Six

THE time that Luki got up the next morning could in no way be called early, but he did roll out of bed before Sonny. Which made him jealous. Nevertheless, he took advantage of it to smoke without guilt. *Well, sort of without guilt.*

He called for service, and twenty minutes later they had a table full of food and two carafes of coffee, hot and almost as good as Margie's.

He called Margie, who predictably brushed off his concern.

"I don't know why I got so upset over this. I mean, poor Sonny, he worked so hard, but you took care of everything, Luki, and it's fine now. Don't you worry about me."

Luki had trouble understanding how she could have convinced herself that she'd overreacted to her home being invaded and vandalized. But he didn't try to disillusion her. He figured maybe that's what she needed to do to move past it. He also called the agents he had watching her place.

"Nothing, Luki. Absolutely nothing. Well, we did see a couple of seagulls get into a scuffle, but—"

"I get it, Bartlett," Luki said, and delivered a few supervisory words in a chilly manner.

On the other hand, Kaholo's voice, when he answered Luki's call, sent warmth straight through the phone line. Something in Luki always softened when he heard that heart-deep Hawaiian bass. And he had good news. Josh and Jackie were safe, eating like horses, sleeping like the dead, and even acting like boys now and then.

But when Kaholo said, "They're down at the river just now," the words hit Luki like a fist to the gut.

But Luki's uncle knew him well. He soothed it over. "Don't worry, Mili, there ain't nobody gonna hurt 'em. I got my eye out."

Soon afterward, Sonny opened his eyes and sat up, looking like he had no clue where he was. Luki took him coffee. Another first. *Sweet, thoughtful, mild-mannered Luki. Right.*

"At last I've been able to test my theory," Sonny said, as deadpan as he ever got. "And I was wrong. It is, after all, possible to sleep on a mattress that doesn't tilt to one side and have lumps."

Luki realized he had made a wise choice attending to business before Sonny got up, because now he had trouble doing anything but watching Sonny. He thought he might be able to make Sonny-watching into a serious hobby. He watched Sonny while he looked askance at the clothes Luki had procured for him, while he dressed in said clothes, while he brushed his teeth and tied his hair back and drank coffee.

But pain lay like a fault line across Sonny's features, spoiling the perfection.

"Did you take any of your pain medication?"

"Just now. I took one. After this I'm only taking Tylenol. If you don't mind stopping for some."

"No problem," Luki answered, but he hoped Sonny wouldn't be too stubborn about it. Pain was likely to show up full force after a while. But… "What else is bothering you, Sonny?"

He sat down, taking a seat across the table, but only met Luki's glance fleetingly. After a silence that went on just a beat too long, he dropped his head in his hands and sighed. "I think I remember something, Luki. I remember it or I dreamed it. My brain has been a little mushy ever since last night."

Luki waited, but no further words came. He prompted, "What did you remember?"

"Or dream," Sonny said. "It's making my head hurt trying to sort out which."

"Just tell me about it, and we'll figure that out later if it's important." He refilled Sonny's coffee, and then drained the last half-cup in his own mug, mournfully peering into the pot before putting it aside.

"You're really cute sometimes, Luki."

"Cute!" He didn't know whether to protest or laugh. But he was saved from having to decide, because Sonny chose that moment to explain.

"That piece of metal that cut me at the armory yesterday?"

Luki nodded. "What about it?"

"There might have been someone holding the other end of it."

THEY left the hotel around two thirty, Luki having decided that, in light of last night's debacle, and even though Kim would do a good job, he needed to do some reconnaissance of his own at the armory before mounting a second attack on the castle walls. The ride from Old Fairhaven took only minutes, but during that time, Sonny chafed under Luki's silence. Luki had put on his game face—perfectly cool, impenetrable, ice fortress.

Sonny gave him directions, turn here, up there, next light, etc., etc. Luki followed them, silently shifting gears. Sonny didn't know how a chasm had developed between them, and he wasn't sure how much longer he could stand to leave it in place without doing something drastic. But relief came from an unexpected quarter.

"Squalicum." Luki kept his deadpan face.

"Yup," Sonny said. "Samish. Lummi. Nootka. Tlingit. Mililani."

He watched Luki from behind his shades. He didn't think it likely that many people could see the tenacious smile, never quite defeated, behind the ice mask. But at the moment, someone would have to be blind not to see him trying desperately to keep it from blooming.

"Mililani, huh?"

"Of course."

"Do you remember anything about this person at the armory?"

"I'm not even sure he—or she—is real."

"Pretend. You said it was a woman?"

"No, a man."

"And he was about my age?"

"No, young. Like fresh out of high school. A street kid maybe."

"Hispanic."

"White, I think."

"Blond."

"I don't know."

"As tall as me and wearing a blue hoodie, looked like an athlete."

"The hoodie is right, but it was dark. I couldn't tell what color. I don't think he was athletic—he had that smell about him. You know, like when a dope fiend gets sick. He wasn't tall. Leastways he pushed upward when he stabbed me.... Luki, how the hell did you do that?"

Luki chuckled without smiling. "Tricks of the trade, sweetie. And you were easy."

Sonny lay back against the seat. "Left here." He pointed, and as Luki followed his instruction, he put his hand on the seat close to Luki and said, "It might sound weird, but I feel better, knowing he was real. It's a little crazy-making trying to figure it out. Well, you know."

"Yes. I do know." Luki took hold of the offered hand and gave a gentle squeeze. "And I'm glad you feel better."

"But I'm still scared."

Luki nodded. "Of course. Who wouldn't be?"

AFTER their failed attempt to assault the fortress by crossing the moat of thorns, Luki refused to take chances. He set up to watch the front of the building from a block away until he was satisfied he knew that part of the exterior, as well as who went in and out—college students, mostly, he thought—and where the entrances were. He left then, partly because it was mid-afternoon in summer, thus bright daylight, and he didn't want to draw attention. Partly because he hadn't eaten much at the hotel, what with circumstances and wishing he was asleep, and his noteworthy appetite had caught up to him.

Sonny had decided he needed the other half of his pain medicine dose and subsequently had been asleep in the car. Luki had cursed himself for not bringing a pillow from the hotel because he felt obliged to use his jacket again, and he was almost certain Sonny would drool this time. *Spiffy*. But he did figure out why he had let Sonny come along in the first place—he'd know where to get some good food.

"Umm," Sonny said when Luki first woke him up, and then he closed his eyes again.

Luki hoped that was just part of his waking-up process, but when he started to lightly snore even in the upright position, Luki decided to take action. He shook Sonny's shoulder and called his name.

"I'm awake," Sonny insisted.

Luki wasn't sure, so he kept shaking. He probably shouldn't have, wouldn't have, if he hadn't been hungry.

"I know, I know." Sonny started to sound downright irritated.

Sort of sweet, on drugs, Luki thought, then wondered if he'd finally crossed the crazy line.

"What," Sonny asked, scowling. "Do you think you're being cute or something? What do you want anyway?" After Luki repeated his original question, Sonny looked thoughtful. "Umm… where are we?"

Luki groaned.

"Just kidding," Sonny said. "There's a place on Samish Way that has great hamburgers—it's also a drive in, has carhops, but I'd rather go in because you've kept me in this car far too long—"

"I've kept you—"

"Kidding again."

"In bad taste."

"Speaking of which, there's a place in Old Fairhaven that serves dynamite fish and chips. It's a trailer. Or a bus. Or something that they've set up permanently, so you pretty much have to eat outside, but it's sunny today. It's all touristy down there, so if you want to be inconspicuous, that's the place to go."

They did. Sonny ate half his food; Luki ate the other half along with his own. Then he called Kim and asked what she and Brian had learned about the armory's neighborhood and exterior. As for the interior, he'd decided to trust Sonny's firsthand knowledge, even though he prefaced his description with, "Well, it's been a while, but if I remember right...." Luki assumed that was only a figure of speech. Or at least he hoped so.

He parked on the opposite side of the building this time, again about a half-block away but with a good view. He saw Kim, looking like an angsty goth, sullenly get into an ugly, squarish van fairly well hidden behind a stand of nut-brush that didn't belong in suburbia. A minute later, he couldn't see her at all; she'd disappeared into the back where she was set up for surveillance—not quite state of the art, but usable. He spotted Brian outside, looking like a homeless person and wiping his nose on his sleeve, or so it appeared.

Luki tuned a radio that looked just like a cell phone to the frequency he knew they'd be on, checked that everyone could hear everyone, and clipped it to his belt.

"Like on TV," Sonny remarked.

Luki patted his hand.

He had never seen a place with so many entrances, or so he swore after a half hour or so of observation.

"What time did I take those pills?" Sonny asked.

"Are you going to take some more?"

"Hell no, never again. I thought I'd take some Tylenol, though."

"But it hurts?" *There I go again, little old grandmother me.*

"A little."

Right. Like I believe that. Luki got the bottle of Tylenol out of a compartment—after he figured out which one it was in. When had his car become so messy? "Lean up; let me look at it... Bleeding a little again. Skin's kind of red around the edges of the bandage."

"It's fine."

"Do you feel like you have a fever?"

"Luki." Sonny's expression managed to say "I'm annoyed" while at the same time shouting "I can't believe you're doing this."

Point taken.

"STAY in the car," Luki said, after he finished his first burger and started on the second, which Sonny refused to eat. Sonny also refused to stay in the car.

"Sonny, as I mentioned, you're in pain, and your wound is oozing. In addition, you're weak because you've been on drugs and won't eat. You're going to get us both into some kind of trouble."

"Luki," Sonny replied, trying not to sound rude while mimicking Luki's tone, "I know the place, I've only taken Tylenol, and if I was hungry I'd eat. And even if I hadn't eaten, I wouldn't be weak."

He waited for Luki's reply. None came, but Sonny saw him fingering the nylon cuffs that always hung from his belt. Still, he didn't balk even when Luki gave him his iciest and, Sonny was willing to admit, scariest stare. He reached for the door handle. "I'll go in by myself." He opened the door and put a foot out, hoping Luki would be too stunned to stop him.

"Okay," Luki said, sounding none too pleased. "Fine. Now close the door, you stubborn little shit."

"I hardly think you could call me little."

"But first"—Luki may have given in, but he was damn sure going to lay down the law—"first, take a bite of this." He held up the half-eaten burger, pointing it at Sonny's face like a weapon. "You heard me."

Sonny bit, chewed, swallowed, very confused.

"Another one."

After Sonny obeyed, he began to feel hungry, so he took the hamburger back and ate it on his own.

"Do you feel better now?" Luki looked quite satisfied with himself.

"Do you?"

"Yes. And here's the rest of what you're going to do: stay behind me, do anything I tell you to do, and don't do anything else. Be quiet—

that means your feet, your breathing, and your mouth... which I'd like to kiss first. So get rid of the damn hamburger."

Sonny swallowed, a little frightened, and washed the last bite down with Coke.

Luki carried out this threat, and he didn't laugh even though Sonny did.

"There you go, bubbling again," he said.

"*Bubbling?*"

"I'm not explaining right now; we've got something to do. Let's go."

"But," Sonny said, "I do want to mention that the kiss spoils the tough-guy image." Sonny could have sworn Luki was smiling, though he wasn't sure how he could tell by looking at the back of his curly head.

After Luki looked around one more time, they got out of the car, and Luki took a few drags off a cigarette, hiding the brightening tip with a cupped hand and blowing the smoke out slow when there was a breeze to take it away. He put it out on the sole of his classy shoe, and then they made their stealthy way down the hill to the armory.

Luki turned a serious gaze on Sonny, his bright, pale blue eyes glistening in the dusk. "Careful now, Sonny. Quiet and careful. I want you to stay safe."

GHOSTS could be quite comfortable in a place like the armory, full of cubbyholes and closets, corridors and large, echoing chambers. Sonny found a few of his own ghosts: shades of youth, hours of work, moments stolen for trickster substances and dark, secret sex. Discovery. Not of what he was—queer, artist, vulnerable—but of what he might make of those materials. Most of the Sonny Bly James that had come of it, he liked. Some things he'd do differently. Some things he'd change now if he could.

Like Delsyn. He'd take better care of the boy if he could go back. He wouldn't let him run wild. He wouldn't let him take chances with his life. He wouldn't have to worry and wonder if this time he'd come back in time, or never again.

He stepped through the corridors almost blindly, remembering his days at Western, the university that technically owned the building. Remembering the way he'd neglected his young cousin while he spent time there at the armory. With every step, he fell deeper into that past, seeing everything in the old, oddly-used ruin not as it was, but as it once had been, until Luki gripped his shoulder and turned him around to face him.

"Slow down," Luki whispered, so quiet the sound fell away before it reached Sonny's ears. "And stay behind me!"

Feeling guilty, Sonny nodded and let Luki pass. His ghosts vanished as he marshaled his attention to the here and now, treading carefully, feet—even breath—as close to silent as he could make them.

A flash of movement behind a half-lit, half-glassed door. Luki put his hand out to hold him back, stepped toward the door, gun in hand, and pushed it open. The man fled, but not before Sonny, closer behind Luki than he should have been, got a good look.

"That's him," he said. "That's the guy who stabbed me."

LUKI registered Sonny's meaning before he finished speaking. In motion immediately, he laid a forearm across Sonny's chest, stopping him before he could step out, then flying after his target, relaxing his body, freeing his muscles to move without hindrance. Without ever increasing the tension, he reached his target and kicked, striking behind the knee.

The man—*no, another kid, maybe as old as Josh*—went down and rolled over, putting an arm over his face as if fearing a blow.

"Mr. K? Are you Mr. K? I'm sorry I ran. I got scared. Please!"

"Damn," Luki said. And wanted another cigarette. "What's your name?"

"BJ. I'm BJ, like I told you before. That's what everybody calls me, I mean. Please, I did what you asked. I did the best I could. I—"

"BJ, just shut up for a minute." He locked the safety on his gun and holstered it, looked at Sonny, who was staring at him and looking a little out of his comfort zone. "What are *you* looking at?" he asked, which drew a little smile from Sonny but apparently confused BJ.

"I'm not, I mean, please, Mr. K—"

"Not you, BJ! And stop calling me that. I'm not Mr. K. Now stop talking until I ask you to start."

"Okay, Mr.— "

"What did I just say?"

BJ got the message and made a lip-zipping motion, which made Luki want to laugh. He didn't, of course. He gentled his voice a bit. Here he was again with a kid who wasn't likely to be the real bad guy. "Is there anyone else here, kid?"

"No! I did like you said, Mr.— "

"I'm not Mr. K!"

"I came by myself!" A shred of a sarcastic adolescent attitude peaked through, and he added, "Whoever you are."

"Whoever I am, I'm probably not as sleazy as Mr. K," Luki said, "but I could probably be scarier. Information, BJ. For now, that's what I want from you. First, are you still expecting this Mr. K?"

"I don't... I don't think so. I got here late. I think maybe he was already here and left."

"Lyin' little shit," Sonny said, his voice not at all patient or kind.

It wasn't hard to understand why Sonny might be less than happy with the boy, but Luki was pretty sure a modified game of "good cop, bad cop" wouldn't get them what they wanted. He gave Sonny a glare. When BJ started to edge away toward the door they'd just come in, Luki kept his glare on Sonny while pulling his pistol smoothly, slipping the safety, and pointing it unwaveringly straight at BJ. "We're not done, BJ."

The boy went still, but Luki's glare seemed to have no intimidating effect on Sonny at all. He began to wonder if he should have played it the other way—gun on Sonny, glare at BJ. *Too late now.*

"Sonny, perhaps—"

"Don't bother, old man. I get the message. But I won't be listening to you comfort that junky scum."

"Sonny, stay close," Luki said, but the door had already closed behind him. Luki turned his attention back to the "junky scum."

"Why do you think that?"

"Think what?"

"Why," Luki said, the strain on his patience about to surpass what it could handle without a cigarette, "do you think he was already here and left?"

"Because," BJ whispered, wide eyes shining in the dying light. "Because of what I saw in that other room."

Luki had it on the tip of his tongue to ask what he saw, but he thought twice. Whatever it was, it had the kid so frightened he could barely speak of it. And when he spoke of it, he gestured with his chin toward the door Sonny had just gone through. Luki holstered his gun and in a fluid motion reached behind him and snapped a pair of nylon cuffs from their concealment on the inside of his belt; without even hesitating, he gathered the kid's arms and slapped the bindings on.

"I'm under arrest?"

"I'm not a cop," Luki said as he pulled the struggling boy toward the door. "But listen to this: if you can't be still with those cuffs on, I can hitch your hands to your ankles behind your back and string you from a coat hook." *Nice, creative, empty threat*, Luki congratulated himself, *especially since BJ seems to believe it.*

He pulled his captive out into the corridor, where he found a lot of shadows that were not harboring Sonny and some crates that Sonny was not sitting on. Luki held his breath, fighting down an uncharacteristic blast of adrenaline—something close to panic. *Which I could fight down much easier with a cigarette.* But there was no time for that. Mouth gone dry, he rasped, "Take me to this other room."

BJ pointed with his chin again. "It's that door, right there."

Following that direction, Luki strode down the hall, heedless of the stumbling teen he was practically dragging behind him and making no effort now to keep his feet silent on the hardwood floor. Pushing open the wide, heavy door, he found a cavernous space that must, he figured, be against the building's outer wall. Blue light, streetlamps or moonshine, flooded in from a bank of high windows to his right. The high ceilings were lost in darkness, and in the opposite wall, wide double doors, the kind you might see on an old garage, stood almost closed against the cool night air.

Which had nothing to do with the chill that crept up Luki's spine.

Sonny stood like a marble statue in silhouette against the almost-light flooding the room. At the sound of Luki entering with BJ, he let out a long, slow sigh and turned his head so slowly he might have been an apparition, the only break in his dark form a hard glint in his eyes. Luki recovered his power of thought and sat BJ down in a corner.

"Don't move," he said.

"No, sir," BJ answered, teeth chattering.

Luki knew exactly what had the young man so frightened. He could smell it. He switched on his flashlight, careful to keep the light low and shielded.

A slick on the floor as if someone had been dragged through a puddle. A smear on the partially-tiled wall under the windows—with a double handprint clearly visible near the baseboard. And almost at Sonny's feet, a small pool of dark liquid, drops splashed around its edges.

And smeared across the wall: FAGGOT. FAGGOT. FAGGOT.

Luki, for all his experience, all his professional and personal chill, felt his temperature soar with adrenaline, and then plummet with real fear.

"Blood," he said.

"Not that." Sonny nodded toward the puddle.

"What do you mean?" Luki stepped nearer the substance in question as he asked.

"It's not blood."

"I get that, Sonny, but why do you say that, and what do you think it is?" He shone his light across it, started to add that it looked like blood to him, but as he drew near he noticed a faint acid odor. And it looked odd too. Instead of clotting at the outside edges as blood would do, it seemed to have a layer of liquid sliding over gel.

"Dye."

"Die!"

"Dye."

"Speak in whole sentences, Sonny," Luki said, knowing it was an odd command coming from someone whose policy, overall, was silence.

"It's mine," Sonny responded.

"Yours?"

"Speak in whole sentences, Luki."

Luki inwardly smiled, strangely glad for the return of Sonny's smart mouth.

"Yes, it's mine. That's a dye made from cochineals—little insects—and some other ingredients. I make it. I use it for dying silk. Other people might use similar components, but that dye is mine; no one else makes it just like that. It produces a signature color, something that's in all my work, unique enough that it's part of the way buyers verify that a piece at auction is mine. I can tell by the smell, by the way it separates, and when you shine your light on it, I can see the color. People call it Sonny James red. They compare other reds to it. It's mine, Luki. I could recognize it anywhere." Suddenly running out of words, he began to shiver.

"It came," he said, "from my studio."

Luki, for the moment, could do little more than stare. He touched Sonny's arm, an effort to calm him. Or perhaps to calm himself.

Sonny held out a square of paper, drops of liquid gathering at its corners.

Dear Faggot,

You stole something from me. I want it back. Follow the clues, and we'll do business. No police, or I'll change my plan. And that would be a bloody shame.

Luki put an arm around Sonny's shoulder, partly to comfort him, partly to keep from falling over. As soon as he could breathe, he called Kim.

"Come in here, bring a print kit—you'll need acid yellow 7 and some gel lifters. And… hold on a minute."

"Sonny?" When Sonny continued to stare at the small pool of dye as if he hadn't heard Luki at all, Luki shook him and called again, louder. "Sonny!"

"What?"

"This dye, in a puddle like this, can it be identified easily?"

"I don't think so. No one knows my formula."

"Okay, then… what's the best way to clean this?"

"Just sop it up."

"It'll stain."

"Right."

The exchange seemed to be at a dead end, so Luki let it drop. "Kim," he said into the phone. "You got rags in the van?"

"Um, why do—"

"Never mind! Do you have some?" Kim did, and Luki told her to bring them, Brian, and a camera.

Orders given, Luki turned his attention back to his stunned lover.

"Sonny," he spoke softly. Once again, Sonny gave no indication that he heard. Luki touched his shoulder. "Sonny, sweetie, look at me."

He did. His eyes had a distant, half-hooded look that Luki found disturbing. If he'd been anyone else, he would have found it frightening. But he had no choice but to forge ahead.

"The note says no cops. Up until now, keeping the law out has been a clear choice, for Josh and Jackie's sake. But there's blood here, and as a condition of my licenses—all of them—I'm supposed to notify law enforcement." Sonny looked so blank that Luki thought he'd better check to see if he was hearing him at all. "Do you understand what I'm saying?"

"Why me, Luki?"

Luki shook his head, feeling—and probably looking—less cold, less confident than he could remember feeling for at least twenty years. "That's a damn good question. I don't know the answer. Yet. But listen, Sonny, there are two ways to go about this, and I need you to choose."

"You're calling the police?"

"That's what the choice is about. I need you to tell me what you want. You've already been hurt. Clearly the writer of that note is implying that you're at risk for something worse. And... well, there's blood, a threat as well, whatever else it might mean. Obviously the goal is to find this person and stop him. Police have a lot of resources and power—most of them are good at what they do. They can probably catch this... monster.

"But, in my experience, that doesn't necessarily happen before someone innocent gets hurt or even killed. Bad guys go to great lengths to make good on their threats. What I'm trying to say is, there's lots of reasons to say, yeah, let's call the police. And there are reasons to do what the bad guy says, for now, and keep the cops out of it. It's a tough choice, but this seems to be about you, and I'm asking you to make it."

"You'll lose everything, if we don't call them."

"Not everything. And that's not as important as it sounds."

Sonny was quiet, looking down into the pool of red at his feet as if he could find a vision there, a vision with all the answers. He sighed. Looked up toward the doors with their horrible message. "What do you think I should do, Luki?" He turned his head and met Luki's eyes with a weary simplicity. "I mean, I'll choose. But... maybe you've been here before. I just need advice."

"Yes, I've been here before, more or less." He chewed his lip, troubled by one factor. *Never before have I cared more about my "client" than about my job.* St. Christopher's medal lay cool against his chest, counterweight to his skipping heart, calming him.

Finally, he gave Sonny the same advice he'd give to anyone else. "No one can predict the outcome. But in my experience, when the bad guy is holding the cards and says no police, it's safest to agree for as long as possible."

"And if we do that, then what?"

"Then we work like hell to make sure he's the one who makes a fatal mistake."

DECISION made, and Luki in action, Sonny remained where he was, squatting on one knee next to the pool of dye, staring into its viscous depths. One thought ran reel-to-reel and back again in his mind. *This came from my studio.* The import of that sank no farther than his brain cells, and that's what troubled him the most. He knew it should have his gut quivering in fear, but it didn't. The closest he could get was a detached sort of mild anger. He looked up to find Luki studying him.

"Are you all right?"

When Sonny started to answer, the words caught in his throat, which seemed odd considering their complete lack of impact on his emotions. He cleared his throat, worked up some saliva, and tried again.

"This came from my studio."

"Oh." Luki slowly nodded, apparently not meaning that he hadn't known that. "I see. I understand. I don't know how to make that okay, Sonny, but I'm doing what I can. I've got people on the way to take a look outside your place, and we'll go as soon as we can. But we have to finish this here. It's important."

"Whatever." Sonny returned immediately to staring at the puddle of dye.

"Whoa," Luki said, and took Sonny's chin in hand to turn his head, looking worried and staring into his eyes.

Sonny stared back, emotions blank.

"Maybe it'll be best if you're busy," Luki observed. "Would you clean up the dye?"

"Plastic bags."

"What?"

Anger came over Sonny all at once. "For my hands! For the towels!" He refrained from adding, *you idiot.*

Brian, still breathless from trudging in with all the equipment and supplies, spoke up from across the room. "Kim brought some. They're in this bag with the towels."

Sonny went to get them, and the towels. "At least," he said, still bristling, "someone's thinking straight around here." He was glad, though, when Luki didn't respond.

What Luki did do was scratch his head. He looked vaguely puzzled, though his typically expressionless visage had dropped back in place. "Not a single person has come near us. Is that unusual for this place?"

"Wasn't when I was around here," Sonny snarled. "Ask the kid."

"He does have a name."

"Yeah, but he stabbed me."

"Good point." Luki turned toward BJ, assuring himself that he hadn't actually forgotten the young criminal. "Hey, kid. There hasn't been anyone around. Is that normal?"

"Yeah, at night. A lot of people think the place is haunted. And the people that are here… they don't want to be seen." By this time, BJ was beginning to sweat. His nose was running.

"While we're on the subject, why did you stab my friend, here? Did Mr. K tell you to do that? How did you know we'd be here?"

"I didn't… I mean, no—"

"Didn't what? Stab him? Everyone here knows that's a lie."

"No, I mean it wasn't Mr. K—he didn't tell me to do it. It was… an accident."

Sonny stopped sopping up dye to glare at him.

Luki raised his eyebrows.

"Please, I mean I only did it because I was scared." BJ was trembling now, his voice shaking. "I wasn't supposed to be here; it wasn't a time I was supposed to come. I thought maybe he'd be here— Mr. K—and I could talk him into helping me. Then I got scared, and I was running out that door, and there he was." He nodded toward Sonny. "I couldn't see… I just stabbed him. Please, I was scared."

Luki didn't say he understood, didn't condemn the kid, didn't respond. Sonny had gone back to feeling numb and cleaning up the dye, *his* dye. Luki had sent Kim outside on patrol. Brian had already taken pictures of everything, in great detail, and now, while Luki lifted the prints, Brian would be cleaning up. Despite BJ being covered in smelly sweat and gagging now and then, Luki ordered him to help.

"You'll have to work in exchange for me helping you out," Luki said. He gave no hint about what his kindness would look like. Sonny decided not to make wishes he might later regret.

With limited supplies and equipment, they couldn't remove every trace of the crime. The police could find signs if they were looking, but when the job was done they wouldn't have cause to check here. There did remain, however, a fairly strong residue of the writing on the wall.

FAGGOT.

"But the whole place is graffiti and rot," Sonny said. "Who's going to care?"

Chapter Seven

LEAVING the armory, they saw only a handful of homeless people in the shadows—mostly asleep—and one young couple backed against the wall in a corner of moonlight. Sonny had started to wake up, as he thought of it, as soon as they had left that horrid chamber. Now, seeing that couple in clandestine sex, he was glad nobody could see him blush purple with memory.

They took BJ to the van, sending Brian and Kim on some whispered errand in Luki's car. The back of the van, while technologically interesting with listening devices, etcetera, crowded Sonny to an uncomfortable degree. It probably would have under any circumstances, but with an unwashed teenager sweating the sweat of the withdrawing junkie, it was all he could do to hold down that hamburger he'd eaten. He promised himself that the next time he didn't want to eat, he wouldn't, Luki's coercion notwithstanding.

To his annoyance, he was left alone in the van with the kid while Luki went for his traditional puke, cigarette, mouth rinse, and breath mint. Apparently refreshed, and also apparently not planning to beat around the bush, Luki started in on BJ as soon as he stepped into the van.

"Why are you here?"

"H-He told me to meet him here—Mr. K. He said he'd fix me up, you know, help me out for a while if I did what he asked one more time, and he'd tell me tonight what he wanted. It seemed easier than… well, some other stuff."

"He was going to fix you up."

"Yeah."

"Smack."

BJ nodded but hung his head.

"And though you know he's a creep and generally a scary fucker, you'd be willing to shoot whatever he gave you into your veins, no questions asked."

No response, but it seemed clear Luki hadn't expected one.

"Because you've done it before, and you're not dead yet. At least not so it would show."

"HOW old are you?"

Luki felt frustration mounting. He knew his iceman exterior already showed some cracks, and when BJ said he was sixteen, he had a hard time maintaining anything that looked like disinterested cool. Josh, Jackie, now BJ. Kids... desperate kids, and this Mr. K used them to commit his crimes. Violent crimes. Hate crimes. The kind of crimes that disgusted him, that angered him more than any other. Crimes that hurt people he lo... cared about.

Perhaps these boys weren't generally as innocent as they should be—especially BJ. Maybe they couldn't be held entirely free of blame, but what could Luki do? Not turn them in to the police, not in this case, at this time, and he damn sure wasn't about to beat sense into them. Besides, they'd been used; they were tools. How could he call it justice to punish them, even though the guy holding the hammer over their skulls might slide?

"Alright," he said to BJ. "Relax. Just tell me how this all happened. How did you meet the infamous Mr. K? I'm still not real clear on how you ended up stabbing this man—"

BJ shot a terrified look at Sonny, and to Luki's surprise, the look Sonny shot back was every bit as cold as Luki could have made it.

Well, I can't blame him. He's the one with the six-inch slice. Still... "Sonny."

"Yeah," Sonny said without taking his eyes... his dark, brooding eyes off of BJ.

"Damn it, Sonny, stop!"

"What?"

Luki almost wished he hadn't gotten Sonny's attention. When provoked, it turned out he had a glare that could slay the beast. Luki didn't say anything, but held Sonny's eyes. He won. But just barely.

Sonny sighed and shook his head. "I'm tired, Luki. I'm going to take a nap."

Luki watched in something like awe as he managed to find crooks and crannies for his long limbs. Reluctantly, he returned his full attention to the kid cowering on the floor at his mercy.

He thought, *cigarette, damn it!*

He said, "Sit up straight, kid."

BJ did, but it looked like it was hard to do. Luki was pretty sure his stomach was already cramping from drug withdrawal. And he said, "I'm not really a kid so much anymore." He sounded wistful.

Luki sighed. "Yeah, you are. Regardless. So tell me about Mr. K."

"What do you want to know?"

"Start at the beginning."

BJ seemed thoughtful for a minute. He looked up at Luki, frowning and serious… really serious. "Which one?"

Luki arched a brow, confused. "Oh, which beginning, you mean. Pick one."

"I've been out here a while, you see. On the streets—"

"Why?"

"I… I can't tell you that, mister."

"All right."

"So at first, I used to panhandle and dumpster dive, sleep in the park, or wherever. But then it got cold—it gets really cold up here—and I couldn't stay in the shelters because I'm too young. I thought they'd turn me in."

"Is that true?"

"I don't know, but it's too late, anyway."

"Go on."

"So one night I'm standing out on the street downtown, trying to decide what to do, wishing for a ride south, maybe to Seattle or something. But this guy drives up and asks me if I want to get out of the cold for a while." The kid stopped, swallowed hard. "I had a bad feeling." His voice had begun to shake, and he'd doubled over his arms again. He made a retching sound when he tried to speak.

"Oh, stop, damn it." None too gently, Luki took one of the boy's arms, and then the other, inspecting tracks. "Anywhere else?"

"No."

"You haven't been doing this too long, then. Did Mr. K give you your first fix?"

BJ nodded.

"And the next? And the next? And then bingo, BJ's a dope fiend? How convenient for him."

"But mister—"

"Vasquez."

"What?"

"Mr. Vasquez."

"It was so cold out there, Mr. Vasquez. And Mr. K… I didn't have to be scared all the time. And I didn't have to—"

"I get it."

"I'm going to puke."

Once again, Luki considered saying *me too,* but instead he checked to see if anyone was near the van, then opened the back doors enough for BJ to roll out, hide behind the van, and dump the contents of his stomach—which didn't amount to much. When Luki pulled him back in, nasty stuff was still running from the corner of his mouth. He lay on his side, arms clenched across his belly, rocking and crying.

"My pills," Sonny said.

Somewhere in a corner of his mind, Luki had known Sonny wasn't sleeping. Still, he almost jumped when he spoke. "What," he said, "you want one?"

"Don't be stupid, Luki."

Nobody had said such a thing to Luki in a long, long time. He almost choked. "What—"

"They're oxycodone. Opiate. They won't cure his itch altogether, but if he can keep them down, they'll help."

"I probably shouldn't ask how you know this."

"Right. Give him one at a time until he can keep from barfing them back up."

Luki rummaged around in the van. "The only thing I can find in here for him to wash them down with is flat Coke."

"Actually, that's perfect."

"You amaze me, Sonny."

While the pills began to do their work, Luki called Jude. Jude was sleeping. It was the wee hours in Chicago, and Jude made her displeasure evident.

In response Luki said, "Find a drug treatment center with medical detox, a locked-down, six month program, and a bed available now for an anonymous teenager. Within a hundred miles of Bellingham, Washington."

"How do you expect—"

"Every faith, Jude. Call me back when you've got it. Better yet, call Kim."

Just before Luki turned van, pills, and BJ—who was feeling considerably better—over to Kim and Brian, he shook the young junky out of the lethargy that had already begun to overtake him as withdrawal receded. "The hospital, BJ. What do you know about that?"

"Hospital?"

"Where did you go after you ran away from here last night? Did you see Mr. K then?"

"I was afraid to come back here. I went to find… a way to get fixed. A place to sleep."

"You don't know anything about an incident in the hospital parking lot?" BJ shook his head, eyes beginning to take on that vague look that said there was something fuzzy between your voice and his brain.

"I'm not the only… person Mr. K uses," BJ offered up.

Luki decided not to question him further, not so much out of compassion as out of an unwillingness to waste his time. The kid was telling the truth about the hospital, and Luki had pretty much known that before he asked. And he was busy, anyway, kicking himself. "The car!" he growled. "Why didn't I think of prints?" But he knew why. He'd let his emotions run away with him and thought of nothing except trying to wipe out every trace of the damned, hated word.

"You forgot, boss," Kim said, "but I got 'em."

Luki chuckled, and shook his head. "You see why I hired her, Brian? Study up. You, too, can be a Kim someday."

Fifteen minutes later, the Mercedes had been stocked with gas, and he and Sonny were settling in with their very large coffees. Luki, who also had a very large hamburger to consider, didn't start the car. He looked at Sonny.

"Are you feeling okay?"

"As okay as I'd expect. Why?"

Luki pictured Sonny driving the rusty pickup and inwardly cringed, but decided to risk it. "Would you mind driving for a little bit?"

"So you can eat? How can you eat so much, anyway? You're eating all the time."

"Not all the time. And besides, I'm a big guy, and I'm quite active. And I puke a lot, in case you hadn't noticed. And yes, I want to eat my hamburger, and I also want to make some notes for myself, a couple of calls."

They switched places, then switched their coffees' places, then Sonny fixed the seat and the mirrors and held out his hand. "Keys?"

Luki held them out, but just when Sonny was going to grab them he took them back.

Sonny raised his eyebrows.

"Before I take a bite of this hamburger, would you kiss me?" *Oh, hell. I'm turning into a freaking cupcake… a needy freaking cupcake….*

Sonny's lips, sweet and somehow grateful, effectively put a stop to Luki's self-abasement. When the gentle kiss was over, something inside, something sad, happy, and brilliant pulled up a chair in his solar plexus. He didn't recognize it, but he sort of knew what it was. He thought he might like to share it. Unfortunately, he could not find a single word to put in such a sentence.

Sonny clearly had more sense. He smiled a little, in spite of everything, rubbed a thumb across Luki's bottom lip, and then leaned across and kissed him once more, a little more than a friendly peck, a little less than sex. Then he snatched the keys out of Luki's hand.

After the hamburger, Luki fell asleep, which surprised him when he woke up. The nap couldn't have been long, though. He stopped wondering about that almost immediately when he realized the Mercedes was flying past everything on the road, flying around everything in its path, flying… *damn! This car shouldn't be flying at all!*

"Shit, Sonny! How fast are you going?"

"This is a seventy-mile zone."

"I repeat, how fast are you going?"

Sonny glanced down at the speedometer. "Eighty… seven, no eight. Eighty-eight."

"Shit!"

"Don't worry, we won't get stopped. I have freeway karma."

"I'm not worried about getting stopped, Sonny, I'm worried about getting broken!"

"Besides, your car likes it."

"My…"

"This is a German car, Luki. Fantastic engineering."

Luki had the feeling he was being lectured.

"And it's built for the autobahn. You drive it like a granny. A good gallop is good for it now and then."

"Like a granny!"

"Yes," Sonny said, and then, in a much different tone, "Trust me, Luki. I won't get pulled over, get in a wreck, or cause one.

"And I need to get home."

SONNY handled the car so skillfully that before long Luki relaxed. He went to sleep again, this time deliberately, and he didn't wake up until Sonny pulled in at a Chevron station with a mini-mart attached. From the number of gas pumps, Luki judged it must be a busy place at times, but at four in the morning, they nearly had the place to themselves

One thirtyish woman sat behind the counter. She looked experienced and war-weary, but when he walked in wearing a muscle T-shirt and his curls—judging by his reflection in the door glass—frizzed out around his head like Jimi Hendrix, she stood up and reached under the counter.

The movement made Luki wary, so he straightened and turned on the chill. She seemed more nervous yet. When Sonny walked in, wild-eyed but with an easy stride, she relaxed a bit.

"Don't worry," he said. "We're the good guys." She smiled. Luki thought maybe someday he could take a page out of Sonny's book.

Luki pumped the gas, and Sonny walked out of the store with a dozen donuts, smelling fresh out of the grease, and two breakfast burritos, smelling like bacon. He passed Luki the keys and the burritos without a word and settled into the passenger seat with feet on the dash and the box of donuts on his lap. On the one hand, Luki was glad to see him eat. On the other, he wanted to scold him about sugar versus protein. But he said nothing.

After cramming a burrito down in three poorly chewed bites, he took to the road.

It wasn't long before Sonny reached back to deposit the donuts on the back seat, pulled his hair out of its braid, and said, "I'm going to sleep now."

He woke as Luki negotiated the bumpy dirt road that led to Sonny's sprawling, ramshackle house. They still had the dregs of cold coffee, and Sonny downed his, dragged his hands through his hair, and stepped out of the car before it stopped.

Luki ran to catch up with him. "Wait, Sonny," he said in a stage whisper. "Let me check it out first."

"No," Sonny said. He picked up a tire iron by the door as he swung it open.

Three things happened in Luki's brain. One, he wondered why he hadn't seen the tire iron… the large, visible tire iron before. Two, he realized Sonny had the ability… the obvious ability to take care of himself. Three, he realized that shouldn't have surprised him, and wouldn't have if he hadn't had this strange… very strange drive to be the one to take care of him.

He didn't chew on those thoughts for long, though, because Sonny had pushed the door open. After a moment, apparently listening, he stepped in, Luki on his heels with gun drawn and held in two hands, nose down. Again, Sonny waited, then reached around Luki and pushed the door closed gently and took a few more steps into the house. A few more seconds.

He flipped the light on and began to walk noisily into the house.

Luki coughed. "What are you doing?"

"Put the gun away, Luki. No one's here. I'd smell it. Just like I can smell that they *were* here, a while ago."

What can one say to such a statement? Luki followed Sonny through the house, down a hallway he hadn't seen, past a bathroom that wasn't the one he'd showered in, to a door he would never have guessed was there. Sonny stopped in front of it, tensed in a way that said anger rather than fear, then snatched a scrap of paper from the door and passed it back over his shoulder.

> *Good morning, faggot,*
>
> > *I've had my fun. No more games. I'll see
> > you around. By the way, Dr. James, that red dye
> > is absolutely beautiful. I adore red anyway,
> > don't you? Such a lively color.*

Luki was stunned as much by the reference, "Dr. James," as by the note's message, but he let it go. Sonny stepped through the office beyond the door and through another door, not even waiting for him.

Just when he began to feel superfluous, Sonny—hidden behind that second door—called out, his voice a breath-starved whisper. "Luki?"

Inside the studio, the gray of dawn fell in through a bank of tall, north-facing windows, sinking the long, narrow space into a gloom more black and mournful than a moonless night. Wooden structures stood or huddled in various corners. Skeins and piles of yarn and string, all deep shades of purple in the gloom, lay strewn across the hardwood floor surrounded by liquid, lightless pools.

Two upright looms stood along the wall across from the bank of windows, each with a partially woven piece slashed across like a cut throat. Between them, on a space of wall that should have been blank...

FAGGOT.

FAGGOT.

FAGGOT.

Chapter Eight

SONNY walked through the world in a haze for the next three weeks, disturbed by the crimes that had been directed at him, worried about the absent Delsyn every minute, waiting for the hammer to fall. Despite the surreal quality that threaded itself into every ordinary movement, Sonny and Luki began to grow together. The artist in Sonny saw it as if from a distance, each of them changing orientation the way plants move imperceptibly, but fast, until all their leaves face toward the sun.

Ostensibly, Luki stayed at Sonny's house for security, and Luki did stay vigilant, weapons safe but at the ready, alert—it seemed—even when sleeping. He set a schedule for agents to be on surveillance at all times, watching and checking a perimeter about a quarter mile in all directions, including the back of the house—where, Kim complained, the trees and brush grew so thick they might become mired in them and never come out.

"Right," Luki said and smiled. Not widely, but a little.

"My God, boss. You're smiling."

"Maybe."

"Wait a minute…. Okay, I'm done choking on shock. Now, have you ever been back there in those trees?"

"Once, and I'm not going back, but you are."

Sonny laughed, overhearing the conversation from the mud porch where he was working on combining dyes for a project he needed to recreate after the vandalism of his studio. The piece was more important in his mind than anything he'd ever worked. Happily, he was more pleased with it this time than he'd been with the first effort. He appreciated Luki's concern and—he would readily admit—felt safer with all the precautions. But while he loved having Luki there nights and mornings, he was glad Luki left during the day to do whatever it was he felt he should do to find the "doer." He was glad to have his days alone.

Almost alone. The agents never bothered him. They stayed pretty much out of sight and made no noise, but Sonny felt *watched*, and he didn't like it. He threw himself into work in order to forget it, but he didn't go walking and he didn't bathe in the sea come dawn, as had been his habit. And he worried all throughout the daylight hours. Not constantly, but whenever he let his hands fall still at the loom. He could put the crimes, the ugly words, the notes and threats out of his mind fairly easily—Luki was on it, and by nature Sonny wasn't a worrier. But Delsyn had not come home. That worry, he couldn't quiet.

"What's eating you, Sonny?" Luki asked, one night when Sonny was pacing back and forth across the front of the house. "I haven't found the hater, and I'm sorry about that. It makes me feel pretty useless, but at least you're safe here."

"Don't be sorry, and that isn't it. It's Delsyn."

"Your nephew."

"He should have been home weeks ago. I've had him with me ten years. I haven't been the best uncle, and he's a little wild, but he always comes home."

"You filed a missing person report?"

"No. Yeah. I mean I tried to, not long after you and I met. But when the police found out that he was usually gone more than he was here, they told me to wait a few more weeks. Now, with everything that's going on...."

Luki nodded, chewing his lip. "Yeah," he said. "It's complicated."

After that, Luki started looking for Delsyn too, and he was coming up just as empty-handed. So tension ran through their days like stretched fishing line, ready to break at any minute. For Sonny, Luki's nightly homecoming—which is how he thought of it—kept him from crawling out of his skin. Despite everything, their days and evenings fell into a pattern that could only be called domestic.

They had dinner, played cards, and had sex, easy and sweet. And one day Sonny knew. He understood, all at once, what he felt when their hands joined, when Luki did some small, kind thing for him, when Luki, still in bed, cringed from the morning light but thanked him for the coffee anyway. And he understood, all at once, why he slept so soundly in Luki's arms, and why after sex he needed to curl into the shell of Luki's broad chest, and why their sex left him always wanting a next time. He loved Luki Vasquez, pure and simple.

But he thought it wise not to say so, just yet.

SONNY felt wrapped in heat, and filled with it too. They lay together in an almost sideways position Sonny wouldn't have imagined, much less believed possible. Luki's gentle motions reminded him of the rocking of waves in the straits on a calm day. It made him drowsy, but it felt a little too good to bring on sleep. He was glad Luki didn't seem to be in a hurry.

Luki's tongue and teeth teased at his ear, and Luki's breath flew past it, drying and cooling the tender lobe. "Does it feel good, baby?"

"Mmm," Sonny responded, spellbound, unable to speak more clearly.

Luki ran his hand across Sonny's chest, flicking past the hard nipples, playing in the light growth of hair. His hand moved lower and, with a light, firm touch, stroked down the shaft of Sonny's erection, brushed across the glans with his thumb, gave his testicles a slow squeeze. "Have you ever had an orgasm this way? With a man inside you?"

"No," Sonny managed to breathe. By now Luki well knew about Sonny's lack of experience, and Sonny had relaxed and become easy with the idea of Luki teaching him—something Luki clearly enjoyed.

"Do you want to?"

"Y—ah!—Yes."

Luki's chuckle felt nice. Sonny felt completely enveloped in care, and it was a sweet, seductive feeling; he wished he would be there in Luki's arms forever.

Luki's raspy voice turned to silk, somehow, in this loving, his words coming slow and smooth. "Let's make that happen for you then, baby." He turned Sonny's face toward him and stretched up enough to kiss and lick across the corner of his lips. "Are you ready? Listen to what I tell you, sweet. I'm going to be still, for a while. I want you to move against me—find the place, the stroke that feels right. You're strong; you can do that. Right?"

Sonny answered in an undecipherable syllable. No way could he articulate through the haze of sex in his head; even the sound of Luki's voice, the simple direction he gave, tantalized like the slip and pressure of flesh over flesh. But Sonny's body followed Luki's instruction without need of decision or will. And for the first time, Sonny found that the fullness of a man inside him, always pleasurable, could take him higher. That it wasn't just good, it was everything—at least in this moment. He found that place, that rhythm that was just right for *him*, for *his* body—a place he'd come close to before but hadn't actually known existed.

Fever. Sweat. Working it and becoming afraid, oh so afraid, of losing it, this magic place. Luki clamped one of his strong hands onto Sonny's thigh, effortlessly held it firm.

"Okay, baby. I have it now; you've shown me what you need. Relax and let me do it. Just feel it." He turned them both slightly to a position that would let him work, and then slowly started to stroke. Perfectly, matching exactly the pressure, the rhythm, the twist, that Sonny had found. The catch in his voice made it clear that, though Sonny was getting the attention, Luki was loving it—beyond turned on. "That's it, Sonny," he said. "God, yes, baby. That's it."

The sheet that had covered them had long since found its twisted way to the floor. Moonshine modeled their sweat-slicked bodies, so intertwined they might have melded into one. Sonny, feeling more open, more vulnerable than he'd ever felt in his life, had taken refuge in the curl of Luki's arms and broad chest. He needed the safety of that place because what was about to overtake him rolled like a tidal wave, and he didn't think he could stand in it alone.

Gradually, Luki increased the speed of his strokes and the pressure of his smooth glans running against the slick pad of pleasure inside Sonny. He held Sonny tight, stroking and soothing. "That's it, baby," he crooned again. "It's good, right?"

Sonny still found words beyond his reach, but he knew Luki understood; he could feel Luki smiling. The hard shaft of Luki's erection grew hot inside him, and little frissons and jerks of pleasure, like friction sparks, left him gasping. He started to push Luki back, wondering even at the time why he would do it, but he'd begun to feel afraid, overwhelmed.

"Sonny," Luki whispered through his own ragged breaths. "Baby, don't stop it. Let it happen, let it come."

A moan started somewhere deep, and Sonny—who always stayed nearly silent during sex—couldn't stop it. As it rose and stretched out, his pleasure possessed him. Then, just when he would have fought to regain control, Luki pushed a little harder. Firecracker-quick, perfect strokes, and at the same time he reached around to stroke Sonny's sex.

Sonny disappeared, or so it felt, enveloped in something beyond good, beyond pleasure. Something he didn't dare try to name. It was the sex, the pleasure, the incredible orgasm; and it was the care Luki took in taking him there. And when Sonny came back to himself he still lay in Luki's strong arms. Luki was still inside him, still hard, rocking Sonny gently and holding on to him tight.

"Beautiful," Luki whispered across Sonny's ear. "You're okay? It was good?"

"Mmm," Sonny said, which was the closest he'd come to saying something in a long while. He grabbed for Luki's hand, and Luki took his, and Sonny reveled in the hard-muscled feel of it.

Luki lifted his head and, when Sonny turned toward him, kissed him. Softly at first, but then harder, hotter. The gentle rocking once again gave way to strokes. Luki nipped at Sonny's ear, his shoulder. "Stay open for me, baby. I want more. I want to fuck you hard this time. That's okay?"

"Yes," Sonny whispered, surprised at the way his own desire responded to Luki's words.

"Good, sweetie. That's good. But don't let me hurt you, okay?" He panted, starting to quicken his movements already. But he said, "If it hurts, I'll stop."

Sonny didn't respond, except to feel a shiver of a new kind of excitement sweep through him, tensing his nipples again, beginning to tighten his balls. Luki slid out, flipped Sonny full onto his belly and pulled him back toward the foot of the bed where he could stand behind him. More lube, and then he pulled Sonny's ass up against him and wrapped demon-strong hands around his thighs. Sonny's excitement surged, maybe higher than ever. Never in his life had he so badly wanted to give himself to someone—no, not to give, to be taken.

Luki strengthened his strokes, plunged into Sonny just hard enough, again and again. Sonny was wide-open, body and soul, craving it, and even in the midst of this flame, Luki kept control, never crossed the line and hurt him. "Sonny?" he said, barely able to talk between hot breaths.

"Yes," Sonny answered. "Yes." The words were punctuated by deep thrusts. He groaned, braced himself against Luki's drive with one hand, and with the other hand reached down to touch himself lightly, tentatively. Miraculously, he began to harden.

"Stroke it, Sonny! I know you want to. Do it, baby, stroke it."

Sonny did, falling quickly into his long-practiced rhythm, then adjusting to a sweet counterpoint with Luki's rhythm. He stopped, squeezed out some pre-cum, and lifted it to his tongue—a habit since adolescence, but something he'd never before done in company.

Luki saw, and it seemed to drive him toward the edge. "Damn, baby," he said. "That's it. That's beautiful." He quickened his thrusts again, then reached around and clamped his hand over Sonny's, helping him stroke. "Oh, Sonny," he panted. "Sweet man. Sweet, sweet man!"

More fucking, more stroking, more sweet words, and Sonny felt himself disappearing again. The sounds they made turned primal; their bodies jerked and clenched, out of control. And then they dissolved into a moaning, gasping, quivering tangle of limbs and sex.

Luki fell back, pulling Sonny over to lay by him, curled on his side, sweaty and hot, but once again ensconced in Luki's strong, safe arms. For once, he'd held nothing back. Luki had coaxed from him complete trust, in opposite extremes. He didn't regret it. *This*, he thought, *is how it's supposed to be.*

Luki untangled the St. Christopher medal's chain from his curls and reached across to hang it on the lamp on Sonny's side of the bed. On the way back, he paused to kiss Sonny's brow and whisper in his ear, "Good sleep."

LUKI got up early, just on the edge of a yellow-gray, salt-beach morning. In the nights they'd spent together, this was the first time Luki had woken before Sonny except in Bellingham after the hospital. He sat up, skin prickling from a chill in the air that spoke of summer's end.

Appropriate, Luki thought, extracting himself from Sonny's arms and legs. He rolled off the mattress and snugged the blanket up around Sonny, brushed a long, heavy lock of hair out of his face. Sonny turned over, curled up tighter under the blanket, and sighed, but he didn't wake. He looked content.

"Damn," Luki muttered, revisiting the self-torture that had kept him awake nearly all night. He'd let it go too far. He'd broken all of his own rules with Sonny. He'd pursued him, come to know him, *slept in his bed,* for God's sake. More than once. Lots more than once. He'd let it go on too long, let it go too far. And now he had to end it—this thing he never should have started. Because he couldn't do this. He wasn't made for it. And it was far too dangerous.

"I shouldn't have done it," he whispered. "I shouldn't have stayed.

"I need a cigarette."

"DO YOU want more coffee?"

"No," Luki said. "Thank you." He could feel Sonny's tension. Sonny would have made a good detective. His intuition, his sense of a person's intention, was stronger than his own. *I should just speak up,* Luki told himself. He thought a cigarette would make it easier, but he didn't have any handy. He'd quit smoking—just yesterday. He tried to swallow so he could speak, but Sonny took the matter out of his hands.

"What's up with you this morning?"

"I'm leaving, Sonny."

"Hm," Sonny said, pouring his own coffee.

He wasn't smiling at all, which was so unusual that his face looked strange—like a face Luki had never seen. He stirred flavored creamer bit by bit into his cup until, apparently, the color of his coffee matched the color he'd imagined. He carried his cup to the other end of the great room, the open space that served as everything except bathroom, studio, and woodshed. The bank of windows on that side looked out on sand running up against a wall of second-growth fir. Sonny studied it like a subject for silk and wool. Possibly it would be, or had been.

He didn't turn to meet Luki's eyes when he spoke to him. "I'm getting the idea," he said, "that you don't mean you're running out for a pack of smokes. You're *leaving,* leaving."

"Yes." He fought the shake in his voice. Saying this, doing this, felt impossible. But staying *was* impossible. "I'm not going to desert you; I'm still working on the case. I'll still help you find Delsyn. We'll figure it out. But I—"

"The case," Sonny said, his own voice steady but low, obscured in a sheath of breath. "Tell me about last night, Luki. What was that?"

Luki found it hard to unclench his teeth. He never should have stayed with Sonny, never should have *slept in his bed*—not even once. But he had, and now he had to cut the strings—as he'd known from the beginning he would. It was the hardest thing he'd ever had to do, short of burying his dad. And it felt about the same. Something precious on one side, and in the opposite corner, a great big hole. But this time the choice had not been made for him by something as inevitable as death. This time he was making the choice. Because his defenses couldn't tolerate the "something precious."

"Answer me, Luki." Sonny's voice had gained strength. His words commanded.

"It was... Sonny, I have three talents, three things I've learned how to do for someone, anyone, you. I can protect, I can cook, and I can do great sex—"

"You can cook?" Sonny turned and glanced quickly at Luki. The expression on his face belonged so completely to Sonny that Luki almost smiled in recognition before he remembered the moment. And Sonny's glance didn't linger.

"Yes," Luki answered faintly. He swallowed and went on, hating himself for what he was doing, hating even more that he felt he had no choice. This togetherness... daily and committed togetherness, was outside his repertoire, and he couldn't afford it. He'd already let down his safety guard too much, for too long.

"You haven't answered yet, Luki. Last night..."

"It was—" He saw Sonny's shoulders tense. His own voice turned to a plea, something he hardly recognized. "It's the best I have, Sonny. I wanted to give you the best I have to give... how can I make you understand? Look at me," he said, but Sonny didn't.

"But I can't do... *this*, Sonny." Even though Sonny didn't turn around, Luki gestured in a way that took in everything: the sky, the bed, the house with their torn hearts inside it. "*This*, it's not in my range. I can't do it, and I don't want it. I'm sorry, Sonny, but I don't want... I don't want—"

"You don't want!" Sonny shouted, snarling. He pivoted, took three long strides toward Luki, and threw his body against him, backing him up against the wall. The move stopped just short of violence, so quick and certain and unexpected that Luki, for all his skills and practiced strength, didn't react, didn't even see it coming. Though Sonny stood only a few inches taller than him, at the moment it felt to Luki that he towered overhead. Luki stood in a position he'd not been in for twenty-eight years—he was pinned.

But Sonny wasn't holding him against the wall. Sonny leaned with his elbows on either side of Luki's head, his face twisted into an expression blurring the borders of bitterness and rage and pain. His eyes bored into Luki's. Sonny kissed him, kissed his forehead, his cheek, his neck, interrupting the kisses with raging, hurting words.

"You don't want what? *Me!* You don't want *me*, goddamn it." He pressed his lips against Luki's, pushed hard, pressured his tongue past lips and teeth, and, God help him, Luki kissed him back, just as desperate. Sonny broke the kiss off suddenly. "How can you do it, Luki? How can you build my love for you brick by brick, make me want you more than my own life, make me *need* you for Christ's sake, and then tell me *you don't want me?*"

He lifted his arms from the wall as if to turn away but then slammed them down again on either side of Luki's face, kissing him, pleading, commanding behind the kisses, "Don't leave. God, Luki, please don't."

Luki hadn't thought Sonny was ever capable of real violence. Now he wasn't sure; maybe he was. Maybe Luki had pushed him past that point.

And I might not fight back! That thought, that *fear*, struck like a bullet.

Sonny had buried his hands in Luki's hair, where they'd been so many times before in passion, and this was not a lot different. He pulled, but not hard, and pressed more kisses against Luki's face. Then, "How? How can you do it?

"How can you leave, you son of a bitch?"

Luki tasted salt. Sonny's tears. But there was nothing soft, no flex, no give even in Sonny's pleas. In the space of an instant, Luki saw the man in front of him as never before. For all his gazing, all his scrutinizing and desiring, he'd been blind. Now he saw Sonny, and it was like looking into some strange mirror. They both guarded their hearts, Luki with guns and ice, Sonny with beauty and smiles.

But the difference, now: Sonny had stripped his armor and laid it aside to let Luki in; Luki had felt the cracks in his ice shield spreading, and he'd beat a retreat.

All that figuring in a fractured second, and then Luki broke through his shock. He didn't push Sonny back, he didn't move at all. "*Stop*," he said.

Instantly, Sonny lifted his arms, turned away, and walked across the room to stare through the window, looking across a sink full of dirty dishes to the cloud-covered straits, tears and rage apparently spent.

"Leave," he said.

"Sonny—"

"Get out." His shoulders lifted and fell in a deep sigh. His voice softened. "I'm going out for a while. Be gone when I come back. Take everything you brought here with you. Including your guns. Your silence. Your *fucking* cigarettes."

"I quit smoking." *Why did I say that? All the things I want to say, things that might somehow, magically, make a difference, and that's what I come up with?*

A rough, almost certainly painful laugh forced itself from Sonny's throat. "Just go, Luki. This is my house, and I want you out of it."

Luki whispered, "Sonny."

"Open the windows on your way out, if you would be so kind. This place smells like you."

"Sonny," he said, and silently he begged. *Look at me, please. See me.*

But Sonny didn't look at him, just walked out and let the screen door slam behind him. Luki stared after him, numb....

Until he saw Sonny drive past the door and the kitchen window in a teeny Honda Civic that must have been the first one ever made, white paint splotched with rust, two little mirrors mounted near the front of the fenders. The car sat so low that Luki could see inside, how long-legged Sonny had to drive with his knees on either side of the steering wheel, which might explain why he was having such a hard time shifting. The little car putted away with Sonny looking like he would burst its seams, and Luki couldn't help himself.

He laughed. He laughed hard, uncontrollably, from somewhere deep in his gut. He laughed like he never had—at least that he remembered. He laughed like his life depended on it, which maybe it did. He stopped when he couldn't laugh anymore. The cobwebs had cleared by then. He understood his sorrow, and he thought perhaps he understood Sonny's sorrow, too. The insight had come too late. He sighed, remembering the taste of Sonny's tears.

He went through Sonny's house—Sonny's home—gathering his things. A shirt. Flip-flops—something he'd never owned before, bought for exploring the beach with Sonny. Underwear, by God. He looked at the St. Christopher medal he'd hung over the lamp by the bedside, lifted it, but let its weight fall from his fingers. He'd leave it for Sonny.

I want him safe, he thought.

He headed for the bathroom to gather his toothbrush, hair pick, and dressing for the curls he was so vain about. But before him, Sonny's studio door stood open. Luki hadn't been in there since the day after they'd come back to find it desecrated, half of Sonny's work destroyed. Sonny was right, he realized now; the house did smell of him. He knew that because the air coming through the studio held not a trace of him.

It was all Sonny. Sea salt and coffee. Sun and dyes and wool. Beneath it all, a trace of I'm-too-into-my-work-to-stop-for-a-shower sweat. All of it sweet. Even the sweat. Luki stepped down into the one room into which he'd never been invited. Sonny's haven, his sanctum, his kaleidoscope world.

Nothing could have prepared him for what he saw. Sonny hadn't cleaned the hate words from the wall, but he'd painted a thick, black line through them, crossed them out. Next to the scrawl, on a huge, complicated, upright loom, hung an almost finished tapestry of light-filled blues and sun so bright it blurred the lines of everything it touched. He recognized the place and the time. The street in town with the strip of park against the long sand beach, and people walking in bright clothing, some standing in line for pizza-by-the-slice at Manzetti's. A child in a stroller.

The day they'd met.

At the focal point: Luki. Larger than life.

It stole his breath, and he sank to the arm of the couch that he hadn't even noticed behind him. Some time after that—Luki didn't know if it was minutes or an hour—he heard Sonny's boots on the porch, the screen door open and this time close more gently. Sonny would of course know Luki was still there, would have seen his car outside. Luki gave the thought a corner of his attention, wondered distantly whether Sonny would hate that Luki had breached his private domain, on top of all the harm he'd already done.

But he couldn't look away from the tapestry.

Sonny came to stand just inside the studio door. Luki felt him there, heard his breath, noticed his faint shadow falling over him. He didn't turn his head.

Sonny didn't speak.

Luki asked, his voice no more than a thin scratch, "Is that how you see... saw me? You thought I was beautiful?"

"Yes," Sonny said, and then he sighed. His voice had lost its edge, melodious and rich again. "That's how I *see* you. I *think* you're beautiful. How could that change? I see what's there. I always see what's there."

Something tightened in Luki's throat, something foreign, something painful, and with a shock he recognized what it was. Tears. *Oh my God, tears.* They welled up in his eyes and flowed over. His face felt wet, and heavy drops ran down his scar like a river bed, like that was the reason the scar was made, to give the tears a place to run.

He wanted to howl, to sob, to bury his face in a pillow and scream, but he didn't. He sat stock-still, holding back the screams, and it hurt.

Sonny stepped forward, quieter, more sober and capable than Luki had ever seen him. With a thumb he wiped gently at the tears under each of Luki's eyes. Again, he sighed. "What do you want to do, Luki?"

"I'm not beautiful, Sonny." The words forced themselves up and out.

"You are. I see what's there. I always, only, ever see what's there, and I weave what I see—or at least as close as my fingers and materials can come."

"I—" Luki stopped, choking on the words. They cut like diamonds when he forced them. "I don't want to go, Sonny. I don't want to leave."

SONNY knew Luki was waiting for him to respond, but he couldn't bring himself to say anything at all. He laid a hand on the back of Luki's neck, feeling tension like fear stretched across his broad shoulders. Tension that didn't belong there. Fear that Sonny shouldn't make him endure.

But his own terror and the memory of the humiliating way he'd revealed it hung too fresh in his mind, and he just couldn't force the kindness. His eyes roamed over the tapestry, his most precious work. More than a tribute; he'd wanted to make it a message of love, for Luki. For beautiful Luki. His eyes stopped at the empty weft in the only corner left unfinished.

It was to be a pool of dark night sky and scattered stars, one star brighter than all the rest. In the finished piece, it would become clear that the bright star high in the sky—Sonny—was the source of the brilliance in Luki's pale blue eyes.

Wishful thinking, Sonny told himself now. But he kept staring at the emptiness, kept turning it over in his mind. He belonged there, woven into that tapestry with Luki. For Luki, the work meant that someone saw him as beautiful, an eye-opener. And Sonny agreed: Luki's likeness gave the tapestry its beauty. But the star in the corner reflecting in Luki's eyes, that gave it meaning and wonder. Luki had *seen* him—that day on the boulevard; he'd looked into him, not past him. And since then, even when Luki wrapped himself in ice, Sonny had always been able to find himself reflected in Luki's eyes, a tiny gleam of warmth.

Except today. Today he hadn't been able to make Luki see him at all.

He let his hand drop and stepped around Luki, who still sat immobile on the arm of his old sofa—the daydreaming sofa, he called it, or the planning couch, depending on his mood. He switched on the bank of expensive daylight fluorescents, then started to sort out the bobbins of colored silk hanging from the back of the weaving, only a few left now at the end of things. When everything was ready, he put his hands and feet to work.

He took a deep breath. "Go smoke a cigarette, Luki. We'll talk later."

Luki's answer came delayed, and then tentative. "I'd rather watch you work."

"I never let anyone watch me work."

"I never cry." He tried to smile, to pretend it was a joke.

Sonny turned around to face him. "Yes, Luki," he said. "You do. You're crying most of the time, and everyone knows it but you."

Chapter Nine

LUKI had stayed, slept in Sonny's bed one more night, sexless and nearly silent. Sonny sat beside him, watching him search for sleep. As the long, late summer dusk deepened, he gazed more closely at Luki's face, running the side of his thumb down the long scar that split the left side of his face. He watched the rare light play across the faint marbling that flanked the line of the cut; slightly raised and corded, it made the wound look braided together rather than simply healed. Luki pulled away and turned his head, hiding the scar against the pillow, rolling away in his almost-sleep to put his back to Sonny.

Sonny knew that the scar represented something much deeper in Luki's soul than a mere injury. Luki had never allowed Sonny into the intimate past of that secret wound. But Sonny had always known that if he wanted Luki to be there in the morning, he had to let him keep his silence. And he had wanted that. He couldn't have sworn to it, but he thought it might be true that he'd never wanted anything quite as much.

He reached across and turned out the light, then curled his body up right against his lover's skin. Feathered his hand gently through Luki's silk-soft curls until Luki's respirations finally slowed and deepened into real sleep, and his muscles relaxed into the cradle of Sonny's care.

The moment tasted sweet, but Sonny knew—and he'd have bet his own blood that Luki did too—that if they were to have a tomorrow, they weren't going to find it for a long time.

THE last night he spent at Sonny's house had been almost impossible to bear. Afraid that the morning would be worse, Luki held on to sleep as long as he could. When he finally forced himself to leave the warm, tangled sheets that smelled of Sonny, and of him, and of that fabulous night of sex that he had tried to tell Sonny was some kind of parting gift, Sonny had gone.

Cigarette, Luki thought. But he'd quit, just two days ago.

He left his toothbrush, his flip-flops, his hair cream and pick, but he knew it was an act of blind hope. Magical thinking: *if I act like I never said I wanted to leave, it shall be so.*

He rolled his eyes, laughing at himself and crying out for Sonny but all of it inside. He placed his well-used mask of polar ice firmly over his face. He rolled out of Sonny's home, down the gravel road, the paved cut-off, the highway, and back to town. Stopped at Margie's.

"He's already been here, Luki. I don't know what happened to you two, but I'm sorry, dear." She put his black coffee down before him and passed him the sugar and a spoon. "But you know, I've always had a feeling you two would get on fine. Maybe you want to give up, I suppose. But if you don't give up… well, you never know."

So Luki didn't give up. He showed up at Margie's nearly every morning. He stood on the street outside Manzetti's pizza, even though the weather had turned windy and wet and the color-clad tourists stayed hidden. He called.

At first, Sonny would answer the phone. "Sonny James."

It seemed an odd way for him to answer, and Luki said so, which earned him a terse reply.

"I do business on this phone, Luki. What's on your mind?"

"You," he answered, on that first call.

"Don't be a jackass." Sonny hung up.

Twice more, Sonny picked up. The exchanges between them were not quite so curt as the first, but they weren't exactly love songs, either.

At the end of the third call, Sonny said, "Just leave it be, Luki. I'm still hurt. You're still just as scared as you ever were. I don't want to talk about it." Sonny hung up.

Luki called the next day. "Sonny," he said.

Sonny hung up.

After that, Sonny set his answering machine. Aside from the usual business greeting and a direction to sonnyjameswovenart.com, he recorded two personal messages: "Luki, hang up now and add this number to your do not call list. Delsyn, let me know how to get in touch with you. Please come home. You're scaring me."

But Luki couldn't put Sonny out of his mind. *Someday,* he told himself, *I'll find a way back.* In the meantime, he hadn't forgotten his business.

Technically, Sonny had hired him to solve a crime, and he hadn't yet discharged that obligation. He kept it at the top of his agenda, and he realized that with a burning need to keep his mind occupied he was finally giving the case the attention it deserved. He put all resources not otherwise obligated on the task. He got up early in the morning. He freed up money for unforeseen expenses. He applied all his know-how, and pointed all his people toward this, the James case. He had agents and junior staff in five major cities—even if they were working something else, he wanted their eyes and ears aware. He had sub-contractors and a host of connections ranging from the ATF agents he used to work with to street informants in every major city in the US and not a few small towns. Whatever he could buy of their time and effort, he pointed toward this job, gladly footing the bill.

After the desecration of Sonny's studio, he'd dusted for prints and other clues, done as much as Sonny would allow to collect evidence. But, at the end of the next day, Sonny had firmly evicted him and his agents from the suite of rooms that constituted his place of business.

His agents hit the streets, looking for clues to Mr. K, street news about queer-haters, and anything about loose kids getting picked up and taken off the streets—other than in the usual way. In particular, anything about ratty, white vans driven by middle-aged men with more than the usual amount of bling. Mr. K's trail led from Bellingham south again to Seattle, and then east along the I-90 corridor. No criminal events that Luki's people could track down. His name had turned up on the streets but, though there were the usual number of haters out there, nothing they did appeared to be linked to the target. The bling was still there. The white van had disappeared. Word was, the creep was cruising in a BMW.

For Jude, Luki set the task of searching recent news stories and crime data for look-alike incidents, especially anything about traces of the dyes taken from Sonny's studio. He had her check for vandalism of Sonny's art in galleries and public installations. A child had spilled chocolate milk on a tapestry he'd donated to the Washington School for the Deaf, but nothing else of note had taken place.

For himself, he reserved the toughest job, the one that took the most skill, the one only the senior agent could do. Asking, begging, pleading, cajoling, promising, guilt-tripping every consultant and agent—current and former—that might remember his name to help him ID prints.

One set, lifted from Sonny's studio wall, had been easy—the ID was in his own database. They belonged to a thug named Danny Jordan, a penny-ante pair of fists who had never left behind any evidence of more than a rudimentary brain. Kim had lifted partials of what certainly appeared to be Jordan's prints from the Mercedes too. The timing had been a little difficult to figure out, but it was possible and appeared likely. Jordan hit the car and Sonny's studio in the same night. Luki appreciated the fact that they had, at last, one solid clue. But it seemed impossible to line up their note-writing, threatening, slippery quarry with an oaf like Jordan. Probably, Mr. K had just been resourceful when his supply of homeless teens had run dry.

On the other hand, the prints left on the bloody tiles in the armory haunted and eluded him. Everything he'd tried had come up to a dead end. PI's, attorneys, data geeks, consultants, Luki had just about exhausted his virtual rolodex, shelled out a pretty substantial sum to have every private and publicly accessible fingerprint data base searched. Zilch.

He thought he should let it go, try to find some other angle, but the problem scratched at the back of his brain, begging him to put two together with some other two he couldn't quite grasp. It kept him awake, and when he did sleep, he saw Sonny, and when he woke, he needed all the more to find the hands that printed themselves in blood.

Desperate measures.

"Katie," he said, when ATF special agent Sullivan returned his third call.

She whispered into the phone. "What is it, Luki? I told you I can't help you out anymore. My ass is still in the fire from last time."

"Okay," Luki said. "I understand. But hey, listen, how's Jenny and the kids? Did that deal go through on the five acres?"

"They're fine. We're fine." Her voice softened. "Jenny and I went to Hawaii and got married. Doesn't mean a lot legally, but still. It's a good feeling."

"Congratulations, Kate," Luki answered, something inexplicably dropping to the bottom of his stomach like a brick. "That's... that's wonderful. I'm glad for you."

"Luki? You all right? 'Cause I was pretty sure you were only trying to butter me up so you could slide into one of your famous irresistible pleas, but now you're sounding a little mushy. Melt down?"

Luki didn't answer that. Didn't seem to be any point. Apparently Sonny had rendered him transparent, even over the telephone. "Kate," he said, "you know I care about you, all of you. But yes, I was trying to butter you up. Did it work?"

"Sure, damn it. But this is the last time. And if I get the boot from ATF, you're supporting my family until Social Security kicks in."

"Deal," he said. "All I need is to run some prints through IAFIS."

"Hey, no big deal. I'll just put in my code so they'll know exactly who it was that ran an unauthorized, *illegal* fingerprint search, and then I'll—"

"*Katie!* Look, I'm sorry. I know I'm asking you to put your neck on the block, here, and I know there's not much I can do to repay you. But this no ordinary job, for me. An ugly... slime-filled ugly set of crimes that I can't give officially to law enforcement. One, I want the crimes solved, and I don't feel all that sure they'd try real hard; and two, some kids... vulnerable kids stand to get hurt real bad if I do, and three, someone I care about... care about far too much will get hurt, which scares me more than it does him. If you think it's too much risk, tell me so and I'll back off. But if you can help, Kate...."

"Luki, do these really ugly crimes have anything to do with, say, haters? Maybe, say, queer-haters?"

"Yeah. Yes, they do."

"And does this person whom you care about in any way resemble a lover?"

"Well—"

"Past, present, or future?"

"Yeah, Katie. He does. He was."

"I see."

Kate cleared her throat several times, a habit that used to drive Luki crazy when they worked together—nothing ruins the ice cube effect when questioning a suspect as badly as a short, blonde, tri-athlete sounding like a chain saw that wouldn't start.

"Stop it, Kate."

"When's the last time you vomited, Luki?"

"Point taken. So…?"

"You heard about that woman in Seattle. Cat Bronwyn, I think her name was?"

"I heard."

"Cops did a fine job with that, right?"

"Oh yeah."

"It was obvious, after all, that she was a random victim. Didn't have anything to do with her being lesbian."

"Etcetera."

"So, did you get good prints?"

"Excellent. It was almost like the person who left them did it on purpose. Stamped his—or her—hands, both of them, into a slick of blood on a tile floor. I fixed, stained, lifted, and got the pictures. They're a masterpiece."

"Acid yellow seven?"

"Yeah, great stuff. Got part of a shoe print, too, but I don't think that's going to help much. So, how do you want me get these to you? Upload?"

"God, I don't know, Luki."

"Listen, I've got actual photos, besides the digitals, so I'll courier those to you—sound safer?"

"Best we can hope for. I might have to wait a few days to slide these in... somehow. Meantime, you know where to find me."

Luki hung up feeling like a stone was slowly being turned to take the weight off his chest. Like maybe at last something was cracking about this... he wasn't sure what to call it. To him, it wasn't just a case; the crimes were all about Sonny. About somebody hating Sonny, the most perfect... the most gorgeously perfect man Luki had ever met. And those prints had stood like a roadblock against his efforts to make him safe.

But if the prints had ever been taken or lifted, anywhere in the country, for any reason, they would almost certainly be in IAFIS. And Luki hoped—really, really hoped—Kate would lend a little of her generous Irish luck. He'd cross his fingers if he didn't have to drive.

But he did have to drive because there were two parts to the James case, and he'd left one alone too long, in order to tend to the other. Luki was supposed to keep Sonny safe, at least until they could take the hater down—hopefully in cuffs and a squad car, but in a body bag if necessary.

That meant keeping watch. Standing guard. Scanning the perimeter.

Luki, with backup nearby, held vigil much of the time when he wasn't following up other aspects of the case, and a trio of ex-cops staked out the rest of the time. He always had agents patrolling the beach, the road, and the single, traversable trail down the ridge and through the trees. He kept everybody a good distance away, and concealed their activities as much as possible, though he couldn't have guaranteed that Sonny wouldn't see, given his instincts and artist's eye.

Although the stakeout became melancholy at times, the task also had significant entertainment value. He had been there when Sonny rode out on a sleek blue Harley Davidson. And he was there again when Sonny came up the gravel road coaxing his truck the last yards to the shed, Harley standing in the bed on a rack. Another day, Sonny backed the silly little Honda out of the shed that was clearly bigger than it looked and parked it, and then backed out a yellow Mustang. One of the really expensive, old ones in shiny show-room shape.

To Luki's surprise, Sonny tooled around—literally—fixing or changing or servicing or doing something more mechanical than Luki could readily understand to his various engines and moving parts. And polished the Mustang and the Harley and put them away. And patted the Honda fondly and put it away. And kicked the truck fender and left it in the yard.

And maybe, just maybe, looked right at Luki where he was hidden.

Luki felt guilty, actually, because when conducting surveillance of this sort—guarding—the object was not to watch your charge, but rather to watch for anything coming that might be a threat. But in Sonny's case, that was difficult to do. For instance, how was Luki supposed to look away when Sonny walked down to the water's edge in the morning when the sun was shining through shreds of fog wearing a loose cotton shirt and his boxers. And when he stripped off those clothes and waded into the straits—the almost certainly frigid straits—submerged himself under rolling, angled waves, and then rose up from the water stretching his arms wide, gold sunlight shining off of him like he was some kind of god. How was he supposed to look away then?

Sonny surprised him, repeatedly. One afternoon he walked into the thick-sown firs and came back hours later with cedar fronds and long strips of red bark. He spent a whole day splitting firewood, shedding his shirt when the sun warmed the day, sweat slicking his chest and arms, highlighting corded muscle. And some evenings, for hours at a time, Sonny sat in a metal chair by his unprotected door with nothing at all in his hands, staring past his rusty truck at the road. Like he was watching for someone, waiting.

Luki wished that watching and waiting was for him. But he knew better.

SONNY pressed the record button on his answering machine and tried to speak. The first part came easy, but when he came to the personal messages he wanted to leave for Luki and Delsyn, he choked. He'd tried twice already. He hoped the third time would be the proverbial charm.

"Delsyn, damn it. Please come home, nephew. If you need money to get here, you know I'll send it." He swallowed, then pushed on.

"Luki, I'm sorry about my last recording. It was mean. I'm still not sure I want to talk to you but, well, you know. Leave a message."

There, that should do it, for now.

He could hardly sleep nights, worrying about Delsyn. Sonny knew he couldn't keep his nephew home, but Del knew he had to get back every week or ten days; his life might very well depend on it. Sonny had called all his relatives, the few of his nephew's friends that he knew how to contact, and with dread weighting down his heart, every Indian Health medical center he could think of from Oklahoma to Neah Bay. On the one hand, he was glad to glean no information about Del's whereabouts from the hospitals. On the other hand, that might mean something worse.

"Damn," he muttered, and he repeated it at frequent intervals, running his fingers through his hair. He haunted his own house, wandering in the early morning hours from corner to remote, dusty corner, down hallways that shouldn't have been connected, linking clumps of rooms that once stood alone.

Delsyn liked his independence, and just after his twelfth birthday he'd talked Sonny into letting him live in an unlikely set of rooms in the section farthest from the great room and studio where Sonny spent his time. One night when Sonny's mood felt as black as the clouded, new-moon sky, he wandered there, not realizing that's what he was doing until he set foot through the door. A mess, Delsyn's usual.

"Del, goddamn it," Sonny said, his voice sounding muffled as if swallowed into the planed log walls. He began to tidy up, hanging up shirts that seemed clean, folding socks, making a pile of dirty clothes to be carted away.

"You don't even have your jacket, you little shit." He bent to pick up the forgotten item, but as he did, he caught sight of something silver peeking out from under the bed. Medical ID tags. "Don't tell me… Delsyn, I thought we'd been through this. You have to wear the damn things!" Sonny felt despair nipping at his heels, so he pivoted, snapped the light switch on his way out, and shut the door.

He might worry, but he wouldn't despair, wouldn't believe something bad had happened. He believed Delsyn would come home; he insisted on it. He composed the thorough scolding he'd deliver when that happened. Because Del was okay. He *would* come home.

But something about that visit to his nephew's private domain bothered him. Something felt wrong. Maybe it was the tags. Certainly that troubled him, but something else too. Something he should see, but couldn't quite grasp, even when he went back. "I'm imagining things," he told himself and decided to leave it alone.

Oddly, and annoyingly, when he closed his eyes at night and tried to forget about Delsyn so he could sleep, thoughts of Luki surfaced, and he still couldn't sleep. Sometimes because he was overcome with anger, sometimes hurt, and sometimes even shame because he was sure he should have known better than to fall so hard and fast for the man. He'd spent the last ten years avoiding that kind of mistake—sex rarely and casually, no sweethearts and no steadies. On the few occasions when he met someone he *might* have fallen for, he ran the other way.

Just as, apparently, Luki had wanted to run away from him. That's the only way he could make sense out of Luki's sudden split. All that manly "I wanted to give you the best screwing you ever had, and now I'll be on my way" crap was just that. Crap. Reality was, the man was scared. The question that troubled Sonny: *what the hell could he find in me to be afraid of?*

But, of course, that hadn't been where the nightmare ended, had it? The man had to change his mind, beg to stay, so now it was Sonny who looked like a mean cuss. And he felt like one too.

Damn it!

And he still couldn't sleep. He'd spent a day splitting wood. He slept five hours that night. He spent a day in the woods, which ended in another five hours. He tried to work on his cars—which Luki, the detective, was too unobservant to have even seen while he was around—but he'd had too little sleep and ended up smashing his thumb. Thus couldn't sleep.

Eventually, he took up the habit of sitting out by the door instead of sleeping, then going in and weaving all night. He stuck to making simple throws with jacquard patterns, way too tired and grouchy to weave a decent tapestry. He suspected even the stuff he was turning out on the jack loom would have to be undone.

One early morning, he woke to pounding on the door. The first thought to come to mind was *Oh my God, I've been sleeping.* Yes, he'd fallen asleep leaning across the loom with his foot on the treadle and the shuttle in his hand. He'd drooled on his work. When the pounding came again, Sonny reclaimed his wayward brain and instantly thought, "Delsyn," not taking time to remember that Delsyn had a key.

When he swung the door open, Luki stood there, steam spitting off of his icy surface.

Sonny stepped back and started to close the door again, too shocked and groggy to think of a better response.

"No, Sonny. Damn it," Luki put a foot across the threshold and kicked the door out of Sonny's hands. "You need to either let me in there or come out here because I have something important to tell you. I've been calling you every hour for the last twenty-four, and you *never* pick up, and I can't even leave a message because your 'messages have exceeded memory'. And then, I couldn't even get my car past the lake in your driveway, so I walked through it, and I've been standing out here for the last half-hour in the *pissing, pouring* rain, knocking politely and waiting." He stopped for breath—and apparently to calm himself. "So, whatever you think of me, whatever you do or don't want where I'm concerned, you're going to listen now."

He met Sonny's eyes, and even though Luki's were ice, something soft gleamed inside of them. Sonny's heart tumbled for a beat or two at the sight of it. He stood back and let Luki in, started to help him take off his soaking wet coat.

"No, wait," Luki said. "Remember the hand prints in the blood at the armory?"

Sonny nodded, a cold fist of premonition forming inside his belly.

Luki stalled, or perhaps took a moment to gather fortitude, chewing his bottom lip. In a stressed whisper, he said, "They belong to Delsyn James."

Chapter Ten

"THEY what?"

Luki watched Sonny closely, stayed behind him as he stumbled to the sink and turned on the tap. He looked like he might fall, but he didn't. He drew water in a plastic tumbler with a cartoon Pocahontas, drank it down, and filled it again. He stumbled three steps toward the bed, then turned to face Luki, looking half-mad and half-sick.

"Where is he?"

"I don't know, Sonny." Luki wasn't sure how much he should say, or even how much Sonny would hear. He felt certain about one thing, though: if he'd fooled himself for even a minute into thinking he'd get over Sonny, that he could walk away from what they'd begun to share and go back to his solitary, self-sufficient ice cave, he'd been wrong. He'd do anything, he realized, if he could atone for the hurt he'd caused, anything to have Sonny's hand to hold, anything at all to get Sonny to let him back in.

At the moment, he would do anything just to soothe Sonny's fear. "Listen, baby—"

"He was here."

All the color drained from Sonny's face, and he spoke so low that Luki almost didn't catch it. He pondered; he didn't think Sonny's words were a response to what he'd started to say. He wasn't sure Sonny had even heard him. Taking him by the arm, he led him to the bed—which also served as the room's main seating—moved over a pile of clothes, pillows, and… yes, even shoes, and pushed Sonny down to sit.

Now, in the circle of light cast by the bare bulb overhead, Luki saw that Sonny's hair hung in greasy strings. That his light beard hadn't been shaved since God knows when. That his clothes were… well, a little worse than usual. He needed a shower, and Luki began to wonder how this beautiful, bright man could have fallen into such disrepair. But it didn't matter so much, now. Sonny looked at him with near-dead eyes and spoke with no inflection.

"Is he dead?"

"I don't know that, Sonny, but I think there's reason to hope not—"

"He was here. I should have seen it. I should have understood." He got suddenly to his feet and strode to a door Luki had seen but never asked about.

Luki followed him, once again finding that it was hard to keep up. Down a narrow hall, to the right and down another, through a door on the left. Sonny took a jacket off a coat hook and turned it until he found a stain. He went still.

"Sonny, what is it?"

"Dye. Two colors. He wouldn't ever do that—mess with my dyes. And this." He held up a set of tags on a chain. "He did have these on. When I found them, I thought he didn't take them, but I knew he did, knew it all along. I was here when he left, and I made sure. He had his jacket and he had the tags. Oh my God, it's my fault. It's my…"

He stopped, breathing hard.

Luki opened his mouth to speak, but he didn't get a chance.

Sonny pivoted to face him, eyes cutting, burning right through him, words slamming his chest like hollow-nose bullets. *"Is he dead?"*

Luki stepped back, under attack. Once more, as he had the morning he'd tried to bid Sonny a casual farewell, the sheer power Sonny could muster, the suddenness with which he could turn it loose, left Luki stunned. But then, just as quickly, Sonny sagged, deflated, fell apart. He looked at Luki, shaking his head; Luki took it for apology.

"Luki, is Delsyn dead?"

"I don't know. But he hasn't turned up in any…" Luki let the remark trail off. He didn't think it would be a good idea to say "morgue." But how to put it then? "…any crime reports, or as a John Doe. And we have no reason to believe he was badly hurt. The blood we lifted the prints from—it looked like a lot, but Sonny, that was no more than a few tablespoons—"

"You don't understand, Luki."

Luki waited for Sonny to say more but instead he stepped across the room—Delsyn's room, apparently—and pushed back the loose-woven, brilliant curtain to stare out at blank night. "You don't understand."

"What? I don't understand what?"

"He's sick. No, not sick. The blood…"

"What about the blood?" But Sonny's eyes had gone distant. Luki gave him a gentle shake. "Look at me." When Sonny turned his head and met his eyes, lucid for the moment, he repeated, "What about the blood?"

"Von Willebrand disease. Have you heard of it?" Luki shook his head but Sonny was still talking anyway. "It's a blood disorder. His blood doesn't have something called Factor V Leiden, or Factor VIII. Or both, really. He bleeds."

"You mean… he's a bleeder, like with hemophilia?"

"Not quite the same, but yeah, he's a bleeder. Worse when he's not treated."

"Treated?"

"Glue…"

"Glue? Sonny, make sense. What do you mean, glue."

"Fibrin glue. He usually has glue, at least. If he's just cut a little and he can stop the blood long enough, it might clot. Or give him time to get to a hospital." He turned his head very slowly to face Luki, but his eyes shone, flickered unblinking, like those of a sleepwalker. "Do you think he's just cut a little? He needed to come home, Luki. He knew it. He was here."

It didn't take much deduction to see that Sonny had an important chunk of information he wasn't passing along. "He needed to come home for what? C'mon, wake up, Sonny. What aren't you telling me? You said treatment. Are there pills or something?"

"No—yes, nasal spray. Dezmopressin. But for him it doesn't help very much. It's not enough." He shrugged. "And he left it here, anyway. He has to come home. Every other week. Maybe three weeks at the most. They load the factor intravenously. It helps."

"So as long as he has this treatment, he's okay?"

"Yeah. Well, not okay, but a lot better than without it."

Sonny's eyes had cleared; he looked awake. But he spoke without inflection and his spine didn't bend. He might as well have been a robot—an angry robot, perhaps. Luki wasn't fooled. He stepped closer, pushed Sonny's stringy hair back.

"Sweetie, how long has it been since Delsyn's last treatment?"

Sonny dropped his head in his hands, exhaled a long, shaking breath.

"Ten," he whispered. "It's been ten weeks."

Luki wanted to sit with Sonny and hold him, comfort him, rock him to sleep, but he settled for an unreciprocated hug, a kiss on the top of Sonny's head—ignoring the grease—and a promise. "I'll find him, Sonny." He hoped he wasn't lying, and he also hoped that when he did find Delsyn, the young man would be on the right side of Death's door.

"HE'S dead, boss."

Luki's heart stopped.

"You know, the kid with the prints? Let me see... Danny Jordan—"

"Oh, thank God!"

"Uh, boss?"

Once Luki's heart slowed enough that he could speak, he said, "Never mind, Jude—"

"Oh, you thought I meant the other kid? C'mon, Luki, you know I'd never be that tactless."

"Tactless perhaps not. Blasé certainly." He noticed he was sweating, and still wearing his damp coat, which was steaming in the over-warm room. "Hold on a sec." He put the phone down, tugged the jacket loose and stripped it off. "So anyway," he said, picking up the phone. "Who, when, where, how."

"The first question, I don't know—except that a honeymooning couple, or their dog, found him. When? He died sometime in the last twenty-four, they found him about six hours ago. Where? Behind a rest stop, of course."

"Of course." It bordered on cliché, but only because rest areas made such convenient places to kill, or dump a body. "What rest stop?"

"South Dakota, of all places. I-90, right near a little town called Tilford."

Luki's heart skipped. He knew the place. Mouth a little dry, he repeated, "Tilford. Okay. How?"

"I'm not sure of the details. Weapon was found, though, a knife."

Knife. K.

"Boss?"

"I'm here."

"Are we done?"

"Unless you've got more." She didn't. Luki ended the call with a "keep me posted," and returned the phone to its cradle.

He picked up the whole instrument and began to pace Sonny's kitchen, back and forth as far as the phone cord would let him go, trying to decide who to call and what to say. He hated this... indecision, a concept previously foreign to him.

But decision was taken out of his hands when the phone rang. Never stopping to consider that a call on Sonny's phone might not be for him, he picked up. "Yeah?"

"Luki? It's Jude again. I have Ladd on the line."

"Why the hell didn't he—" He remembered he stood in the cell-phone Bermuda Triangle. "Never mind. Can you hook us up?"

"Sure—"

While he waited for Ladd to come on the line, Luki took a look at Sonny, who still sat on the edge of the bed. The look on his face had changed, but Luki couldn't interpret it. One word came to mind: stone. It was a little scary.

In seconds, he heard a couple of clicks, and then Ladd's voice—somehow always youthful and carefree though he was in his fifties and worked every case with so much intensity he sometimes put even Luki to shame.

"Boss, listen I—"

"Wait. This job is about to get a lot bigger, and before it gets crazy, there's something I want done. You're in charge. Get it done. This is *freaking* important. All the teams in the area—and interpret 'area' broadly—need to carry a pharmaceutical product called...."

"What is it called, Sonny?"

"Just say von Willebrand factor."

"Did you get that, Ladd?"

"Yeah, boss, von Willebrand. But where the hell are we supposed to get it?"

"The drugstore? The hospital? Shit, I don't know, Ladd, and I don't have time to find out. That's why I pay you, and if you can't do it, ask Jude. She can do anything. But listen close, I don't care if you have to steal it at gunpoint, you get it, and every team has it with them at all times."

"Okay, fine Luki. I'll sacrifice my firstborn. But are you ready to hear the reason I called? Because I think this might be *freaking* important too."

Luki bit down on his lip, way too hard, and pictured in his mind a burning cigarette, up close and personal. Voice carefully controlled he said, "I apologize, Ladd. This job is important to me, that's all."

"I know that, boss. Hell, we all know that—you're damn near sweating. Most of us didn't think that possible. So we're on it. We'll give it our best, right?"

Hating that his ice shield had cracked in plain view of everyone who knew him, but at the same time grateful for loyalty, he said, "That's a lot. Thanks. What have you got?"

"That white van, boss. It showed up, if you can believe this, at a gas station off I-90, outside a little podunk town called Box Elder, South Dakota—"

"Box Elder. East or west?"

"West of town, heading east."

"And…?"

"This is the crazy part. Not more than a few minutes after they left, one of the attendants went into the head and found a handprint—in blood. Like the one you found."

Luki's chest clamped down on his lungs, but—after stealing another quick glance at Sonny—he forced out the logical question. "They called the law?"

"That's just it." Ladd sounded mystified, which was strange enough all by itself. Nothing ever took Ladd by surprise. "They did call," he said. "County jurisdiction, I guess, so they called the sheriff. Sheriff's office is just a mile or so away; they were there in a few ticks. Deputy takes a look, calls for the crime scene folks. He's hot on it, in the car, flasher going. He radios in; the top guy takes the call and tells the boy to stand down."

"What the hell?"

"Official story: no sign of a struggle, no crime. Someone got an accidental cut and accidentally made a handprint. Go figure."

But Luki had already figured, and he didn't want to dwell on what he came up with, so he just started delegating right off. "All right, Ladd. Put a couple people on I-90 east from there, and just to cover the bases, a couple on 63 south. You and the rest of the team are heading south on 83. Stop wherever it looks likely and look around, stay in touch with each other, check with store clerks, ranchers, whatever— you know how to handle it. Any word about the van, the blue BMW, any sign of a young man—"

"Sonny?" Luki had been so absorbed that he didn't even notice his lover… former lover had left the room. "Hang on a minute, Ladd."

He put the receiver down a little harder than he intended. He called Sonny's name again, searching the house; he glanced outside, shielded his eyes from the sun, and scanned the shore. Nothing. Stepping back inside, he bit his bottom lip cruelly, which he thought might be a more dangerous habit than cigarettes, and resolved to invade Sonny's territory, again. He hadn't known there was a bathroom off the studio, but that's where Luki found Sonny. The shower was running, but when Luki called out, he got no response.

"Sonny," he tried again, pushing the door open. "Sonny!" He could see his tall shadow behind the curtain, but Sonny still didn't respond. Luki pushed the curtain back enough to see inside, ignoring the spray soaking his face and arms. Sonny was standing with his back to the spray, head bowed like a man on a crucifix, both arms braced against the tile of the far wall. It looked as if Sonny's senses had fled. Luki reached toward him.

"Don't touch me."

Luki jerked his hand back, feeling as if he'd touched flame. He cleared his throat of whatever it was that suddenly blocked it. "I need to know how old Delsyn is, what he looks like."

"He's seventeen. He's freaking seventeen. He's kind of... smallish, I guess. Brown eyes, brown skin—my color. His hair's almost pure black, usually long." He started to say something more, then sighed and wiped his hand down over his face. "I can't think. He has a bad knee—he limps. There's some pictures of him in the top drawer of the cabinet next to the stove."

Reluctantly, Luki let the shower curtain drop closed and marshaled all his brain cells into single file, thinking only of the task. Knowing that Sonny needed him, that Delsyn, whether he was an innocent or not, did not deserve whatever was happening to him. Ignoring the niggling itch at the back of his brain that told him there was no such thing as coincidence, that he might have already made the worst mistake of his life.

East on I-90. Tilford, Box Elder, then another hour and a half, maybe two, to Highway 83. Head south. A few hours more; through White River and Rosebud, across the State line into Nebraska and on into Cherry County. Then a quick jaunt west at the North Loup. To Oak Flats.

To my hometown.

THE plane crowded everyone, as they always do, especially in coach, which was all they could get, despite money and influence, on such short notice. Luki and Sonny, big men who were trying to avoid touching each other while occupying adjacent seats meant for people the size of rhesus monkeys, found the cramped space crippling. When Sonny took the window seat, Luki wondered if that was something he always did, or if he was subconsciously letting Luki take the position of guard.

Either way, it suited Luki just fine. Gave him a little more room and, yes, made him feel better positioned for action. Though, off the bat, he couldn't think of anything likely to occur during the flight that he'd be able to fix. After his carry-on was stowed above, he sat, trying to make himself small. A ridiculous proposition. He huffed an annoyed breath a minute later and stood again, stripped off his shoulder holster which, bereft of its usual comforting weight, only served to make him sweat.

After that he plunked down in the seat again, drawing a recriminating glance from Sonny. He decided that, since Sonny was likely to be silent and possibly rude during the flight, he'd read. He refused to remind himself that this wasn't a vacation and he had other things to think about. He had a book in his carry-on, though he had no memory of its nature, its title, or when he'd purchased it. Standing up to get it, he could feel not only Sonny's stare sticking to him like boiling pitch, but that of the passengers in the seats behind.

The eyes burned, but not nearly as hot as the desire for a cigarette. Even though he felt early withdrawals coming on, he felt smug at the idea of smoking. Like thumbing his nose at Sonny.

I can smoke a cigarette. So there.

Which was stupid. In the first place, he couldn't have a cigarette. Second, Sonny had made it clear… excruciatingly clear that he couldn't care less. And third, he was the one who had wanted… thought he'd wanted to break it off with Sonny, not the other way around.

He took his seat once again, book in hand, jostling Sonny just enough to make him glare. It amazed him that sweet, laid-back Sonny could, when the time was right, display that masterful glare—so cold it made his own perpetual ice look like a snow cone at the fair. He didn't, of course, let on to Sonny that he felt that way. He simply opened his book, which he still didn't know the title of, but at least he wasn't holding it upside down.

But he couldn't read it. Because he needed his reading glasses. Little pince-nez jobbies that sat halfway down his nose, which he would be far too young to need if it weren't for the damage sustained to the Bowman's layer in his left eye when his face got sliced. And of course a monocle made him look like a sitcom Nazi commandant, so he'd opted for third-grade-teacher glasses that Mr. I'm-Twenty-Nine Sonny James could have a field day with. *If* he deemed it worthy of his notice. Luki couldn't decide if he hoped Sonny wouldn't notice or wished he would. Either way, if he was going to read, he needed the glasses.

Damn.

He got up again, unzipped and re-zipped compartments until he found the cursed things, and re-planted himself in his seat. This time the roundish, sixtyish lady in the seat in front of his turned around to add her sneer to the glares.

Sonny leaned forward and caught the woman's eye. "What," he said very quietly, "are *you* looking at?"

It left the woman looking shocked as she swiveled her head around front and center. It left Luki with a lump in his throat. Hesitating, he turned toward Sonny with his almost invisible smile— the one that Sonny could always see—but Sonny had already turned away to stare out the window.

The engine noise increased to a high whine, and as they taxied to the runway, everyone received instruction on how to breathe while dying in a plane crash. A steward walked by, making sure tray tables were stowed and seats were in the upright position. Sonny dug in the pocket of his badly worn leather jacket and pulled out some gum.

He offered a piece to Luki. "It helps with the whole eardrum thing. And it might help with the not smoking thing too, I suppose."

Sonny's glance had barely touched Luki's eyes while he spoke. Their fingers barely grazed when Luki accepted the offer and said thanks. Crumbs. Somehow, though, for Luki it felt like a feast of intimacy.

But, curling the gum stick into his mouth, he reprimanded: *don't be stupid, Luki. It was civil, no more than that.* He felt certain that a cigarette would help him see things clearly, but for now it looked as though he was stuck with emotional fog.

In the air, at cruising altitude. Sonny reclined his seat as much as possible without crushing the multiply pierced teenaged girl behind him, and leaned his head against the wall. "I'm tired, Luki. I'm so *freaking* tired."

Again, that fist squeezing in the middle of Luki's chest. "Well," he dared to respond, throat far too dry. "Well, on top of everything else, you haven't slept." Sonny didn't speak or move—long enough for Luki to decide he wasn't going to. Then he did, nodding his head and favoring Luki with another glance.

Within five minutes Sonny had fallen soundly into sleep in the most uncomfortable position for sleeping Luki could imagine. Gradually, though, he shifted to the side. Luki collapsed the armrest between their seats, and Sonny shifted again to take advantage of that small space. When the steward came around, Luki asked for two coffees and two pillows. He drank the coffees and used the pillows to pad the hard places under Sonny's head and shoulder.

He raised his tray-table, forgetting to read, and also to take off his ridiculous reading glasses. Over the top of them, he watched Sonny sleep. Watched him gradually consume all the floor space in front of both their seats with his long legs. Watched him, finally, lift one of those legs and drape it over Luki's knee, leaving the other foot planted firmly on the floor. He slept like that for the entire flight.

Which Luki thought wonderful… miraculously wonderful except that he'd drunk a cappuccino at the airport and two coffees at the beginning of the trip and was more or less stuck in his seat. To take his mind off his misery, he thought about the case. Which he should have been doing anyway, but watching Sonny sleep soothed him. Thinking about the case did not.

He knew his hunch would prove to be right. He knew as sure as he knew the weight of his gun that Delsyn was in that white van and that whoever sat in the driver's seat was headed to Oak Flats.

With a jolt, he realized he'd made another mistake. Apparently being in… well, whatever he was in with Sonny, being in it caused him to screw up left and right.

Kaholo. Why didn't I call Kaholo?

He tried his cell, got nothing, hung his head and sighed. Let a hand fall comfortingly to Sonny's knee—comforting to him that was, not to Sonny, who apparently hadn't noticed it at all. He wished he could comfort Sonny.

How in the hell would I do that?

He'd jilted him, spied on him, failed him, delivered the worst news in the world to him, and most horrible of all, though Sonny didn't know it yet, he'd dragged him and his beloved nephew into a nightmare. Because this bloody trail they were following wasn't about Sonny at all. All this time Luki had been diligently trying to find out who would want to hurt a weaver who went everywhere with an easy smile on his face and eyes always ready to laugh. Well, of course, the answer was no one. Nobody wanted to hurt Sonny.

They want to hurt me.

And they must have known Luki better than he knew himself, because they saw right away that Sonny wasn't ever going to be just another chance-met man he'd hook up with for a bit of mutual satisfaction. Whoever was behind this scheme was certainly cruel, but not stupid, and not likely to stop at half-measures. He was either no stranger to Luki, or he'd done his homework and knew who was who. Hurting Delsyn would hurt Sonny. Hurting Sonny would hurt Luki. And the only hope Luki could hold out, at this point, was that if he kept the cops out long enough to keep Delsyn alive and could somehow get a step ahead of the enemy, he could call down a miracle.

And as if all that wasn't enough, he'd put Kaholo, Josh, and Jackie at risk—played right into the creep's hands. And he had to go home, where he'd long ago decided never to go again. To Nebraska, Cherry County, a little neighborhood of ranch workers outside of Oak Flats on the North Loup River. Where his nightmare had begun the first time around.

Luki took a deep breath and let out a sound, louder than he'd intended, halfway between a groan and a growl. The steward happened to be near and he leaned toward Luki solicitously.

"Are you all right, sir?"

Luki glared at him over the tops of his *fucking* reading glasses and was instantly sorry. The steward had been concerned. He looked like a nice man. Luki snatched the glasses from his face with one hand, let the other caress Sonny's thigh, and nodded to the steward—Peter, his tag said. "I'm fine. Thank you." Then he let his head fall to the back of his seat and refused to think any more.

He might have even slept. Except he really had to pee.

His cell phone—which apparently had come back from the dead zone—buzzed against his hip. *I hate that bloody buzz. I'm going to get a Patsy Cline ring tone.* "Vasquez."

"Luki, it's me, Kim."

"I know."

"Shut up."

"I get to say that, Kim. I'm the boss. You're not."

"Okay, boss. Clap your trap."

"That's better." Luki felt the tiniest smile begin, like fresh air sneaking through a loose windowsill into a room full of poison gas. Focus. "What do you have?"

"It's that boy, BJ. The one you had me take to lockdown treatment? Well, someone in uniform flashed some ID and a warrant and carted him off in cuffs."

"When?"

"Yesterday, wee hours. But that's not all. He was found—"

"I'm guessing dead?"

"Yeah, at a place called the Buck Stop, off Highway 83 just south of the Nebraska-South Dakota line. Town called Valentine, I think. I can check my notes."

"Don't bother. I know the place." Sonny stirred, shifted, but went on sleeping. "How, Kim?"

"Needle still in his arm and all that."

"Classic, eh? White van?"

"Blue BMW."

Luki got a report on Sonny's place and the Cup 'O Gold, where all was apparently peaceful. He told Kim to stay in touch and to remember to sleep. He broke the connection. He sighed. He started to push the speed dial for Kaholo, but no time. They had landed, taxied almost to the gate.

Surprised that Sonny didn't wake up even with the noise, pressure, and jolt of landing, Luki considered the best way to wake him. He should, he knew, adhere to the new "we're not lovers" ground rules and tap his shoulder. Instead, he ran his thumb across Sonny's slack lips a time or two, and when that didn't do the trick he let his hand fall to Sonny's throat.

Sonny took hold of his hand before he opened his eyes, then he let it go.

"We're there," Luki said.

Sonny looked around, noticed the pillows, realized his leg was draped over Luki's. He took it back and sat up, wiping at his eyes and apparently preparing to face the de-boarding crush. But he turned back to Luki, managing his habitual half-smile despite the time, place, and reason for being there. "You know, you're much kinder than you'd like people to think. Much more thoughtful than you look. I hate that." Sonny closed his eyes, and shook his head, still looking weary. "It makes me think I'll be stuck loving Luki Vasquez until I die."

AS SOON as Sonny said *loving Luki Vasquez,* he wished he hadn't. Especially when Luki's eyelids dropped half-closed in that way of his that always made Sonny think of cats or reptiles. Ready to strike. That wasn't it, of course. Luki was protecting himself, as he always did. But when Sonny saw it, chills played his spine like a xylophone—and knowing better didn't help in the least.

Not a minute later, Luki stood in front of his seat calmly letting a parade of passengers go by, even though he probably wanted a smoke more than he wanted to win the lottery. And he probably had to pee. A boy of about eight nearly caused a pile up behind him when he stopped and looked up at Luki with admiration. *So,* Sonny thought, *I'm not the only one who thinks he looks like a superhero.*

"I'll wait, mister," the boy said. "You can go ahead of me."

Sonny couldn't see Luki's face, but he could tell by the sound of his voice that he smiled. That impossible smile. The one that Sonny and children could usually see, while no one else even suspected. And his shoulders, broad and bunched with muscles that Sonny could easily see through his summer shirt, relaxed.

"That's kind of you, young man," he said. "But you'd better catch up with your Mom. If you lose her, who's going to help keep your baby sister safe?"

His voice had changed. Smoother, richer. The way Sonny had heard it before, when Luki talked to children. The way Sonny had heard it before, when Luki made love to him.

If that's what it should be called.

HAVING slept just those few hours left him feeling a little less dazed and dull than before. He silently thanked Luki for letting him do that—helping him do it, maybe. At any rate, by the time they'd gotten off the plane, into the airport, and done with the all-important necessary stop, Sonny felt in charge. He'd been letting Luki feel in charge for a while now, all too easy to do, because Luki was damn good at it.

But this was a race to save Delsyn. Luki or no, Sonny had to step up. By the time Luki was done fetching his guns—plural—from the baggage claim office, Sonny had already rented a fast car and bought two pairs of shades and two cold Cokes. Before Luki quite caught up, he'd walked out the door and trotted out to the car rental lot. He started the car with the remote and was buckled and in gear, ready to go by the time Luki made it to the car.

"Here," he said, passing Luki a Coke. Then the shades. He barely waited for Luki to take them before he let go.

"Buckle up," he said, already out of the parking lot and turning north to pick up I-90 east, about ten miles away. When they'd picked up the interstate, Luki still looked a little shell-shocked. Sonny asked, "What is it?"

"This car," he said.

"What about it?"

"A little… muscular, don't you think?"

"2010 Camaro SS, 6.21 liter V8, 422 horses. Yup. Muscular. But don't worry, Luki, I can drive it. I'm really not all that soft and juicy."

Luki's eyebrows went up.

"Well," Sonny chuckled. "Juicy, maybe." The moment was sweet, almost like before, almost as if they weren't on a desperate mission to save Sonny's nephew and only living close relative from death or worse. But it wasn't before, and they were desperate, and the moment passed.

"I'm going to call my uncle, then I've got some stuff to tell you." Luki was halfway through dialing when a call came through. He looked at Sonny. "It's Kaholo. That's weird."

Sonny heard a greeting that didn't sound like English, and then Luki spent a long time listening. When Sonny glanced at him, Luki was biting his lip way harder than normal, and he looked anything but ice cube. His right foot had started tapping, and he gripped the phone so hard Sonny expected it to snap.

"Did you see the plates? Kansas…. You're sure…? You saw him yourself, Uncle? You're absolutely sure it was him…. That's good thinking…. Listen, Uncle, I'm on the way. We're about fifty miles or so east of Rapid City; we'll come down 83. Sonny drives like Satan on crack, so it shouldn't be more than a couple of hours. I'm going to see if I've got anybody south of you—if I do I'll let you know what they're driving. You might see them and not me, depending on what I find on the way down. Just stay safe. Okay?" Another long pause, then, in a voice that sounded like Luki was choking: "Kaholo, you know I love you, right?"

A few seconds later, Luki ended the call and sat staring at the cell phone in his lap.

"So what was that about, Luki?"

"Well." Luki's sigh was the weariest sound Sonny had ever heard come out of him. "I think we've found them. At Kaholo's place. A car that keeps coming around. A blue BMW with Kansas plates."

"Mr. K."

Luki shrugged, though it looked to Sonny less like unsure and more like fear. "I don't know. Maybe."

"Josh and Jackie are from Kansas?"

"Yeah. And a couple of days ago, there was a white van—no plates. And one more thing." Luki had chewed his lip ragged. "A guy named Ron Jemison, someone I grew up with who was... hateful, you might say. He hasn't been around for twenty-eight years, but he showed up about the same time as the white van. He's drinking a lot and acting strange, scared. Kaholo says Jackie and Josh are like scared rabbits, and the whole thing has Kaholo worried." He turned raised eyebrows toward Sonny and waited until Sonny glanced his way. "Making my uncle worry is not an easy thing to do."

"But I don't get it, Luki. What the *hell* does my nephew have to do with your uncle? And those boys—what's going on?" Sonny raised his voice, but he kept his hands soft and steady on the wheel, feeling like the car in motion, the road rolling away beneath the tires, these were his only anchors to the real world. If Luki could explain, maybe he'd feel better. So he waited.

Instead of explaining, Luki added, "Kaholo was a sharpshooter in the Army, you know? That's how he met my dad, which is how my dad met my mom."

"Luki—"

"So Kaholo got out his two rifles and his shotgun and took the boys outside for a shooting lesson. He hasn't seen the BMW since, but he's not sure if that's why."

Luki got back on the phone. "Ladd, slight change. Is there anyone near Lincoln or Omaha...? Okay, send them north up 83."

While Luki explained his strategy to his agent, Sonny grew more and more impatient. It seemed, from where he was sitting, that once Luki had heard about his uncle's house, he'd forgotten Delsyn altogether. He would have been angrier if he were able to make himself believe it. "What the fuck, Luki?"

Sonny didn't use words like "fuck" very often, and when he heard it, Luki's gaze jerked up sharply to look him in the eye. Still, when he spoke, it didn't seem to be an explanation at all.

"I'm going to tell you some stuff, Sonny. It's... it's a story I'd hoped I'd never have to tell—to anyone. I know it isn't what you expect me to say, and it's not going to be what you want to hear. But please, just be patient. In the end you'll know why I'm telling you this now."

Luki hadn't been looking at Sonny; he stared at his manicured fingers where they lay, seemingly calm, brown against the pale blue of his acid-washed jeans. He'd taken his shades off, and when Sonny glanced at his face, he saw a twitch, or a tic perhaps, under Luki's left eye. He'd never seen it before. A river of silence passed between them, one that—like all rivers—couldn't be rushed. Sonny knew that short of violence—which he wasn't quite ready or foolish enough to try—he could only wait. Luki took a deep breath, and opened his mouth, but he closed it again without speaking.

Sonny guided the car off I-90 and onto the 83. Ten more miles and Luki still sat looking at his hands. Sonny slowed the car so suddenly the seat belts locked, then drove it off the road onto a dusty turnout shaded by a giant cottonwood. Sonny shut the engine down, unclasped his seat belt, and then when Luki looked at him with eyes almost vacant, he unbuckled Luki's too.

"I don't know what the hell is going on with you, Luki, but this is a hell of a time for you to check out." He put a coke bottle in Luki's hand. "Drink. Then talk."

Chapter Eleven

OAK FLATS, Nebraska, 1982:

Sun sinking golden in the west. Kids, new adolescents, running through the trees, the wild joy of warm summer dusk speeding them along, carrying them onto the bridge, over the rail and into the water. Luki loved to run, loved to dive into the cool, slow current and let it carry him until he had to come up for air. His heart felt huge with life.

But when he came up, laughing and spitting, and slicked his hair back out of his eyes, all of the other boys had gathered in a nervous crowd on the riverbank. Maria—the one girl that had always been one of them—was making her way down the steep embankment from the road to the river. Luki wondered why she hadn't come in to swim. She loved the river the same as he did. But just then, the sun dropped away, and for no reason the familiar waters of the North Loup turned dark and dangerous. Luki shivered, a chill passing up his spine.

"Hey, Luki, c'mon over here, man." It was Ronny Jemison, the oldest, tallest, meanest among them. The boy that bullied Little Jimmy and Maria, the boy that liked to hurt people, liked to kill things to see them die. The boy Luki was scared of sometimes, scared of that night when he said, "We've got something for you, Luki."

Afraid, but not quite believing in cruelty, and not quite willing to let himself be branded a coward, Luki went. Before he quite made it safely to dry land, Ronny smacked him hard in the face with a balled up fist, and yelled one word, spit it at Luki as if it was made of acid and would flay him.

"Faggot!"

Luki's eyes changed, dragging Sonny back to the present with him. "You know," he said, "how people say, 'I knew I was gay when I was in third grade,' stuff like that?"

Sonny smiled—really more of a crinkle in the corners of his eyes.

"Well, I didn't, Sonny. I was thirteen years old, and I'd never given it a thought. I was who I was and, growing up where I did, the way I did, it never dawned on me that I might be different from the kids I'd grown up with—different in some way that they thought important."

"Faggot," Ronny yelled, and at his urging, the other boys started yelling too.

Ronny pushed Luki, and even though it wasn't much of a push, Luki sprawled backward, having been gutted by that one word. It wasn't the way they spit it at him that stunned him. It wasn't what the word meant. Though Ron Jemison had twisted the truth until it turned ugly, the truth itself remained. Luki raised up on his elbows, bruising them on rough granite, staring and breathless. Not fear, not shame, only surprise, and his thoughts like tumbling locks, putting together all the moments that made up that truth, made him who he was, always had been.

But he should have been afraid. Ronny pounced on him where he'd fallen and started yelling at the other boys. "C'mon! You know what he is! I'm gonna put him in his place whether you help me or not. What? Are you afraid of a sissy boy?"

That's when Maria broke for the climbing trail to the top. The other boys hadn't seen her, Luki thought, viewing the whole event now as if he stood atop the bridge looming above, darker against a dark-drenched sky. He held on to calm distance. The cold scent of stone, the warm squish of mud between his gripping toes, the low clank of a rock in the shallows that moved an inch or two along the river bed to rest against its neighbor.

So totally did this false distance claim his awareness that he didn't struggle against the insincere, fearful clutches of the other boys—boys that had been his playmates forever, boys that he would have fought for, but never against. Boys that were as afraid of Ronny as Luki. Perhaps more.

The separation that held Luki fast persisted until Ronny said, "Now we'll take care of this. You're only queer, I'm sure, because you're pretty."

A blade gleamed under a luridly rising moon, and Luki came back all at once to stone pushing hard against his spine and mud stinking like the rot of life.

"C'mon, Ronny," Little Jimmy said, and though it would make no difference, Luki knew there'd be a special place for Jimmy Santiago in heaven, if such a place existed, just for speaking up in that moment. But the small, dark Filipino boy would pay for his courage in this life, without doubt. "Ronny, we'll get in trouble. You've already banged him up good, see, and he ain't never gonna come anywhere near us again. He's gonna have to leave town and—"

"Shut-up, you little bastard!"

Jimmy did as he was told, but in that moment when Ronny took his attention away, Luki wrenched himself free. The other boys let him break their grip, and he pushed back, trying to get to his feet—only to run, not to fight because he knew he would never win. He might best Ronny tonight, one on one, but if he did, he'd never be safe again.

"You little shit-asses! Grab him! I'll beat the crap out of all of you if you let the fag get away."

They all jumped to do what he said, their fingers digging deeper, their hold more sincere than before, because each was more afraid of Ronny than of his own conscience.

"Hold him down. Hold his head," Ronny said, his voice like sleet hissing over glass.

Luki fought and spit and yelled until they held him down tight and he couldn't move. And then he didn't move, didn't try, because the knife—a razor—hung suspended, a half-inch from his left eye.

"That's right, sissy-boy," Ronny smiled, pleasure putting a slight tremor in his whisper. Pleasure that didn't make sense to Luki because he hadn't yet come to understand. "That's right, hold still. Keep very silent and very still, and you can keep your eye, because I want you to have both of them to see the rest of what I'm going to do. But come to

think of it, while I'm up here by your face, BY YOUR FACE, I might as well start."

The knifepoint pricked into the skin at the top of his head, not deep, but as scalp wounds do, it poured blood. It smelled like copper, and trickled into Luki's ear, making him shiver.

"You know, faggot, if you shiver like that, you might make me slip with the knife."

Summoning will from nowhere, will so strong it overcame the imperative of adrenaline pushing him to act, Luki went still again. The knife stroked down over his forehead, driving a little deeper as it went, and then stopped at his brow.

"Now close your eyes, you little punk, and don't open them again until I tell you."

Luki closed them, willing himself again not to shake, not to struggle. His arms and legs were numb by now, and all his awareness centered on the pain of that knife pressing into his flesh. Then all at once it skidded past his brow and, of their own accord his eyes snapped open. The knife nicked the eyelid and Luki screamed.

Ronny let go a whole string of curses, then sliced down the rest of Luki's face, cut deep this time, and all at once.

Then Ronny wasn't there—a loud thump, a boot against flesh, and Ronny disappeared. Maria hadn't run away, she'd gone for help, and Luki's father, Peli, had come, and his uncle Kaholo ran the rest of the boys off. Ronny had fallen into the river and had come up choking and that was the last Luki heard or saw of him.

By this time, blood had flooded Luki's left eye and his ears, dulling his senses, and his throat had flooded with blood, too, so that his screams became garbled coughs. His father scooped him up and carried him, running up the steep trail as if Luki weighed no more than a pup. "Hang on, son," he kept saying. "Please hang on. God, oh God, Luki, hang on."

Luki began to feel numb and sweetly warm, and he thought his father's arms had somehow become so long and enormous that every inch of him was covered in their strength.

"I'll get the truck going," Kaholo shouted as he ran past them on the way back to the house. Luki heard it through a tunnel that stretched

a mile from anywhere, and somehow the sound of his uncle's voice was mixed up with his father's pounding heart, and salt, and his own sticky blood soaking his father's shirt.

Luki rode to the hospital, thirty miles away, lying across his father's lap in the back of the pickup, aware in moments of consciousness that his dad was pinching the wound—hard—in his uncle's borrowed white T-shirt. That pinch hurt, too, but Luki never questioned that his dad knew exactly what to do for him, in a case like this.

At the hospital, Luki flew from the back of the truck while it still moved, or so it seemed, but of course his father had jumped, still holding him. Before Kaholo had even shoved the gearshift into first and shut the old engine down, Peli had crashed through the ER doors and was shouting, "It's my son! Help my son!"

The shouts were so loud and so commanding that they cut right through Luki's fading awareness. It didn't amaze him at all that nurses came running at his order. He felt himself taken from his father's arms—something he did not want to happen at all—and then he felt nothing.

"This thing that's happening," Luki said, jerking Sonny back to the present. "All the attacks on you, taking Delsyn, all of it—it's all tied up with that night, Sonny. I made a mistake. It's not about you. It's never been about you. All the messages—all the scrawls on the wall, all the taunting notes—were meant for me.

"I knew it when the clues finally broke and they pointed toward Nebraska. Then Kaholo called and the minute he started talking my gut churned. All the while, though, I was hoping it wasn't true. That strange coincidences happen. That unrelated horrible things can happen in the same place, that it's like that in the world all the time. But then my uncle said that Jemison—Ronny—was back in town, where he hasn't been seen since that night at the river.

"I can't deny it anymore, Sonny. You've been hurt, and Delsyn, because Ron Jemison hates me. It's my fault.

"Someone, Jemison or someone else, is playing me... playing us and gambling on the fact that he holds just about all of the cards. And I don't know if I can… win. I don't know if I can win, Sonny. I'm sorry."

Sonny felt sick. Silence hung around, unwilling to be shooed away by the sound of voices. Finally, he spoke softly. "How could it be your fault, Luki? You're a jackass, not a monster."

Neither man laughed or smiled or looked at each other, and it felt as though every living thing for a mile around held its breath. Then Sonny let out a breath that bore some resemblance to a sob and wrapped his arms around Luki, twined his hands in Luki's curls, and kissed him. Not hard, not passionately, but full of both comfort and need.

Finally, Luki lifted his arms and held Sonny close in return. They kissed again, holding tight, and then Luki pulled away.

"There's something more, Sonny. This isn't about the crime. I'm not sure, but I think it's about us, and I'm sorry to bring it out now, but I need to say this before God-knows-what happens in Oak Flats. I hope thirty seconds or so isn't going to make the difference. Will you listen?"

Luki spoke with no emotion at all, but Sonny knew him well enough to know that an ocean was boiling inside him. He, Sonny, knew that despite their shared purpose, despite Luki's revelation, despite their moment of mutual comfort, the gulf between them remained and might never be crossed. He got a refresher in the meaning of heartache. It hurt. Physically. He thought he truly might die of a broken heart. But he knew how to hide his feelings, too, when necessary, and he thought if he didn't do that now, Luki wouldn't talk and neither of them might survive.

He put his shades back on, stared out the windshield to the scrub at the edge of the turnout, and said, "Yeah. I'm listening." He marveled at Luki's courage, for in spite of his decades old open wound, and in spite of Sonny's anything but encouraging response, he continued.

"When I woke up in the hospital that day, my father was in a chair by my bed, facing away, so that I could only see his back and his big shoulders. Kaholo sat across the room; he nodded at me and smiled. Maybe it was Kaholo's nod that let my dad know that I was awake, or maybe he heard it in my breathing, or sensed it somehow."

Luki stopped talking, and his hand came up to his face as if he was in trance. He traced the line of his scar with his thumb. It was the first time Sonny had seen Luki touch that damaged flesh or acknowledge it in any way. As if suddenly aware of what he'd done, Luki jerked his hand away and laid it back in his lap.

"I remember what he said to me word for word. I can hear him speaking, feel the blankets weighting down my legs, even smell my own sick-smell. He said, 'I've known for a long time what you are, Luki. And I hate it. But you're my son, and by God, Luki, I love you. And I swear I'll do everything in my power to make sure no one will ever do this to you again.'

"He made good on his word. He did everything he could—and that was a lot—to make sure I'd be able to defend myself. Boxing, Aikido, blades and guns and camouflage. How to think fast and put myself inside an evil mind. And more. So you see," Luki held out his arms and almost smiled, "here before you is the well-defended Luki Mililani Vasquez."

He let silence fall again, but Sonny knew—knew from the slant of his shoulders, from the way he breathed—that he had more to say, when he was ready.

"He took care of me when I was hurt. He made it as sure as anyone could make it that I wouldn't be hurt like that again. He put his whole life on hold to protect me. But he never looked at me, Sonny, not really. He hated *what* I am. Here's what's strange—and what I think might be important for... us, you and me. Even though I remember my mother's sweet ways, and even though Kaholo has always been there, never failed, for me it's what my father showed me that passed for love. Protection, guns, skill. No heart required."

Sonny took advantage of a pause. "And then you added sex."

Luki almost smiled. "Like I said, skill."

A couple of heartbeats, then Sonny, breathless, "Is that what it was with me? Skill?"

Luki at last met his eyes. "I wanted to think so, Sonny Bly. But I can't. It isn't the same at all. But... well, you can see the problem."

Sonny's own words played back in his mind. *I'll be loving Luki Vasquez until I die.* Very likely true. Damn it. But he'd never even tried to fool himself into thinking it would be a smooth ride and all downhill, or even that it would surely turn out well. He cleared his throat and took a drink of his now-tepid Coke.

Luki's phone buzzed. "Kaholo," he said, biting his lip. When he looked up at Sonny his brow was furrowed, a worried look Sonny had never seen on him and wouldn't have expected. He touched the screen twice, taking the call on speaker. "Uncle."

Sonny laid his head on his hands, resting on the steering wheel, and listened to the conversation.

"Mili, I got a call. It was Jemison. He said you need to find him."

Luki stayed silent. Sonny glanced at him and found him still chewing his soft bottom lip, his eyes roving as if they searched for an answer.

Finally, Kaholo said, "Mili, you there?"

"Yeah, I'm here, Uncle. Sorry. Listen, can you tell me his exact words?"

"Uh huh. He said, 'He's supposed to find me. Tell him that.'"

"You seen anybody around your place recently?"

"No, ain't been nobody around for three hours or so, at least not that showed themselves. Boys finally relaxed enough to eat. They're playing Fable."

"Fable?"

"A video game, Mili. Where you been?"

Luki's face softened, almost a smile. It lasted for less than a second. "Kaholo. A couple of my people should be there within a half hour. Look for an army green Ford. Ugly. Looks like a cop car. One of them will come to the door to check on you, so be careful you don't shoot 'em."

Kaholo laughed, straight from the belly. "Ah, Mili. You know me better 'n that."

"I do know you; that's why I said it. I've never seen a shinier 30-30. Anyway, watch for 'em, okay?"

When the call ended, Luki sat unmoving for a moment, then said, "It's not Jemison, Sonny. He's being used pretty much the same way he was using the street kids. Someone's behind him."

"Who else hates you, Luki?"

Luki laughed without a trace of humor. "Probably lots of people. But… not like this."

"Buckle up," Sonny said. "We've got stuff to do." He started the car, then added, "You said you're not sure you can win this time, Luki. But you will. We will. You said you'd find Delsyn. You said you'd keep us safe. I'm going to do whatever I can, but I'm putting my trust in you. You haven't ever let me down."

"I haven't?" Disbelief. Calling a bluff.

Sonny was about to say that no, Luki had truly never let him down. But Luki was right. "Okay, you let me down once. One night you made love to me like I was the most precious human being on the planet, and the next day… well, no need to elaborate. You were there. I let me down that day too. But it doesn't matter. Even on that day, in the worst moment of it, I would have trusted you with my life." He felt tension tightening his shoulders, heard it in his own voice, so he stopped, hesitated a fraction of a second.

"Losing isn't an option, Luki. It can't happen. So let's go." Sonny put the car in gear, and for the next hour they didn't speak. They passed no one on the road. There wasn't a cloud in the sky. Still, to Sonny it felt like they were wheeling toward a wreck in a storm.

Chapter Twelve

IT TOOK a good fifteen minutes, but Luki found his equilibrium again. *Cold*, he kept telling himself, remembering a lesson he'd learned long ago—and not a few times since. The surest way to bring everyone safely out of a hot situation is to go into it like dry ice.

Since age thirteen, he'd never let it melt. Not in front of his father, not for Kaholo, not for any of the momentary lovers he'd known, nor even for true friends—and he did have a few, despite his untouchable ways. But he had chipped the ice away for Sonny until the last brittle coating melted, and now it scared him all over again. What if he couldn't bring the temperature down, couldn't be what he needed to be for work, couldn't save anyone?

But, no time.

He watched, scanning the roadside left and right, looking off to the distance, checking the side-view mirror for someone approaching. But he saw nobody, and he felt the need to check and ready his weapons.

"Keep your eye, out, Sonny? I want to tend to my tools."

"I'm looking."

Luki checked his holstered handgun—his weapon of choice—and then retrieved the case that held his other weapons. The sniper's rifle he'd have no use for, and Sonny's eyebrows raised when he saw it out of the corner of his eye. So after he took out a smaller pistol, another even smaller pistol, and two knives, each with its own wearing device, he locked the case back up with the rifle inside. He'd just begun to check the small gun when Sonny took his ruthlessly lead foot off the gas, tapped the brake, and started working down—quickly—through gears.

Sonny had his window down and had to shout to be heard over the sound of the wind and the big engine. "Blue BMW. Minnesota plates."

Luki shouted back. "You saw it?"

"Not 'til I'd already gone by."

Before he finished speaking, he'd executed a clean one-eighty— the kind they do in the movies involving brakes and moving sideways, the kind Luki had never seen even during his years with ATF. He devoted a tiny portion of his brain to admiring the driving, another larger portion to trying to stay seated and in the vehicle, but most of it looking for what Sonny had seen and preparing his mind to face the next level of threat.

"There," Sonny said, heading the Camaro straight for the dusty, dented vehicle half-concealed in a stand of scrub about ten yards past the shoulder.

Luki worried hard for a few seconds, thinking the Camaro was going to fly over the ditch alongside the road, but Sonny clearly did know how to drive, as he'd said, and he came to a neat, almost gentle, stop three feet away from its edge. He once again proved that he could move fast, but he stopped as soon as he jumped the ditch. Right behind him, Luki stopped, too, hearing the noise of a two-legged animal crash very noisily through brush. Two possible reactions: *One, follow the animal immediately; two, find out what I can from the car first, then try to catch up with the animal.*

Suddenly, in the instant he took to ponder, he realized exactly where he was. Now that he looked around he saw the remnants of the old road, which had already been half grown over when he and his friends played here, having ridden their bikes from town—thirty years ago. The road's remains ran back into fields about a quarter mile and ended at a tractor shed. They had never known who owned it, and it had held nothing but an old rusty tractor and crates of rusty tools. Now, it looked like the road had all but faded away, but the shed would likely be standing much as it had then. Things disappear slowly in dry Nebraska fields.

He knew exactly where he was, and he knew for a certainty the two-legged animal running through the brush was Ron Jemison, none other. He turned to find Sonny poised to run. "Wait," he said.

"What?" The look Sonny shot him could have wilted lettuce.

"Just for a minute." Luki jogged over to the BMW, tried the doors—locked. Looked in the windows—dirty. Came away knowing nothing more than he had when he started. He called Ladd, told him the location of the car and the shed, and told him to check out the car but then get on with whatever they were doing—leave the shed to him. He'd call them in an hour, and if he didn't they should worry.

"Sonny," he said. "I don't suppose you'll wait in the car."

Sonny's answer was an eye-rolling look that would have been comical if the circumstances were not so very serious.

"Fine. Then listen. I'm the one who does this sort of thing for a living—"

"Playing with guns and all."

"So I'm the boss."

A nod. "I trust you."

He trusts me. Which, just like the first time Sonny had said it, wrenched Luki's gut six ways.

But, no time.

"There's a shed about a quarter mile out this way." He pointed perpendicular to the road. "That's where we're going. Stay behind me, watch where you put your feet, and when we get there, let me handle it. I expect we'll meet up with my old friend Ron Jemison in the shed, but no matter who it is or what they say, leave it to me. All right?"

"Okay. C'mon, let's go."

"One more thing, Sonny." Luki chewed his lip, but only for an instant. "I can get really ugly, when necessary. Just letting you know ahead of time."

"And just so *you* know ahead of time, Luki. I'm scared."

"Of course," Luki said. "Who wouldn't be?"

"But I'm going anyway."

"Yeah. Me too."

SONNY stayed calm and patient, moving quietly through the grass where Luki led. Luki hoped he seemed as calm, but inside he felt anything but patient. Instead, he hoped to find Jemison in the shed. He wanted violence. Wanted not to use as much as needed—which had always been his maxim—but as much as he could muster.

No, shit no. I can't go for cruelty, can't go for vengeance, can't hate him back. If I go there, I'll never return. Damn, where are the cigarettes when you need them?

He'd discovered that, actually, he had some in his pocket. *Now is not the time*, he told himself, but that argument didn't seem to hold water. He stopped, lit up, and squatted down to one knee, feeling a little weak in the stomach. No surprise. He looked up to see Sonny waiting behind him, looking confused and concerned.

Luki shook his head. "It's nothing," he said quietly.

Sonny squatted down beside him and leaned close. "Luki, I know you really want to hurt this guy. It's obvious, and if I were you, I'd want to murder him. You're having trouble getting past that. Am I right?"

Luki breathed deep and sighed, but he said nothing.

"But you're way too good at what you do to fall into that trap. I'm not like you—I'm a weaver, for God's sake—and I'm pretty sure I can't handle this, can't get Delsyn back, safe, on my own."

Luki opened his mouth, but what could he say. Sonny had read his mind.

"Please."

That word, and the sincerity in Sonny's eyes, woke up the lover and the friend in him—but also the professional. He stood, pinching the cherry off his cigarette in the same motion and grinding it into the dirt. He pulled the handgun from his shoulder holster and slipped the safety. Gripping it gently but firmly with both hands, he pointed it down in front of him and turned to Sonny. "Stay close but directly behind me. It's difficult to be really quiet in the brush, but don't make any extra noise."

"Hey," Sonny said, holding his hands out, palms up. "I'm Native, right?"

Taken by surprise, Luki actually smiled. He wondered how someone twenty-nine years old had gleaned the wisdom that Sonny showed him time and again. Maybe that was genetic too. However he'd done it, his quip had broken the tension that had Luki strung dangerously tight. When he turned back to the task at hand and started forward, he found the calm, cool confidence that had saved his ass uncounted times in the past.

Still, when he stopped outside the clearing around the shed and saw Ron Jemison standing in the wide doorway, sweating, some part of him rejoiced at the sight of a shotgun. Celebrated the fact that Jemison had a weapon, gave him cause to lash out at him before ever a word was spoken. The gun would have been little threat even if Jemison had held it at his shoulder ready to fire, but was even less so with the butt braced against the dusty ground and Ron holding it upright beside him, his hand white-knuckled on the barrel.

Luki could easily have taken him down, disarmed him with a leap and a kick. Instead, he raised the handgun, braced in two hands, and stepped out into Jemison's view. Jemison stared, panicked, eyes as glazed as if he'd actually been shot. But Luki placed his bullet to put a hole through the shotgun's wooden stock, knocking it from Jemison's hands and not hurting him at all but for possibly a bruised hand and a broken finger or two. *So much more rewarding than saying "Drop it."*

Jemison started to run forward, but it wasn't clear if he was attacking or making a break to get away. Luki didn't want him to succeed at either, so he made the leap—a kick to the back of the knee and a foot against Jemison's larynx once he was down. The shotgun lay at Luki's feet—unharmed except for the damage to the stock. He picked it up, broke the barrel and emptied it, called Sonny over and passed it to him. "Put that somewhere," he said.

"And you, Ron, get up." He reached down and grabbed the front of Jemison's shirt, "helping" him rise. Then, startling even himself, he lifted his handgun and held it to Jemison's head. *Not* necessary. Stupid. *St. Christopher, help me. I'm an idiot.* Dragging the man through the shed's wide doors, he said, "Walk, Jemison. Go stand against the back wall."

He backed his pistol away from Jemison's temple and slipped the safety on. Instead of returning it to its holster, he passed it to Sonny, just as he had with the shotgun. "Put that somewhere too." He met Sonny's eyes briefly but long enough to see a flicker of warmth in them. He resolved anew to use the least force necessary, as per all his training, which set much lighter on his shoulders. He'd start with an interview, not a fight. *Ice, Luki. It's your best weapon.*

"Jemison," he said, "after all these years." He walked toward his quarry, steps slow and smooth. He watched Jemison cower back against the planks. Satisfying, but possibly not a good omen for success, and he had twinge of regret for his trigger-happy approach. "I found you, as instructed. Tell me why you're here."

"Go to hell, Vasquez."

Luki smiled carefully, coldly. Just enough to frighten; not enough to overwhelm. "You have something for me? Information, a message, directions?"

"Like I said. Go to hell."

"Ron, you do of course have the right to remain silent, according to the law. However, as you may know, I'm not a cop. I'm not granting you that right. I need whatever information you're here to give me."

"And I've just recently decided not to give it to you. To hell with you, all of you."

Jemison seemed to think he had nothing to lose. He had the synthetic-diamond bling of a prosperous, if tacky, man. *Undoubtedly Mr. K.* But he reeked of booze. Apparently, whatever he'd thought he had before, he'd recently been taught that he had nothing. A fair bet he'd be happy to die. A threat to his life might yield information just out of spite—though that was far from a sure thing. Luki needed leverage, and he could think of nothing to fit the bill. Nothing other than pain. And he could provide that. Better than most.

He stepped closer, and Ron's breathing became shallow; his heels dug into the dry dirt floor and pushed him back against the wall. His voice shook. "I wish I'd never done it, Vasquez. That night at the river. I wish I'd never been there."

Luki turned his back to Jemison, an intentional insult, and briefly caught Sonny's gaze. He saw nothing there worse than mild apprehension. But uglier things would come, and then what would he find in those dark eyes? Fear? Disgust?

But, no time.

He kept his back turned to Jemison, though, had no fear at all that his captive could move fast enough to do harm before he could turn to stop him. And it made Ron nervous, talking to Luki's back. Luki could just about hear his spine chattering like an old blues man playing the bones. "Why do you wish that, Ron?"

His voice tore through his throat, harsh and loud and clearly painful. "You ruined my life, Vasquez. Ruined it! Maria wouldn't even look at me after that. And that little prick, Jimmy Santiago—"

Luki pivoted, and moved, and in less than a blink he had Jemison face-to-the-wall, hands jacked up past his shoulder blades, his neck pinned so tight by Luki's forearm he could scarcely breathe, much less talk. Luki felt disgust crawling over him; his nostril's flared, and if he could, he would have breathed fire. "Never forget, *Ronny*, that you are not fit to say Maria's name, not even to think it, and Jimmy Santiago was more of a man at twelve years old than you have ever been or ever will be.

"But never mind," Luki said, letting go of Jemison's limbs. "That's not what we're here to talk about. Not at all. I've got some questions for you. But first I'm thinking you want to make a move, so you might as well get it over with." He stepped back. As Luki had expected, Jemison hadn't even registered his meaning and, as expected, he reached behind, tugged something free of his belt. A knife, the knife Luki already knew was there, a longish, nasty blade. Probably the knife that put the *K* in "Mr. K."

Under his breath, Sonny said, "Shit."

Luki said nothing, didn't jump, didn't hurry. He pointed the toe of his designer shoe at the man's hand and, just as easily as he had with Josh's switchblade, kicked the weapon away. "No," he said very quietly, hearing a familiar, deadly chill saturate his words. For that instant, hatred took precedence over purpose. "This time we're not going to play with knives. We did that before, remember?" He pointed at his scar.

Showing a vestige of wisdom—or else paralyzed by fear—Jemison held his tongue.

For seconds that felt like hours, Luki forced the anger back in its cage, shoving it away. He breathed deep, and when he'd regained his emotional footing, he addressed Jemison again. "As I said, I have some questions for you, and I'm sort of pressed for time. Best case scenario, you could just cooperate."

"Go to hell, Vasquez."

Things got worse for Ron as Luki began to demonstrate the soft tai chi fist. But Ron's answers never changed, refusal time and time again. "It's obvious you're not the *big* bad guy, right, Jemison?" Luki started to pace, hands behind his back, looking thoughtful. "At first I thought maybe you were, but that was just silly. No way you could put all this together into one giant crime. Right?"

"Fuck off."

Luki reached out an arm as he paced by and tapped Jemison's temple. The man's nose started to bleed. *Yes, now's the time.* "Fuck off, is not an answer. And just for the record, you do realize I could kill you, right? It wouldn't even be a challenge."

"Piss on it! Go ahead. My life is shit. Take it if you want. You don't have a clue, Vasquez. You don't know shit about it."

Luki turned to look at him, gave him someone to talk to. Breathing hard, nostrils flaring, Jemison presented a dictionary illustration of anger. Spit rolled down his chin. Veins bulged at his temples. His face had blotched red and sickly, jaundiced yellow. "That piece of crap owns me. Fucking owns me. I can't get a job, can't leave town, can't even tie my shoes without *goddamn, fucking* permission. The creep has me rounding up boys on the street like I'm some kind of perv, and there ain't shit I can do. I can't say no. You know why, Vasquez? Because even though I'm crap, I got a sister, and some nieces, and my mother. Need I explain?

"I hate the bastard, Vasquez, but you know what? I hate you more. It's your fault, all of this. He doesn't give a shit about me, never would have bothered with me at all, except he thought I could help him get to you. So like I said before, Vasquez, fuck off."

Luki stepped back to lean against the rough, splintering planks of an old worktable in the center of the shed. He crossed his arms in front of his chest and looked at Jemison. "Just curious, Ron. What does he have on you, that he could threaten you so?"

"What's it to you?"

With a light blow to Jemison's ear, Luki drew a little blood; harmless but possibly alarming. He said, "Humor me."

"I like women, Vasquez, it's only natural, right?" *Balls*, Luki thought, with something close to a shred of admiration, because Jemison actually sneered. "But I like expensive bitches, lots of them. And I like to gamble, a little cocaine now and again. The bastard owns all the vice in three states. I owe, shithead. I owe, and that was supposed to mean I either pay or I die. I can't pay, don't mind dying, but instead, because of you, I get to be the dog."

"You're not a dog, Jemison. You're a piss ant." Luki took a few steps away, toward Sonny, then deliberately turned back and said, "Now, don't move, okay Ronny? I've got something to show you."

His gut crawled inside him. He both hated what he was about to do and yearned to do it. He needed to push Jemison a little past the edge, to break him down, make him lash out. He needed to make Jemison give him a reason to scare him, to hurt him, to break him.

He hoped it would work. He hoped that *he* wouldn't be the one to break. He hoped that he could make Sonny understand.

Because I'm going to use him.

He stood in front of Sonny, his back to Jemison. Inside, his lungs felt aflame; he prayed to keep his cool exterior intact. Knowing he likely asked for more than he deserved, he whispered for his lover's ears only, "Sonny. Sweetie. Forgive me for this."

He looped Sonny's long hair in his hand and, before he could respond, pulled him close and kissed him. A long, hard, hot kiss that delivered exactly the right reaction.

From Jemison.

"Faggot!" He lunged for the dropped blade, which Luki had left laying where it fell. "You always were nothing but—"

Luki shut Jemison's fountain of ugly words off, letting fly—not quite out of control—with fists and feet. But once he started, something welled up from inside him, something very much like the tears that had erupted that day in Sonny's studio, something that had been there for twenty-eight years and wouldn't stay down.

"This is for every time in your life you've used the word faggot."

"This is for what you did to my face."

"And this," he said, following the words with a flurry of blows that left Jemison doubled over, spitting blood, and crying for mercy. "That was for every time you've hurt someone who was innocent, someone who was scared, or someone,"—he thought of Sonny—"someone I love."

He stopped just in time to save himself. Sweat dripped off him, not necessarily from exertion. Striving to put himself back in order, he dusted his clothes, tried to comb his curls with his fingers, hoping he didn't look as laughable as he felt.

"We're just about done here," he said, and took hold of Jemison under the armpits to stand him up and prop him against the table. "The only thing left on the agenda is for you to tell me who the *hell* the big dog is. And I believe that's right on the tip of your tongue…?"

Jemison laughed, if that's what it should be called. "But I thought I told you," he said. "The bastard! I'm sure I said it before. You're the golden boy, and the big dog is the bastard."

Luki had come too close to the edge, but in the end he won. It was Jemison who broke. In another three minutes he had the message Jemison had been charged with giving him, and the name of the man behind it.

"Your daddy's by-blow, golden boy. Your big brother. Mariano Royce."

He cuffed Jemison with the soft cuffs to the footrest on the old tractor. He found a bottle of water on a crate in the corner. "Yours?" he asked. Jemison nodded so he put it where he could reach it.

"I *am* sorry, Vasquez." Jemison said. "I'm sorry I was there, that night at the river."

Luki, by now fighting bile, rasped. "Yeah. I know."

He stepped out of the shed, glanced at Sonny and walked past him, and then a few strides beyond the permanently open, sagging door. "Give me a minute."

No time for deep breaths. He vomited. *Damn.*

He popped a breath mint, sucked and spat repeatedly, then walked back toward the shed where Sonny waited. Leaning back against the door with the burning sun on his face, he fished in his breast pocket for the cigarettes and lighter he'd *accidentally* put there some time earlier. He held the flame to the tobacco and inhaled slow and deep.

Sonny stood across the doorway, watching him smoke.

Luki met his gaze, trying to see if all of it was gone—whatever it was that Sonny had felt for him. Should he say something? Between drags he worried at his lip until it hurt, trying to find something that would pull life from the ashes he'd almost certainly made of what he and Sonny almost had. Feeling certain that the stare he got from Sonny meant that he now loathed him, feeling he had nothing to lose, he took a chance.

He held Sonny's eye, sent him one of his hidden smiles. Then he narrowed his eyes and scowled just the tiniest bit. "What," he said, "are *you* looking at?"

Chapter Thirteen

ON THE way back to the car, Luki called Ladd, let him know they were clear, and told him to get Jemison out. "Hold on to him somewhere safe for now. Take care of his bruises. We'll give him to the law later, when it's safe to do so.

"What Jemison told me is that this piece of crap, our friend Mariano Royce, wants me to bring Sonny out to the old mill shed—allegedly to get Delsyn. Sonny won't not go, and I can't blame him. To be honest, I agree that it's the only way to go at this point. The place, as I remember it, is off of Highway 20 after it crosses the North Loup, about ten miles south of Oak Flats. I can't be more precise about the location. As a kid I didn't go there much—it was a little farther from home base. I remember the mill, but not how to get there, exactly, and things change. Not much in Nebraska, but some."

"Can we find it from the air?"

Luki bit down lightly on his lip, remembering. "Yeah, I think so. The clearing is pretty big, as long as it hasn't grown over—and I don't think thirty years is long enough for that to happen out here. And the roof is aluminum. Rusty, but still ought to be visible. What are you thinking of?"

"Sherriff, staters, FBI? What do you think?"

"I think… explosives. And I think the FBI will fuck it up."

"Why do you think that?"

Luki raised his eyebrows, surprised. "About the FBI?"

"No, boss," Ladd answered, sounding annoyed. "That's clear. I mean why explosives?"

"Well, the way the creep works, for one. And the way Jemison described him—smart, cruel, likes to make his point in a big way. And it seems to me he wants to hurt... someone, more than he wants money." Luki went back to chewing his lip and paced outside the car, both actions mostly to keep himself from jumping out of his skin. This, he knew, was the most important case he'd ever worked, *and I can barely think straight.*

"Boss, you there?"

Ladd had apparently been talking, but Luki had momentarily checked out, which proved his point. He looked through the windshield at a very antsy-looking Sonny. *Get it together, Vasquez,* he ordered himself. *God, Luki, if you can't do it for yourself, do it for him.* That cleared his head—some. He opened the car door and got in, still on the call.

"Yeah, I'm here."

"So ATF? Local?"

"Go through our old unit. Kate."

"They won't be able to work out here."

"Maybe, maybe not. But Kate will make the right approach either way. And I already owe her. Might as well make it big."

"Yeah, she'll take it out of your hide if...." Ladd cleared his throat, and Luki filled in the blank: *if you live.* Ladd continued, "So you want them to delay, rush in, what?"

"I don't think we have to worry about delay. They'll take a while to get here. But no, tell 'em, ask 'em, beg 'em, don't rush in." He put the phone on speaker while he buckled up, hoping Ladd wouldn't say anything that would scare Sonny.

"They wouldn't anyway, boss—it was a sick joke, me saying that. You know as well as I do ATF does bombs more than anyone else. They don't want to blow up any more than we do."

"Right, Ladd. Sorry, I'm just nervous—"

"Which is a little scary for the rest of us, Vasquez."

"So, no delay. Cautious approach. Kim and Brian and a couple of juniors are still in Port Clifton. Jimmy is with Jude. Leave the coverage at my uncle's place. So that gives us, what, six agents and some newbies in the area? Bring them all in, wide perimeter—my bet is Mariano will guess ATF, but he might not know you'll all be there, and it's best if we keep it that way, right? You're the boss on this. Make sure they all know it. Anything else?"

"No, I don't think so. That's plenty, ain't it?"

"Keep your skin together, Ladd."

It was an old—and rather sick—private joke, but Ladd's chuckle sounded a little sad. "Right, Luki. You do the same. You keep your skin together too."

Luki gave Sonny starting directions, and then stopped to consider the arrangements. He'd trusted his gut, committing all his free resources to this plan, but his gut had an uncanny knack for being right on the money. It was a good plan, he decided, after giving it a little more thought, but he'd forgotten one thing. He got Ladd back on the line. "Don't forget that... blood factor stuff."

He hung up the phone and looked up to get his bearings. They still had a good forty miles to go before he had to start looking for landmarks. He started to work through the methodical process of checking his weapons and securing them, but he was waiting for Sonny to speak. He knew what was coming.

"Bombs," Sonny said, almost accusing.

"I don't know, Sonny. It's just my gut. Maybe a little more than that. When I put the pieces we have together, that's what I come up with."

He finished talking at the same time he finished holstering his weapons, and then his phone buzzed. "I hate that bloody buzz," he muttered. "I'm going to download a Stevie Ray Vaughn ringtone just to mess with people's heads."

Into the phone, "Yeah?"

"Mariano Royce," Jude said. "That's who the Kansas plates belong to."

"Yeah, I guessed as much. I've recently heard the name. Know anything about him?"

"Sleazy," Jude answered. "Sleazy, borderline-legit businessman."

Luki only half-listened. Ever since Jemison had said the name, something about it had nagged at him. It had a familiar ring. He hadn't had time to think about it, but now he dug at his memory. And then he had it.

"What's your last name?" he'd asked.

"Royce," Jackie said.

"And your father's name?"

"Mariano."

He thanked Jude and ended the call, gears spinning in his head. Two possibilities existed. *One, recent events involved a lot… a hell of a lot of coincidence. Or two, all these strands are woven into one big picture, and this Mariano is a criminal mastermind.*

"Two," Luki whispered. "Damn it, it's two."

"What?"

Luki hadn't realized he'd spoken aloud. When Sonny spoke he looked up and saw where they were. "Turn here! Right, right," he directed. "Sorry, I wasn't watching. So, from here out the way gets tricky, and I might not remember everything. Be patient with me, and we'll get there."

Sonny followed his directions, last minute as they often were, hurtling around corners, dodging rocks and the occasional scrub tree, and running over way too many rabbit holes and rotting fence posts. The Camaro held together despite being bent and twisted; the engine roared like every one of its four hundred and twenty-two horses had been whipped to a full gallop.

In the passenger seat, all but choked by the locked seatbelt and dust driving in at him from his now broken window, Luki called upon his long ago memories of the sand hills, hayfields, and stone outcroppings that had been his boyhood playground. He shouted over the engine to guide Sonny, and Sonny responded as if their thoughts were hard-wired in tandem.

Around a bend and past a green depression that housed willows growing up around a hidden spring, over a ridge sharp and sudden enough to make the Camaro jump, and then, up ahead—

"Stop! This is it!"

Luki already had the door open and his feet on the ground by the time Sonny hit the brakes, jammed the car into first, and cut the ignition. Sonny's long legs got him close enough to see over Luki's shoulder as the van came into view. When Luki stopped, he didn't.

"Wait, Sonny!" When shouting had no effect, Luki tackled him. He had no choice. Even from this distance he could see the wires on the van that undoubtedly meant explosives. Sonny fought hard—harder and a little more well-practiced than Luki would have expected. He was no match for Luki, though, not even when Luki was trying not to hurt him. When he finally had Sonny contained, he spoke slow and easy, repeating until he knew Sonny had calmed enough to hear him.

"Sonny, listen to me. There are explosives rigged to the van."

A new flurry of fists and feet. "Delsyn! I'm getting him out."

Luki shifted his hold. "No. Wait. Listen to me. We'll get Delsyn out, but if you run to that van and blow it up, it's very likely no one will make it out, Delsyn least of all. A bomb, Sonny. Are you hearing me now?"

Sonny's breath came ragged, slowing down bit by bit. "Let go of me, Luki."

"There's a bomb, Sonny. You cannot go running to that van. Do you hear me?"

"*Yes!* Yes, I hear you. I won't run to the van and set off the *freaking* bomb. *Get up off me!*"

Cautiously, Luki backed away, a step at a time, watching Sonny closely.

"I'm sorry, Luki." Sonny sat on the rock where Luki had dropped him, his head in his hands. "But what *can* I do? I can't just leave him there. I can't... I don't even know he's there, don't know if he's...."

"Hold on, Sonny. We're going to find out. Jemison's message was that this guy would contact us. We've got to play along until we have a chance to do something smart. It won't be long until ATF gets here, and they're the bomb people. They know what to do about explosives. In the meantime, let's just keep our heads up and play it as smart as we can."

"So we wait."

"We wait. Or we move, but we do it carefully." After a few seconds, Luki thought a little pep talk might be in order. Unfortunately, it was going to have to be a scary pep talk. "This Mariano guy," he said. "He's probably not quite living in the real world. I can't promise an outcome, baby. But I'm asking you to have faith anyway. No matter what. You said you'd trust me, right?"

"Right." Sonny said, sounding like he wished the word was a bullet.

"I'm calling you on that, Sonny. Right now. You—we all—have a better chance of making it through if we believe there's a way out even when we can't yet see it. Yeah?"

Luki's heartbeat straightened out when Sonny met his eyes, almost as levelheaded as his baseline. "Yeah, Luki." Though he sounded like his emotions were barely controlled, he nodded his head. "I hear you. I understand."

They sat for what seemed like hours in the dry heat of a Sand Hills summer, but when the call came, shadows hadn't moved. Unexpectedly, Sonny's phone chimed, not Luki's.

Luki signaled for Sonny to put the phone on speaker. Sonny showed him the screen. Instead of a number, the screen showed that the call came from "YES IT'S ME, M." It gave Luki the creeps.

"Ah," Mariano said. His voice, Luki thought, was like vocal swagger. The Midwest and the mob. "Mr. James. A pleasure to meet you at last."

Sonny remained silent.

"I've been wondering about you. Now that I've had a chance to see you, I can see where a fellow faggot might find you attractive. The fact is, my world has no room for faggots. If it were within my power, I'd give every single one their just desserts. I'd teach you and my brother why it's not a good idea to go around kissing boys. I tried to teach that to my misguided son, Jackie. I'm certain I would have succeeded if his faggot-loving brother, Josh, had not spirited him away. I thought about going after them, but in the end, I let them go. I've always spoiled those boys, given them exactly what they wanted. Especially Jackie."

Luki was certain he would puke. He just hoped he could wait until he'd heard everything the monster on the other end of the line had to say. To Sonny's credit, though his face was screwed up into a vicious looking snarl, he didn't say a word and didn't break a sweat.

"But I forget myself," Mariano said. "That's not why we're here at all, is it? Listen, I'll call back. I've got another call to make. Don't go anywhere, 'kay?"

The connection broke. Luki puked. Sonny sat still, clenching and unclenching his fists.

Now, Luki's phone rang. Message in the screen: "YES. IT'S ME." Not sure why, Luki felt a flash of anger at that little jibe. He breathed it down and opened the connection. Said nothing.

"Speaker off."

Luki switched it.

"Luki Vasquez. Your fame precedes you. We'll chat later, but right now how about we do a little team-building exercise. Here's how it's going to work. Your friend Sonny would like to get a look at the van. Your task is to get him there without blowing anything up. Are you up for it?"

Luki didn't respond.

"Oh, now, don't be that way. Be a good sport, and you'll get your turn to follow directions later. So, I'm going to text you information. You need to figure out what it means and tell your sweetheart what to do so he can keep his pretty skin together on the way to the van. He's got a present waiting for him there. Simple! How can you lose? Oh, and don't worry. If he gets there in one piece, I promise not to blow anything up for a while. It would spoil our reunion, anyway."

Luki worked some saliva into his mouth and said, "Fine." He wanted to puke again. "Sonny," he said, the sound of his rushing heartbeat all but drowning the sound of his voice in his own ears. He swallowed. He breathed.

"Sonny," he said again, then tried to put some reassurance into his voice. "Sweetie. Remember what we said earlier, about having faith? Now's the time. You're going to have to get from here to the van without tripping a detonator. This cockroach on the other end of the line is going to text me enough information for me to figure out what to tell you, step by step. Do what I say, exactly, and nothing else. Okay?"

Sonny nodded. Didn't waiver, didn't betray the least nervousness. Luki said a quick, mental *gratia* to St. Christopher, finishing just in time for the first text to come through.

"1st is ezy. Stp 2 gren 4 go."

Luki scanned the ground. The message said step, so it should be near Sonny, but he couldn't find anything green. He tried to figure if the text could have meant anything else, and dropped his gaze. There it was. He hadn't seen it because it was so close and in the wrong direction. "Sonny, behind you. That smooth rock that looks kind of blue-green. You see it?" When Sonny nodded, he said. "Step over to it."

The next text came through almost instantly.

"Yelo Yelo Red"

Luki narrowed his eyes. Something was just not right about this. He scanned the ground around Sonny, and sure enough there the pattern was. A patch of yellow weeds, a yellow rock, and a rock covered with red sedum—a little trail leading off to Sonny's right. It didn't track. But, not sure yet what was going on, he gave Sonny the instructions.

"Stairway," the next message said.

Sonny saw right away the row of rocks the message referred to. They led, once again, back away from the van, toward where they'd left the car. What the hell?

Damn! The slime ball is playing with us.

No freshly turned earth, no suspiciously piled detritus. No hidden detonator. He hadn't rigged a trip wire. If he had, there'd be no safe path to talk Sonny through. And if someone was looking for it, they'd see it. No such thing as an invisible wire in a clearing on a sunny afternoon.

He said aloud, "That creep. You know what, Sonny? Just wait right there." Then he stepped out boldly and walked to the shed, a huge, three-sided building with corrugated aluminum walls that once held equipment for milling lumber. It hadn't taken long for the area's usable lumber to run out, midway through the last century, and the shed had stood empty since then.

Luki's cell rang. He felt a little nervous about answering it near an explosive device, but he did it.

"Bravo," Mariano said, and ended the call.

Clearly, Mariano had eyes on them. He looked for a place that he might be hiding. When he didn't find him, he searched for cameras. He found them, or at least some of them, decorating the walls, no effort made to conceal them. He stepped back out and saw cameras mounted outside too.

He moved more cautiously to the side of the van, which was about ten feet inside where a section of roof had blown away, parked broadside toward the open side of the shed.

Through the side windows, Luki saw explosives. Again, no effort to conceal them. The bomber had rigged them under a makeshift cot where a young man—who surely must be Delsyn James—lay covered to the shoulders with a black sheet, bleeding into white porcelain bowls under each of his outstretched hands.

Drip, drip, drip, with a long pause between but steady, still driven out by a slow, but beating, heart. The bowls each held only, maybe, a quarter cup of blood—probably less, but Delsyn's pallor matched the van's dirty white, and his lips, though not yet blue, had lost all color. Inside or out, he'd been bleeding for hours, maybe days.

Another call from Mariano. "Have your boyfriend join you. I'm going to need a babysitter while you and I visit."

For the first time, Luki noticed a low, hollow roar behind Mariano's voice, like water running through a tunnel. *The river.* The river, where his nightmares still lived. He tried to keep the shiver that ran through him at the thought from showing. Now wasn't the time to think about it anyway. He looked up and met Sonny's questioning gaze across the mill yard.

He nodded. "Come on, Sonny. Don't worry about wires; there's nothing between here and there. Just come stand with me—in front of me."

By the time he finished speaking, Sonny was there.

"Stop, Sonny. Wait. First, there is a detonator here on the ground. We have no way of knowing whether it's live. Best to assume it is. Don't step on it, don't even step by it. Second…. Sweetie, Delsyn is there. He's alive. You're not going to like what you see, but please, do your best not to show how you feel. He's got eyes on us, and he's tripping, this Mariano. He's getting off on our fear, and the more we look terrified or even pissed off, the more he's going to drag this out and screw with us."

Sonny gave Luki a look that said he was both insulted and impatient, and then pushed past him.

Luki held his breath.

Sonny turned back toward him, away from Delsyn. His eyes were completely flat, his breathing deliberately loose. "He looks like a corpse," he said, without a single change in facial expression.

"He's alive," Luki whispered back.

Sonny nodded, then they both stood motionless until the call came—on Sonny's phone.

Once again, Sonny said nothing when he opened the line. Mariano came on, laughing.

"Hello, faggot two. How do you like that joke. My brother is faggot one, but you're a faggot, too, or faggot two, get it? Oh, you have no sense of humor whatsoever. You do have a sense of aesthetics. How did you find my arrangement? I'm calling it still life with Delsyn. The black sheet to show off his pale skin, the white bowls for the red blood. Makes a statement, yes? But it's nothing without the tapestry. I absolutely love that red, Dr. James. I believe that's a trademark dye of yours? And the design: blood red rose petals on snow. Perfect!

"Back to business. You're going to wear the detonator, take care of your nephew and the bomb while Luki and I have a brotherly heart to heart. I'll call right back."

Luki's phone chimed immediately. He picked up and listened for thirty seconds while Mariano gave him the how-to on handling the detonator assembly, explaining why for each move. When the call ended. He looked at Sonny, gauging his state of mind. *Disturbed, but calm. Distant and calm. Okay.*

"You know what I'm supposed to do, right?"

Sonny nodded.

Luki set to work, talking low as he busied to the task—for Sonny, but just as much to pin his own thoughts somewhere other than on what he was doing to the man he loved. "This man is crazy, Sonny, sick. Even if I knew enough about explosives to disable this, I couldn't do it. He says he has another detonator. A remote set up to blast with a signal from a cell phone that's set up on a closed circuit with that detonator. If this one is cut, or if the cameras get blown, he sets that one off. I have no choice but to believe him."

"It's okay, Luki. I understand. Faith and all that. We'll win."

"We're not alone, Sonny. ATF is out there by now. Even though we can't see them, they're working."

"Sure. And your people, too, right?"

"Ha! Oh yeah, I forgot about them. They're out there, all right. They might be important later, but for the moment they're about as useful as crows in the corn."

"Corn?"

"Nebraska, remember." He put the last wrap of duct tape around Sonny's waist, locking the detonator to his belly. He commanded his lip not to quiver when he spoke again.

"Sonny. I love you."

Sonny licked his lips and raised deceptively lazy eyes to meet Luki's. "And I love you, Luki Mililani Vasquez. I'll always be loving you." He looked down at the contraption he wore as if it was some strange part of his anatomy he'd just now become aware of. "So how does this work? What am I supposed to do?"

"As I understand, there's a timer on the bomb. If the detonator you're wearing is set off, instead of directly blowing the bomb, it starts the timer. He said it's two minutes. His words: long enough for us to think we can get Delsyn out, but not long enough to do it."

Sonny chuckled—a very out-of-place sound. "The bastard thinks of everything."

"Yeah. He's smart and he's cruel. A bad combination. If you step away from the van, you'll pull the wires and trip the detonator. If anyone tries to disconnect anything, unless they're real smart or very lucky, it will trip the detonator. And there's one more thing. There's heat sensitive rigging in the detonator, and it sits under a lens. If you stand so the sun shines on it, the heat will build up, which will trip the detonator."

He'd have to turn away from the sun, face the van, and Luki knew the moment he registered that because the blood drained away from his face. White-lipped and sweating, a shine on his eyes giving away his desolation he whispered. "I don't want to watch him die, Luki."

"I know. And you might not be able to make yourself close your eyes. But he's *alive*." Luki wanted so badly to be able to say something that made a real difference, but all he could come up with was. "I'm sorry, baby."

Sonny nodded, then turned to face the van, away from the fatal sun, and leaned against it, resting on his forearms. Glancing back at Luki, he said slowly, maybe painfully, "What are *you* looking at?"

Chapter Fourteen

WHAT Sonny felt didn't even resemble what he imagined he should feel. The sun beat on his back and annoyed him. He caught a whiff of his own sweat and felt a bit wistful for this past morning, when he could have put on more deodorant. He noticed the way the brownish rubber floor of the van clashed with the color scheme, and he felt disdain. Mostly he felt bored.

Not the least bit alarmed until he accidently bumped the detonator against the window. Then it all rushed in at once—the facts, the probabilities, the terror.

Shaking—too hard to be a shiver. It started at his knees, and Sonny desperately tried to shore them up, afraid to fall and pull a wire. The tremor climbed until he quivered like a dying leaf in a windstorm, so hard he feared he'd set off the bomb just by shaking it. Heat blew back at him from the van; sweat trickled down his chest, pooling where his thin-worn T-shirt was wrapped tight to his skin by the tape.

Like power running through a cord from the switch through the lamp, he connected heat with light, and realized the sun shone back at him from the van windows. His chest began to heave as he tented his hands over the face of the detonator, picturing in his mind his boyhood experiment—the one that every child tries. The magnifier turning sunlight to flame. In his case, scientific curiosity had resulted in a blaze so flagrant the fire trucks came to put it out.

Remembering, he laughed.

And hated himself for it, until a sensible thought found a roothold in his besieged mind and he realized it was fear; all of it, fear masquerading as a thousand emotions bouncing like a ball in a box.

Get a grip, Sonny. His uncle Melvern's teasing voice from long ago.

You're better than this! Jim Standing Bear coaching basketball at United Indians.

You're strong, you can do that, right? That was Luki, words meant for an entirely different situation but fitting strangely well into the present emergency. Then more from Luki: *have faith... there's a way out... I love you... he's alive.*

Time passed, not by but through him as if he'd been washed thin and full of holes. He breathed. He watched Delsyn's blood drip into porcelain until his eyes burned. He heard a dry leaf skitter in a slight breeze, a current too weak to lift his smothering hair. He smelled a distant hint of manure, brought off the cornfields by that same invisible host.

He heard wires groan in the deadly thing he wore when he shifted foot to foot.

Then all at once he heard the sound of boots on the dry, rocky ground, and in the distance the muffled roar and clatter of vehicles and equipment.

"Mr. James. I'm Sergeant Duffy, ATF. We're here to help."

LUKI had walked away and left Sonny taped to a bomb. *I love you* rang in his ears, his own voice taunting him. The statement had been—would always be—true, but how could it possibly make things better?

He hadn't gone more than fifty yards away, still in the clearing, when he got his first text.

Strip wile I cn C U. Guns, clos. I want no triks.

Well, things are starting off nicely, he thought. And though he could have kicked himself for such a stupid wish, he hoped ATF wasn't there yet to see him naked. *Self-centered jackass,* he accused. *As if ATF glimpsing Luki-in-the-buff could possibly matter.*

He dropped his gun in its holder onto the dusty ground. He dropped his smaller gun in its belt holster on top of that. He pulled his very small gun from its strap on his leg and tossed it down too. Then his two knives from their repositories, brass knuckles—which he never used anyway—last. He felt positively weightless. Jacket, shirt, pants, shoes, undershirt, and *oh my God, way to make a man feel vulnerable,* his shorts.

Text: Ok. Step away frm th wepns & put ur shorts on, shak ur pants out & put thm on 2. A FAGGOT is a trrble thing 2 behold. & u need ur shus.

After he received his first directions, he started east down a broad trail flat enough to be a waterway in the spring. He reflected that, though he didn't feel his words would make a difference to Sonny, Sonny's *I'll always be loving you* did make a difference to him. Made the next step a little easier. Put the task into the right perspective. One step at a time.

Yes. There will be an always, and this is the road to get there.

He kept track of his progress, knowing he might need to remember how to get back. These hills could easily deceive a person into going the wrong way.

Confirming his notion that water ran here when lots of rain fell or during snowmelt, willows and the odd cottonwood lined the sides of the gradually climbing trail. He passed a huge, oddly top heavy, yellow-gray boulder—an erratic—on his right. A nearby nest yielded the sound of squawking baby jays—sure to be the same on the way back; his experience as a kid told him the hungry nestlings never stopped demanding food. He reached a place where the trail split in two. He waited.

His phone buzzed. Wen U R @ th fork, Lft, thn 1st Rt

Luki didn't know why it should surprise him that Mariano couldn't see him out here. Of course he couldn't. Realizing that, though, he also wondered about the remote detonator he said he had. Luki had spent his ATF service in firearms control. When he told Sonny he didn't really know bombs, he was telling the truth. But he'd had the basic training and attended the mandatory updates. He knew that most remote detonators—or initiators—were connected to an electrical power source, which could be controlled with a switch.

Following his instructions, he turned left through the smell of pine resin, taking the time away from his musings to stomp a dusty print on a flat rock.

A hacked cell phone, he decided, was the only way Mariano could have rigged the detonator. He'd not worried about the calls, so he must have set the special cell on a frequency he knew the phones wouldn't ordinarily use. Luki could only hope that having reasoned that out would help somehow when push came to shove with Royce. Taking the path on the right, a track no bigger than a game trail, he held on to St. Christopher's cool medal. *Please.*

Then he concentrated on the trail, burned it in his mind so he couldn't possibly forget it—ever. He desperately wanted to be found if things went wrong, even if he died. Somehow, that mattered. He broke branches along the way, and as the trail dropped toward the river he could now hear, he placed his feet carefully, leaving prints no agent could miss.

Next instruction, cross the river at the rapids. Not easy, especially in designer shoes, but maybe not as hard as it sounded. Rapids on this part of the North Loup meant a stretch about fifty yards long where the water squeezed itself past boulders and old bricks as it lost elevation. The water was high, though, and the stones almost covered. He stepped out to the first one and immediately lost his footing. Stumbling backward to the bank, he admitted what he'd wanted to ignore. He'd have to take his shoes off. He did, and then he rolled up his pant legs, thinking that Sonny would probably laugh if he could see him. Though maybe not just now.

The water chilled him, and the rocks made treacherous footholds, but he made it to the other side. He waited.

The old powerhouse.

That's all that was on the text, but Luki didn't need more direction. He knew the place, just past the elbow bend in the river less than a hundred yards upstream. A dam had once claimed the river—its fallen stones had created the stretch of rapids, but the brick power house still stood. He remembered it quite well—the games and secrets and dares he and his friends, including Jemison, had shared there. None of the walls remained whole, only one side had a roof, and the concrete floor had rotted out in the center. Luki didn't want... really, really didn't want to go there.

Ron Jemison had told him, crude and vicious, who it was he'd meet. *"... your daddy's by-blow, golden boy."* Sonny knew; he'd heard, though neither of them had said a word about it. But that identity made clear that Luki was right. This thing was about him. This was his fault.

"MR. JAMES? Can you hear me okay?"

The agent had kept his distance so far, but Sonny could hear him just fine. The countryside seemed to have gone deadly quiet while he'd been standing here in what felt like a river of his own sweat. He looked inside the van for the first time in a while. He hadn't wanted to see Delsyn like that any more than he had to, so he'd closed his eyes, watched his shoes, turned his head, looked up into the empty sky. Now, he looked in at Delsyn in order to use his new method of measuring time. Not much more blood had drained into the bowls than the last time he looked.

ATF had come quickly.

"Got a couple questions for you, Mr. James—or can I call you Sonny?"

"Yeah." The single syllable scratched his throat.

"Okay, Sonny, and you just call me Duff, everybody does. Be patient with us for a few minutes. We'll try to get you some water for that dry throat, see if we can get you out of this fix. But first we need to know as much as you can tell us about what, and who, we're dealing with. Mr. Vasquez must have got a summons—he's gone to meet with the bomber?"

"Yes," Sonny said, "not too long ago." For the next five minutes or so—*or forever, maybe*—he answered questions about the bomb, the detonator, the cameras, Luki, Delsyn, Ron Jemison, and the man called Mariano. *Luki's brother, for God's sake.*

"Anything you can think of, speak up, any time."

But Sonny had nothing else to tell. Not much room for anything in his mind but Delsyn, the bomb, and Luki. *Wait!* "He… Luki said the guy doesn't care what you do. He doesn't think you'll get close to figuring things out. But don't mess with the cameras. If he can't see you, he'll…."

"Okay, Sonny, we're making good progress here. We'll be bringing some dogs in, some two-legged experts who know way more than me about these things, some equipment that can detect some substances people use in bombs. I'll bring some water for that dry throat, and some agents will come in with me, get started sizing things up. What you've told us confirms some of what we knew already, gives us a better picture. I think we've got some room to move. I figure Royce wants to taunt Vasquez, and he's also scared of him. He won't want us to blow things up. He'd lose all his leverage. So, until he feels like he has nothing to lose, if we get too close, he'll stop us. The trick is to get more information and do more with it than he can see—before he changes his mind. We're going to get busy with that.

"Now Sonny, I've got to ask you something, I'm sorry—it might be difficult to deal with, but I have to know. Your nephew, Delsyn, you're sure he's alive?"

Sonny's breath stopped in his throat. He looked in through the windows. Drip, drip—had it gotten slower? Could he see Del breathing, even the slightest move of his chest? "Yes!" He shouted the answer, appalled at the question, refusing the doubt that came creeping in. "Yes, he's alive! Don't even fucking ask me that!"

He knew his response was irrational, and maybe dangerous, but he couldn't stop it, and when he was done shouting, he sobbed, whispered, "He's alive."

"All right, all right, Sonny." The sergeant had come to stand right by him, laid hands on his shoulders. "I hate to say 'calm down', because it's never that easy, and besides, I sound like my mother."

Sonny smiled a little, despite himself.

"But you know you've got to settle, right? You can't move around too much, or even make too much noise. I hate saying this, but you know the danger. Tug a bit too hard on one of those wires…. Things are desperate here. It's crazy. We need a hero, and you're the only one in a position to be one. So stay with us, help us all out, okay?"

Sonny drank some of the water the man, Duff, held out to him. His fears quieted for the moment, he shook his head. Softly: "Hero. I don't want to be that."

"Then you're one of the best kind," Duff said. "Bobby and Janine, here, are going to check out your designer accessories." He nodded toward the detonator. "They know their business, so not much danger, just be as still as you can and let them earn their pay."

The agents wore bulky, multi-layered suits and bubble helmets with reflective face shields. *Right,* Sonny thought, *not much danger.* He had the ridiculous notion that they reminded him of Buzz Lightyear, from the *Toy Story* movies. When the first one came out, Del was still young enough to want to see it—as long as his friends didn't find out. Delsyn had tugged at his hand, "Please, Uncle Sonny?" Now, in the Nebraska fields, he looked up, almost smiling, meaning to share the memory with his nephew. But of course Del wouldn't recall, wouldn't laugh, wouldn't hear. Not today.

The ATF experts confirmed that, indeed, there were explosives in the van. They confirmed that the hardwired device did appear to be a detonator. They were a little surprised, and alarmed, at the ingenuity Royce had used in rigging the heat-sensitive switch. Maybe it wasn't a first, but this bunch hadn't seen that twist before.

"We don't have any way to be sure about the remote detonator because we could set it off while trying to find the closed signal. Cell phone controlled detonators are pretty common, easily done, and it seems he's got the know-how, so I think we'd best assume it's real. As far as that heat-activated switch, we've got a solution."

Janine helped him pull a cut-off, dark green, insulated ATF vest over his head, which covered the face of the lens but missed the various wires. "There," she said, in a voice like everybody's kid sister. "Now we're all a notch safer and you're more stylish into the bargain."

Sonny actually smiled at that, which he found unbelievable. But it did feel good, like it untied one of the numerous knots in his belly.

"Hey, Sonny," Duff said. "We've got some of Luki's people here—employees, we call them. We're kind of snooty so we don't call them agents even though they're damn good ones. And our folks are calling in from Kaholo's. I'm supposed to be the boss, so I need to hear everything. I'm going to leave Janine here for company. She likes to gossip, so just tell her to button up if she's bothering you. And, Sonny, calm is the word. If it helps, I've done this job for twenty-two years, done dozens of situations, and I can tell you the odds are on our side."

Sonny nodded as the fiftyish man walked away. It surprised him how much calmer he did feel, just having the agents there. *Have faith.* Luki was right of course. There would be a way out, even if it hadn't come into view. He looked into the windows at Delsyn's blood. Still dripping. Still a steady rhythm. He reminded himself that, though it seemed a lifetime, not much time had passed. Del would be alright as long as they could get him out of that van alive.

He saw a black speck in the left hand blood bowl. It moved.

A fly.

Chapter Fifteen

THE Powerhouse came into view as Luki stepped farther out into the stream, clear of overhanging branches. He stepped onto the shore and up the damp trail, barefoot and feeling something like a hobbit.

Completely inappropriate!

Or maybe Tom Sawyer.

Damn, Luki! If ever there was a time to be serious…. Well, shit. Maybe that's why my brain wants to take a holiday.

He thought a cigarette would help him focus.

… in the freaking car!

But then he came to the small, decayed building, and all scurrilous thoughts stopped. No part of him wanted to find something to laugh about. Instead, he wanted to cry. But, as Sonny had pointed out not so long ago, he cried most of the time but hid it well, especially from himself. A poor approach to life, probably, but a useful skill in this moment. He shrugged and breathed, stepped across an old rotting dock and stopped in front of the ruined building. A thin light filled the empty doorway. A now-familiar voice called through it.

"Come in, little brother. Come in."

One look at Mariano, and any doubt Luki might have had about whether the man was really his brother vanished. Whereas he, Luki, had taken his pale-blue eyes from Peli, their father, and not much else, Mariano had been made in his image. The difference: whereas Peli had looked hard and uncompromising, Mariano looked decadent and mean. Not slovenly or lush, not that kind of decadent—he looked quite fit. But something nasty, slimy, seemed to ooze from his pores. Luki imagined him leaving a trail behind like a slug. Beyond that, though, Luki looked at him with a specialist's eye, with the perspective gleaned from years of training and practicing his profession.

The way I look at every stranger. Even my brother. Weird.

He looked, to Luki's practiced eye, like a man who got high on cruelty—and who had been indulging his vice far too long and often. It showed in the way his breath quickened when he spotted his quarry. The way he licked his lips when Luki walked into the broken down building; the way he gave into a little smile, nostrils flaring. Luki had sometimes questioned his own use of violence, judicious though he hoped it was, and limited to the least required force.

Except for Ron Jemison, today. Annoying thought, that. And one he didn't have time for now, though he suspected he'd have to come to grips with it sometime in the future. But for right now, he understood quite clearly the difference between his violent capabilities and the cruel nature of his father's other son. For once, Luki thought he came out ahead in decent-human-being points. *One thing, at least, to be thankful for.*

The slime sat across the small room under the remaining roof. The hole in the rotted floor—which dropped to a rocky, rapid, and nevertheless deep section of river—served as a barrier between them. In Mariano's corner, he had two laptops open and running—obviously for the remote cameras—with an external power source hooked to both. Before him, Mariano had laid out an array of cell phones—seven, no eight, in various colors, sizes, and styles. No guns Luki could see, and no knives. He did have two candles, a bottle of wine, and a pack of cigarettes. Luki's brand.

"I don't suppose you'd join me in a toast to the occasion—long lost brothers meet at last? No? Then how about a cigarette?"

God, yes, Luki thought, but he said nothing.

Mariano threw him two smokes and a lighter with a rainbow decal. Luki didn't even think about not lighting up. Mariano watched him inhale—with what may have been obvious relief—and then pasted a false-cheer smile on his face. "Like the lighter? The rainbow? Got it just for you."

Sick fucker.

"If you're wondering why there are no guns and knives, it's because, whatever else I may be, I'm not stupid. I tried to school myself to be like you, Luki, to turn myself into a warrior so I could fight you. But you had our dear father's help. I had no one. So I don't quite qualify to compete in your class. I'm not sure how I thought you might do it, but if I had weapons, there'd be an outside chance that you could get hold of them. I'd be yesterday's dinner."

Luki took another long, cool drag off the cigarette, not letting his expression change at all, fighting for the ice-cold exterior that had become his trademark and most effective tool. Especially against cruelty. Because cruelty survived on another person's fear, or even anger—any emotion that hurt. Love, for instance. The less Luki responded, the crazier this guy would get, trying to make it happen. He'd make mistakes, which could give Luki what he needed to beat him. Or it could drive the creep to push the button.

A tightrope. That's where Luki was.

The cigarette helped with the whole cool-and-balanced thing. Perhaps it was already a mistake on Mariano's part, or perhaps a ruse. Didn't matter, it helped. *Which positive reinforcement will* not *help when I quit—again—tomorrow.* Which rogue thought helped, too, because it reminded him he believed in tomorrow.

"So was that enough of a hint, dear little brother? You know, Peli never loved my mama. He used her, used the fact that she loved him, and got three children on her. He didn't love her, but he used to love us, especially me, because I was his firstborn. When your mother got sick, he broke it off with mama, but he still came around to spend time, teach me, help me."

Oh crap. Luki followed the logic. It was all Luki's fault, in Mariano's book. Luki's fault, and Ron Jemison's. Luki wondered when that horrible night, that one horrible hour, was going to stop fucking up his life.

"You've guessed it by now. Poor Luki was hurt at the river. Mean Ron Jemison…. Well, you get it."

"No," Luki said. His first word since entering the powerhouse. A lie. A cold, emotionless lie, spoken just loud enough to overcome the sound of the river that rushed by down below, tearing itself apart on the pillars that held up the building.

"No?" Mariano's nostrils flared, and he said the word a little too quickly, a hair too loudly. "No, you don't get it? Well, let me spell it out. You're queer, hence Ronny, hence you became the golden boy— the only thing dear daddy could see. Leaving me with nothing but a cash box. Apparently he knew he owed me at least that much. But then he died and that dried up, and he left you with everything and me with nothing at all. So pay up, brother."

Luki said nothing, remembering that when Peli died he'd left him nothing at all too. If it hadn't been for Kaholo, who knows where he'd have ended up. He took the last drag off the cigarette, dropped it on the ground, and crushed it with a slow twist of his bare foot. *Ouch.*

But the bastard dropped his eyes to watch him do it. His face betrayed him. It knocked him off balance, unsettled him to see his target unflinching at pain. "You're not playing fair," he said. Pouting, almost.

Playing fair.... He thinks it's a game. Like a light in the distance, Luki remembered Mariano's "game" for him and Sonny when they'd first come into the clearing by the van. And the way he had them on a chase, like a scavenger hunt, with his hate scrawls and cryptic notes. And how he'd rigged the bomb, set up everything, like a puzzle. The light grew a bit brighter—Luki thought he might be on to something. Royce liked to play games, liked to play people like a cat with a live mouse, maybe to gamble. *That's it. That's the crack in the wall. Now, how to pry it open....*

"I'll tell you what," Royce piped up. "Let's change the game. Let's play shuffle the cell phones. You see, one of these cell phones is the one that matters. All the others are just for calling people. Like your ATF buddies. Oh, let me show you." He turned one of the PC screens toward Luki. "Can you see from where you're at? See, here's the van— with your cute little sweetheart...."

Luki had to stop himself from laughing. He knew that possibly meant he'd gone as crazy as Mariano, but he thought it was funny anyway. If there was anything that didn't describe Sonny, it was the words "cute" and "little." Luki sobered, though, thinking, *but he is sweet.*

Mariano had his eyes all over him. Had he betrayed himself?

"You confuse me, Luki. I almost thought you smiled."

Luki looked straight at him, dredging ice and deliberately making it glitter in the dead light from the computer. He looked at the screen without ever taking his gaze from Mariano. The bastard narrated what was happening at the rigged van, but Luki let it drone; he could see for himself. ATF—they'd sent Duffy, good. They had a team working over the van, checking all the connections. They had a scope, searching the bomb inside with Delsyn and feeding information to a PC not unlike Mariano's, where they could enlarge the video and stop it to analyze what they saw.

They had an agent talking to Sonny, standing with him. And Sonny was... not scared... a little sad, maybe... and tired, weary, mostly that. *Oh, no, not resigned. Sonny, don't give up....*

"But you know," Mariano was saying, "it won't do them any good. The cell-phone signal, remember. They might disable those detonators, but I can press the button quicker than they can move. Good planning on my part, don't you think?" He spread his arms wide and knocked over the bottle of wine.

Though Mariano laughed, Luki noted a touch of panic as he gathered up the phones. And it gave him an idea. *Water and cell phone signals don't mix.* First he had to be sure which phone was the right one. He'd have no second chance. Mariano was talking, arranging the phones out in front of him and prattling on about guessing games, how he'd liked them as a child, how Peli used to play "that game with the shells and pebbles" with him. Luki swallowed—Peli had done that with him too. It distracted him for just a shred of a second, thinking again, *oh God, this cruel stranger is my brother.*

Luki recovered quickly, still he wondered what that small distraction would cost, if he'd missed his chance. But no. There, he saw the clue he was looking for. One phone, the one with large numbers and a small screen. The kind you never see anymore, with no extras, just for making calls. Oddly trimmed in bright pink. That one, Mariano handled differently; not a big difference, just a tad more care about where he put his fingers. And it was the only one he wiped, patted really, to dry off the spilled wine. Probably, he didn't even know he was doing it.

Mariano's game involved, predictably, laying out all the phones in front of him, and having Luki choose one. Mariano would then pick that phone up and push the call button.

"Each time we survive," he said gleefully, "we'll try again. Nice way to pass the time while we wait, don't you think? Oh, but yes, you don't know that we're waiting! I forgot to tell you about the timer. Not the one hooked to faggot two's detonator. I'm talking about the one I've already started. So sorry for the omission. Let's see… yes, it looks like half an hour left. Hmm, a bit long for us to have to amuse ourselves—you got here quickly—but I think we can find a way."

Luki remained passive, cool, but inside something twisted his gut.

"Oh, one more thing. In case you think you can rush me once your faggot boy is gone—you really don't like that word, do you? Anyway, in case you think you have nothing to lose at any time, remember also that I have nothing to lose, and I have this." He twisted sideways to show Luki a blob stuck to his belt.

It looked like putty. It wasn't. A wire Luki hadn't seen before—*which I should have seen*—ran from the plastics into Mariano's side pocket.

"You get it, I see. Boom, no more brothers." His face gave way from false cheer to a snarl, and his voice dropped. "But first I really want to see you cry when your whore-fag dies." For the first time he let silence compete with the river.

For Luki the silence was louder, and his breathing as he struggled not to move, not to flinch, not to twitch a single muscle and give away his rage. "Whore-fag." Sonny, the best, most beautiful and bright and kind human being he'd ever known.

The false smile returning, Mariano said, "Very good then, shall we play?"

Another choice for Luki. Play? Or let him play alone? The latter, he decided. He was sure to subconsciously handle the pink phone differently, maybe give Luki some kind of advantage. Luki needed every little bit—and even then he might fail. It was a long way to leap, and if surprise didn't slow Mariano down, he'd have time to push a button, maybe both of them.

Or maybe I'll set the damn bombs off myself. Cigarette… no.

He waited.

"Oh, I see, you don't want to play. Well, I can play all by myself. Have you ever done that, say with the shells and pebbles? I did! I used to do that after Dad forgot about me. It's kind of fun. So I'll shuffle, and I'll pass my hand over and choose one, and I'll press the button."

Luki waited. Watched. One turn, two, three. He hoped St. Christopher was hanging out close by. He hoped water really could kill the detonator. He hoped water really could absorb a blast. He hoped cigarettes and moping about Sonny hadn't slowed his reflexes too much. He might even have prayed those things. He wasn't sure.

Mariano, again predictable, didn't close his eyes when he made his choice; he peeked. And when he shuffled, the hot phone always landed a bit off from the others, confirming what Luki already knew. One more turn passed, and then the shuffle brought the pink phone to the end of the line, the last phone on Mariano's right, Luki's left. The closest to the water. No more waiting.

Luki relaxed into his leap and flew. The gap in the floor passed under him, the river loud in his ears. While still in the air, he drew his legs up, cocking the energy like a pistol. Surprise fell on Luki's side, and his foot struck Mariano's neck before the would-be bomber could react. Luki had kept eyes on the pink phone the entire time, and now he landed on his left foot and kicked with his right. The phone flew, almost too far, and at the last minute struck the edge of the rotting concrete on the other side and fell.

Behind him, Mariano recovered and, yes, slapped at his pocket. No explosion. He did it again, but Luki had already jumped—and tried to take Mariano with him into the covertly churning waters below, finding himself unwilling to kill his brother after all, regardless. But Mariano fought and Luki let go. He dropped into the water then went under, deliberately heading deeper. When pressure and current slowed him, he took hold of one of the foundation pillars and pulled himself farther down.

Maybe fifteen feet down, the explosion rocked him hard, shock driving the remaining air from his lungs, confusing him. Only grim determination remained of consciousness, kept him from trying to breathe water, kept him moving toward the surface and air, kept him swimming—or letting the current pull him—downstream.

Toward life. Toward Sonny.

Something fell on him, but he rolled and kept swimming. He scraped over rocks, but he pushed past them and kept swimming. And then a moment came when he knew he hadn't been fast enough or strong enough. He tried to keep swimming, but that was only reflex. He held in his mind a picture of Sonny. *He'll keep loving me.* He knew it would be his last thought.

He broke the surface in time to catch a glimpse of brilliant sunlight. And then it was lost to blackness, like everything else.

SONNY could see nothing but the black fly in the bowl of blood. It had subverted every cell capable of forming thoughts. It didn't move, and Sonny wondered if flies drown. But, still as it was, he soon forgot that it was a fly at all. Just a dot of black on a field of red. Red that didn't quite match Sonny's red, the dye no one could copy, but almost. *Whoever made this red*, he thought, *should be proud*. He wanted that red, wanted to weave it through weft of the same hue....

"Mr. James... Mr. James!"

For a split instant, Sonny wondered why the young woman was bothering him, couldn't she see he was working? He lifted his eyes from the porcelain bowl in order to scold her. On the way to do that he saw Delsyn, then the van, then remembered the monstrous device strapped to his belly, and he came back.

He breathed a deep and quivering sigh, licked dry lips, and focused on Janine. "Sorry," he croaked.

"Mr. James, did you hear the explosion?"

He realized that he had, though he'd shut it away.

The sergeant, Duff, trotted toward them. "Are you holding up okay, Sonny?"

"The explosion?"

"Yeah, that's what I want to talk about. We got a radio call from the agents who went upstream, following the trail Vasquez left, presumably for us. An old powerhouse on the river is what blew." He slicked his hair back, as if stalling. As if he didn't want to say more. "It's pretty clear that the bomber was in there. Since the remote detonator signal, apparently, did not come, we're operating on the assumption that the bomber went down with the building.

"Luki."

"We don't know. We haven't found him, but he's always been crafty. And strong. There's hope."

"Faith."

"Pardon."

"He told me to have faith. In him. In chances."

"Seems like a good idea, Sonny. I'll join you in that. But I need your attention, now. This is about you and your nephew. Hate to be blunt, but we've got to make a decision. Our crew believes they can get Delsyn out without setting off the device, but they can't be sure."

Relief flooded through Sonny like a dam burst, followed painfully soon by fear, augmented now by immediacy. He swallowed and fought for a quiet center. *Delsyn*, he mentally chanted, *Delsyn, Delsyn*.

"It involves cutting out the windshield," the sergeant was saying, "which doesn't appear to have any rigging on it, and lifting him through it. They can check and recheck at every step, using every tool and caution. But *they cannot be sure*. Are you clear on this, you understand?"

"Yes." Sonny meant to speak, but he barely whispered.

"Okay, here's part two. They also believe they can disable the detonator you're wearing. But again, they can't be sure. If they go for Delsyn and all goes well, it will maybe take half an hour. If they start with you there's no telling, could be an hour, could be more. I'm going to leave this for you to decide, Sonny, unless you refuse. You're the one strapped in, so to speak, and it's your nephew bleeding in there. Horrible choice; can you make it?"

ROUGH hands were all over Luki. Every instinct, all his training, told him to fight back and fight hard. True danger, a life at risk, his own. But it didn't work, his hands and feet wouldn't go where he told them to, and his chest was heaving but the air didn't come, and the world was so utterly dark.

His ears came back to him first.

"Vasquez," a voice said. "Luki Vasquez." A woman's voice he didn't know, but it sounded friendly.

Then other voices:

"Get him the rest of the way out of the water. Dry ground."

"He can't get air through, should we do a trach, now?"

"Medics on the way, probably a minute?"

"He's hypothermic. Let's get our jackets over him."

A little warmer, the shiver came in waves. Light happened, somehow, and he saw their faces. Strange faces all around, and every one of them willing him to live. Something that had been clenched inside of him relaxed, and then his throat let go.

Air. Sweet, blessed burning in his lungs. Air.

Questions and facts and fears came back all at once. *I'm alive. And Mariano… gone? And the bomb. Oh no. Oh, God, no.*

Somehow he remembered how to move his arm. He waved it.

No one noticed. The medics had come. To Luki, it felt like they'd brought chaos with them, but he had enough of his wits to know they hadn't. Medics generally knew their stuff. That was all good, but he had something important to say, he had to get someone's attention. He tried to shout, but though he was getting air past his larynx, it still wasn't working for other things. He thought about waving a leg, maybe they'd notice that, but he couldn't feel either one.

They were trying to move him onto a stretcher, apparently, and were counting together to pick him up. A last ditch effort, he concentrated on the muscles of his left arm. He still had them, he found; they hadn't washed away in the water. He reached out once more and this time clamped those rock hard muscles around a fairly skinny arm.

"*Shit!*" the voice attached to the arm said. "Hang on, he's got a hold on my arm. I think he's gonna break it!"

"He's trying to say something. You trying to tell us something, Vasquez?" An agent, one of his. Ladd.

Luki nodded, or hoped he did, anyway. He tried to form a word with his lips, but the face in front of him stayed blank. Chest heaving with desperation, he tried his voice, again nothing. He turned his head side to side—that worked. His eyes locked on the watch at the wrist of the arm he was holding. He slid his arm down and snapped the metal flex band hard against the wrist.

"Shit! Why me?"

"Time, Vasquez? What do you…? There's a timer on the bomb."

Luki nodded, and then in relief, let go. Of everything. Back to black, and welcome. But before he got all the way there, Ladd's voice broke in, and somebody gave him a hard shake. He opened his eyes.

"Vasquez! Luki! How much time?"

He felt warm. He felt drowsy. He wanted to dream, to remember. *Coffee, the ocean, tai chi, and colored flags. The bed. The tapestry.* His eyes sprang open, his breath rushed out. He parted his lips and, miraculously, words came out, low, rougher than ever, but audible.

"Maybe fifteen."

"Minutes?"

"Yeah."

As Sonny saw it, it didn't amount to a choice. Only one answer made sense. "My nephew first."

The team began to move, and though it felt to Sonny like he watched from somewhere else, maybe from the helicopter that was circling overhead now, the bomb specialists' speed, their efficiency, amazed him. They cut the glass neatly, and one of them climbed inside. It couldn't have taken more than five minutes.

A minute later, in a gut-deep voice resonating dread, the agent said, "Boss."

At the same instant, or nearly enough to seem so, a voice called over the radio, "Duff! Can you hear?"

Then both voices at once: "There's a timer on the bomb."

"It's ticking," the specialist inside the van said.

From the radio, "Vasquez thinks maybe fifteen minutes."

Hearing Luki's name, Sonny thought, *He's alive.* Then, following immediately, *We're all going to die. No. Faith and all that.*

The man inside, "Seventeen. It says seventeen—no sixteen—minutes."

LUKI woke up again in time to argue about the stretcher, deciding he was going to stand up and walk.

"Lie still, Mr. Vasquez," a medic attempted to command.

"Screw that," Luki answered, voice now a wisp like ultra-fine sandpaper. He rolled to one side and concentrated on deep breaths. It didn't work, of course. He heaved. "Christ," he said, spitting what, using his imagination, tasted and felt like pond scum. He pushed up on one arm, got a knee under him, and stood. When he reeled, arms came under his armpits, supporting him. Which was good, because he didn't want to fall and have to get up again.

"Luki," said Ladd, who had appeared out of somewhere. "You should let them take you on the board. You've got a head injury. You're gonna fall."

Luki was already walking, stumbling now and then but picking up speed. "I won't fall. You got a cigarette?"

"No, you dumb shit, I don't."

"Testy," Luki said, and then as he broke into a clumsy jog, "I just asked."

With all their gear, the agents and medics actually struggled to keep up with him. He'd apparently managed to swim, or the river had carried him, some distance downstream, and in a short time—heaving and sweating, head spinning—he came to the backside of the clearing, behind the mill shed, and jogged around to the front. Agents everywhere, someone being carried out on a board—must be Delsyn. Duff shouted through a bullhorn, "Clear the area. Move it, people!"

At the same time, the sergeant was adding parts to his own bomb suit, the helmet last. Another agent struggled to strap parts onto Sonny, working around the specialists trying to disable the detonator, trying to trace wires. Facing, Luki knew, the usual, almost cliché, dilemma of which one to cut.

"One minute," came a voice from the rise.

"Cut it now," Duff ordered, and they did.

The agents and medics who had been behind Luki had cut for the clear, assuming Luki would do the same. But he didn't. He stood maybe fifty yards from the van, not enough to be clear of the blast. He didn't care. He couldn't take his eyes off Sonny. "Help him," he said, speaking aloud to St. Christopher, which he'd never done before. "Get him clear."

The person timing yelled, "Forty!"

The detonator fell clear as the agents sliced through wires and duct tape all at once, and two of them took Sonny's arms, heading for the rise.

"Twenty!"

Luki thought Sonny would be safe, would make it, so he turned to run, too, but he'd spent all his false energy, all his adrenaline, and he just couldn't do it. He fell to his knees. Behind him he heard shouts.

"James! Mr. James, Sonny!"

Luki turned to look. Sonny had seen him, maybe seen him struggling. *Oh God. No, Sonny, go on.* But he couldn't even shout, and Sonny bore down on him.

"Eight, Seven, Six…"

Sonny hit him like a blast, knocked him over, and they hit the ground together.

"Three…"

In the middle of the long, silent, three-second stretch, Sonny twined his strong fingers into Luki's curls and whispered, "Loving Luki Vasquez isn't all that easy."

Chapter Sixteen

LUKI knew he wasn't strong enough at the moment to roll Sonny and take his place as protector, but he did wrap his arms and hands around Sonny's neck and head, hoping he could take the brunt of any flying debris that landed there, maybe protect his ears.

Even covered by Sonny, he felt the blast like the breath of Satan, and then he heard it. The noise—explosion, screeching metal, shattering glass—lasted no more than seconds. Then the world spun in silence and heat. Sonny didn't respond when Luki said his name, he didn't move when Luki pushed at him. Panic once again fed his veins adrenaline and he rolled. The ground under him seemed to rock like sea waves, but Luki knew it was only his own body, confused.

He retched while checking frantically for a pulse, so it was good his stomach held nothing to come up. He found a pulse under Sonny's left jaw—not strong, a little fast, but steady. He breathed half of a sigh of relief before he was swept away—a little roughly, he thought.

"You're not getting away this time, Mr. Vasquez."

He was strapped to a board before he could voice a hearty and profane refusal. He couldn't see, but he sensed another pair of rescuers shuttling Sonny alongside. They reached the medic van and loaded them, clamped their boards into the slots on either side, and started moving. Luki would swear the ride was the bumpiest any injured person had ever taken. So it seemed a good thing that he wasn't injured. Still half-drowned maybe, but not injured.

But Sonny....

The EMT had already checked Luki over, catalogued cuts and bruises and—mostly on his hands—relayed information about body temperature, pulse, and respiration to the ER. He moved on, and Luki tried to catch glimpses of Sonny as the EMT moved up and down the narrow aisle between them. He saw bloody patches on his clothes, gashes on his arms, one place on his left shoulder where both shirt and skin had been peeled away. A cotton pad had been laid under his back, and blood oozed into it, blooming along the edge near Luki.

Just when Luki felt despair looming over him, Sonny inhaled sharply, cleared his throat.

"Mr. James," the EMT said. "Glad to see you're with us."

Sonny said nothing. His breathing sounded ragged.

The EMT moved into Sonny's line of sight, which meant Luki could see Sonny too. *Alive. Awake.* Relief struck so fast and hard it hurt. Luki thought that, though he'd survived everything else, this just might stop his heart.

"Mr. James, can you hear me? Do you know where you are?"

Which is when Luki realized that his own hearing had returned. Though a bit muffled, it was acute enough to hear Sonny rasp his answers.

"Can hear. I'm in hell. Delsyn? Luki?"

"You know damn well you're not in hell, Mr. James."

"Sonny."

"Okay, Sonny. Delsyn was airlifted about three minutes before the blast; they got away clean and will be at Nebraska Hospital in about ten, I'd say—"

"Factor?"

"Yeah, that turned out well. Mr. Vasquez's folks had the stuff in spades. Not quite sure how they got it, but I imagine that little breach of legal etiquette will be overlooked in light of the outcome. He's getting factor and red cells, and they'll transfuse him as soon as they arrive at the hospital. I can call and see if I can get an update, if you like, as soon as we clear this mockery of a road and reach the highway."

"Luki?"

"He's right here, to your left—that's the side that probably hurts the most—and he won't stop staring at you. Not sure what that's about...."

It looked like an effort, but Sonny turned his head. Luki crinkled his brow, thinking they should have had a neck collar on him. *What's wrong with these people?* But when Sonny locked his soft brown eyes on him, Luki forgot about his complaints. It felt like forever that they stared at each other. To him, it seemed they floated in a vacuum; nothing else existed but his lover and the small part of him that was good enough to let Sonny love him back. Finally, the ride smoothed out as the aid van pulled onto the highway, and the two of them spoke at once.

"What," they said, "are *you* looking at?"

ABOUT a half hour in a speeding aid car gave Luki time to feel crummy. The backs of his hands burned and so did a place on the right side of his forehead, which he realized had some sort of bandage on it. Probably a butterfly, like the ones he also had here and there on his hands. His head ached and his throat burned and his chest felt sort of full.

And then he started coughing. And when he did, he choked, until the EMT pulled him on to his side, where he coughed more but didn't choke. So that was good.

Sonny got a bit upset when he found out Del was going to Nebraska Hospital while they were stopping at Cherry County Regional, but he managed to sign a release on Delsyn's behalf for various treatment possibilities. The EMT got an okay to give him some painkiller, or sedative, or something, and he slept.

Maybe Luki did, too, because the next thing he knew, he was waking up in green florescent light, propped up on pillows, with oxygen tubes stuck in his nostrils and Kaholo smiling at him from the foot of the bed. Déjà vu. The same hospital, even.

Maybe he had a head injury that changed his personality. Maybe drugs left him feeling mushy. Maybe he'd just crashed after the insanity. Whatever the reason, though Luki strove for cool and unflappable, what he got was desolate and devastated. Probably it showed, because Kaholo came to his bedside. A big man, tall and broad-shouldered like legendary Hawaiian kings, he reached down and drew Luki up to his shoulder, just like he had when Luki was hurt as a child.

"It's okay, Mili," he said. "I got my eye on you. It's gonna be alright."

LUKI and Sonny both spent two nights in the hospital. Luki tried to go outside to smoke, but he choked so hard he was afraid he'd tear the stitches in his face out, so he sat in Sonny's room and looked out the window. He surprised himself by thinking more about the future than the horrific recent past. Things left undone, things that with a little luck could take a lifetime. Sonny, of course. Josh, Jackie, Delsyn. Margie, even. Now there was a thought-provoking development. He'd sent Ladd out west to check things out and clean them up. Shortly after that, Kim called to tell him Margie had the crusty agent roped and tied.

And he decided he didn't want to live in Chicago anymore. He'd go back to see to the details of selling his condo, and then he'd relocate. To Washington State, a place where you had to go south and then west in order to get east and north. A place where impossible sequences of letters spelled place names. And incidentally, a place where reclusive textile artist Sonny Bly James—Dr. Sonny Bly James, whatever that was about—also made his home. Well, maybe not so incidentally.

Once, he dozed in the chair and woke feeling Sonny's eyes on him. He turned to see the familiar half-smile. He spoke softly. "What are *you* looking at?"

"You're gonna have another scar, you know. On your forehead."

"Great. I'll look like the Frankenstein monster."

"No," Sonny said, settling himself gingerly for more sleep. "You're a jackass, Luki, not a monster. Besides, he's more handsome."

Luki laughed. Yes, laughed, and said without even thinking, "I love you, Sonny."

Drowsy eyes already closed, Sonny responded, "Yeah, you do, don't you? Kind of amazing, really."

LOU SYLVRE hails from Southern California but now lives and writes on the rainy side of Washington State. When she's not writing, she's reading—fiction in nearly every genre, romance in all its tints and shades, and the occasional book about history, physics, or police procedure. Her personal assistant is Boudreau, a large cat who never outgrew his kitten meow. The noise she makes with bagpipes should be outlawed, but she plays guitar okay and loves to sing. She also loves her family, her friends, a Chihuahua named Joe, and (in random order) coffee, chocolate, sunshine, and wild roses.

Visit http://www.sylvre.com or contact her at lou.sylvre@gmail.com.

For more of the
best M/M romance,
visit

Dreamspinner Press

www.dreamspinnerpress.com

CPSIA information can be obtained
at www.ICGtesting.com
Printed in the USA
FSHW022031290119
55251FS